LIZZY GOES BRAINS OVER BRAUN

BILLIONAIRE BABY CLUB

NEW YORK TIMES AND *USA TODAY* BESTSELLING AUTHOR

JASINDA WILDER

LIZZY GOES BRAINS OVER BRAUN

BILLIONAIRE BABY CLUB

CHAPTER ONE

I WAS CRUISING THROUGH MALIBU, ON A HANDS-FREE CALL with the owners of a home I'd just finished showing to prospective buyers.

"Tell me you have good news about the showing, Lizzy." This was Gerry, the owner.

"The best news. They're offering eight-point-two-five, with a thirty-day close. Furnished."

A breath of relief. "You are pure magic, Lizzy Stephenson."

"I don't know about that, Gerry, I'm just good at my job. It's why you hired me after all."

"Is this a formal offer?"

"I'm on the way to the office to write it up as we speak."

"I'll be waiting for your email, then." His relief and happiness at my news were palpable. They were mortgaged to the hilt, and this sale at this price was going to free up a lot of cash flow for them.

"You should have it in half an hour or so."

We exchanged goodbyes, and I made it to my office. Pulled into my named, personal parking space behind my adorable little Malibu storefront office. Inside, there were six desks, a white leather couch, a coffee and tea station, several large TVs playing a sequence of nature stills. Four of the desks were occupied: Zoe, Autumn, Teddy, and Kat were all at their desks doing what I presumed was somewhere between working and perusing social media. Laurel had back-to-back showings today and was due back in an hour or so.

Zoe and Autumn were sisters, separated by a little less than a year and a half, what some called Irish twins, and often were mistaken for identical twins. They looked up at me in unison.

"Well?" Zoe asked.

"Spill!" Autumn said, immediately afterward.

Teddy was more laconic about her curiosity, leaning back in her chair, content to wait and listen, while Kat feigned disinterest, pretending to be just totally absorbed by her computer screen.

I decided to draw it out. I sauntered in, purse hanging from my elbow, and fixed myself a cup of coffee. I took a ridiculously long time to add sweetener, nearly going grain by grain, and then almond milk drop by drop, and then stirring it with excessive care.

"OHmyGOD!" Kat exploded. "Just tell us already! Did you sell it?"

I held my mug in both hands, keeping my face straight for as long as I could. Which wasn't long. "EIGHT-POINT-TWO-FIVE, BITCHES!"

There were friendly groans from Kat and Teddy, with whom I had an on-going three-way competition, and squeals of delight from Autumn and Zoe.

"You suck," Kat muttered. "Just wait till I sell the Frasier place."

"There's no way the Frasier house is going for anywhere close to eight-two-five, Kat," I said, stopping to pat her on top of her head. "Sorry, babe, but if you get even a full eight, I'll be surprised. Seven-nine-five is my guess."

She held up her middle finger without looking at me. "Sit on it, Lizzy." She said it with a smirk, though. "Because guess what—I just listed Calder. It's at nine-point-three, it's been up for less than four hours, and I've already had a call to schedule a showing."

I snorted. "Nine-point-three is stupid for that. It's got a shit view, it's under six thousand square feet, and it's got no wow. It'll sit for six months and you'll get seven."

She added another middle finger. "You just hate me. Admit it."

I mussed her long, glossy black hair as if she were an adorable toddler. Or something. I don't know kids. "I don't hate you. I just like to challenge you. That's why I gave you the Calder house: to test your skills."

She batted at my hands, shot to her feet, and scurried to the ornate mirror on the wall. "Of course you know, this means war," she said, fixing her hair strand by strand.

Then, acting as casual as can be, she walked toward me, revenge in her eyes.

"If you touch my hair, Katja Spears," I said, backing away, "I swear I'll give you all the worst listings for the rest of the year."

"Yeah, because you're more of a priss about your hair than I am," she said, still angling for me.

I backed myself into a corner, and then picked up the first thing my hand found: a red Swingline stapler. "I'll staple your face," I snapped, "and then what will you do?"

I was bluffing, though, and she knew it, because she advanced with a grin, hands up, clawed…lunged, and when I moved to block her, she faked one way and then the other, and then her hands shot through my defenses and pawed roughly at my hair.

"Revenge is a bitch," she said, satisfied, "and so am I."

I glared at her. "You're not getting any listings over two, now, I hope you realize." I moved to the mirror and attempted to return my blond hair to the artful waves and loose curls. "Do you have any idea how long it took me to get my hair to look like that?"

Kat stuck her tongue out at me. "That's because you have no volume, boo. You have to fake it."

"I have to write up this offer," I said, waltzing to my desk, sitting with what I hoped was elegant grace.

The desks of the other five girls were arranged around the room, all facing the center, and mine was against the storefront in the focus of the space, since I was the broker and I'd started the firm. Everyone had two chairs in front of their desks so clients could come and discuss options and sign paperwork as necessary, but my desk was just that much bigger and nicer, and the chairs in front of my desk were replica Louis XV chairs.

By this point, with the show over, the other girls had gotten back to work. In short order, I had the offer written up and sent off to the Crenshaws to sign so I could then send it to Gerry and Leanne; I'd had the offer drawn up for days, having had an inkling that the Crenshaws would want this one. I just had to fill in the numbers. I was getting paid two ways on this deal, to boot—I was the buyer's agent for the Crenshaws and the seller's agent for Gerry and Leanne.

Laurel breezed in, dressed to the nines as she always was, her naturally platinum blond hair in a tight chignon, Chanel purse hanging off her elbow, Louboutins clicking down the steps from the back entrance, her cell phone to her ear as she worked on closing a deal.

"Murph, listen—no, Murph, it's *worth* it. It is. I know it needs some reno, but that's exactly what you said you wanted, not a fixer-upper, but something you could put your thumbprint on. The bones are there, you know they are. It's exactly what you said you wanted—in the neighborhood you specified, in your price range—at the top, albeit—with good bones, a great view, and potential for upgrade…you're waffling, Murphy…okay, well, you're not going to find anything else in that specific area for anything less than six, trust me, I know. There are precisely three other properties for sale in a ten-mile radius of the house I just showed you, and of them, only *one* is listed for under six million. And that one is a total gut-job. Like, complete gut, down to studs and subfloor, knocking out walls, replumbing, rewiring, new roof. It's nearly a knock-down and rebuild, you're just paying for the land, location, and view. If you want *that* neighborhood, Murph, *that's* your house. I have another showing there tomorrow at noon, so you have until, say, ten tomorrow morning to put in an offer. I won't cancel with those clients at the last minute, so get your shit in gear and give me a number."

Ballbuster, man. Granted, this guy Murphy was one of her oldest friends, and someone she's sold at least one other property to that I know of. But still, she was a ballbuster.

She was in the center of the room, listening, eyes closed, silently chewing on her lower lip. And then, her eyes flew open and she clenched her empty fist in victory, dancing in a circle.

"Okay," she said, her voice level and cool as a cucumber. "They're asking five-point-two-five, but they haven't had any offers yet, so you could go in at…five even, if you're willing to go up closer to full asking. Okay, I'll send it over. Give me five minutes. Okay, talk soon." She ended the call, demurely placed her phone into her bag, and then began dancing a gleeful little jig, as well as she could in three-inch heels and a crazy tight miniskirt. "Boom, bitches. Top that." She swept her pointer finger around the room.

"Boss lady already did top it," Zoe said without looking up from her computer. "Eight-point-two."

"Goddammit!" Laurel huffed, rolled her eyes. "You are such a chronic overachiever, you know that, Lizzy? Buzzkill."

We were often mistaken for sisters, though were weren't—of a height, both with naturally platinum hair, similar bone structure, similar builds, and even our eyes were close in shade, hers grayish-blue while mine were a swirl of blue and green.

"I'm the boss for a reason," I said. "But good job. Let's get these offers out, because I'm feeling like it's wine-thirty."

"Isn't it always?" Autumn asked.

"No, not until the work is done." I pointed at my computer. "I have to send this signed offer over to the sellers, and then we can tackle the rest tomorrow."

Laurel was already sitting down, filling out the

necessary portions of the offer form. There was little talk for a good half an hour, then, as we all wrapped up our day's work.

I emailed both seller and buyer saying we'd sort out the rest of the process tomorrow, as long as everyone has signed the offer—I received the signed offer from the sellers, which meant we were pending.

A few last odds and ends, and then I put my laptop to sleep, stuffed it into my messenger bag along with a few folders of important documents, and stood up.

"Well, are we all ready?" I looked around at my girls. "I need a glass of wine."

We almost always met for a drink after work, so it was a foregone conclusion that everyone was in. Except...there was hesitation.

I hadn't wanted to point it out, because I'd wanted to think my five best friends in the world, my coworkers, employees, sisters from other misters...would remember that today was my birthday. My *fortieth* birthday, no less.

All I really wanted was a glass of wine with my best bitches.

And here they were trading meaningful glances as if referring to some conversation that hadn't included me.

"Am I missing something?" I asked.

Kat approached me. "We're not going for drinks tonight, Liz."

"We're not?"

She moved behind me. "Hold still." Her hands grabbed my shoulders, holding me in place. "Nope. We're kidnapping you."

"Why would you do that? You could just tell me what's going on."

"Where's the fun in that?" Before I could protest, she had a blindfold around my eyes and was tying it. "How many fingers am I holding up?"

"How the hell should I know? You put a blindfold on me." I snorted. "Knowing you, just one, your middle." I felt a breath of air as someone moved in front of me. "I can't see a thing, alright? For real."

"Good." Kat turned me around. "Now, march. We're going to the back door."

I knew where I was in the room and had more than once navigated the room in near pitch dark, so I headed confidently toward where I knew the back door to be—my toes found the steps, and I followed the handrail up, trailed my fingers along the exposed brick wall to the door, and then waited.

"Now what?" I asked.

I felt Kat move past me—I knew it was her by her perfume: Chanel. "Now…" she took my hand and led me outside. "We party."

I heard a diesel engine clattering. "Is that a party bus?"

"Sure is." I heard a noise that I thought might

a bus door opening. "Hiya, Bill, you ready for this? Because we're fixing to tear this town apart, baby. Up we go, Lizzy."

Step, step, step, and the noise of the engine was muted, and I felt leather seats on either side of me, and then Kat guided me to sit on a plush, deep, comfy leather seat.

"Why do I have to be blindfolded for this? I don't know where we're going, so what difference does not being able to see make?"

"Oh, no reason. We just thought it would be fun to blindfold you." Kat was smirking—I could hear it. "Leave it on. It's more fun."

"Fine." I snorted. "But it's dumb."

"*You're* dumb." She put a bottle into my hands. "Drink."

"From the bottle?"

"Hell yes, from the bottle. You're turning forty, bitch, we're doing this up right. You didn't think we forgot, did you?"

"I was starting to wonder."

The rest of the girls were on the bus by now, filling it with overlapping chatter. I touched the bottle to my nose, sniffed—tequila.

"Oh hell no!" I yelled, shoving it away. "You know what happened the last time I got tequila wasted. I'm not going there again."

"It was the funniest night of my life, is what

happened," Teddy said. "Drink up, boo. We're getting you lit."

"Tequila wasted Lizzy is a walking disaster," I said, feeling my resolve weakening. "Also, I haven't eaten lunch or dinner. You better be ready to babysit me."

"We have the bus, and the driver, Bill, has been promised a hefty tip for being willing to help carry you into your house at the end of the night."

"I have work to do tomorrow," I protested. "I can't be out of commission."

"You're under contract. You have no showings. Laurel got her offers in, so she's pending as well. Yes, we turned off the lights, yes, we locked the door." This was Autumn, on my left. "Just cut loose a little, Lizzy. We have a lot of fun planned."

"Are there strippers? There better not be strippers. The last male stripper you hired tried to get *me* to pay *him* to blow him."

"No, no strippers. We learned that lesson." Zoe answered for the group on that one. "Also, I got an up close and personal look at what he was packing under that G-string, and let me tell you, I can see why he would charge for the honor. It was, like, whoa."

I took a tentative sip of the tequila—Patron, baby. Another, heftier swig. "Chaser, chaser, ohmygod, wow." Somebody put a cold, sweating can into my hand, and I fumbled at the rim, checking to make sure it was open, and then took a long swig—light beer.

"Are you trying to kill me? Tequila chased with beer on an empty stomach?"

"We're eating soon," Autumn said, and then paused, I heard her swallow, hiss.

"Also, Zoe, how exactly did you manage to see the stripper's pee-pee?" I asked. "Did you pay him for it?"

She didn't answer immediately. "I, um. No. Maybe."

"You did! You paid him to suck him off!" I was shrieking already. Drunk Lizzy is loud—Tequila drunk Lizzy is deafening. And I'd barely had any.

"I did not!" Zoe shrieked back. "I paid him to get it hard and show me what it looked like. I didn't touch him."

"Zoe, that's mean." Teddy, laughing. "You got him hard and then left him that way? Have you no mercy?"

"Not when it was going to cost me twenty-five dollars, and besides, who knows if he was clean or how many diseases he had. No way. A random dude at a bar, maybe. A stripper slash prostitute? No way. I was just curious."

"He was big?" I asked, remembering how well the guy in question had filled out the tiny little red G-string.

Zoe snickered. "Um, yeah. Huge. Biggest dick I've ever seen in real life." She lowered her voice. "I honestly don't know if I would have slept with him, if he was a guy I'd just randomly hooked up with. There is such a thing as *too* big. He'd have ripped me in half from stem to stern. And there was no way I could have gotten my jaw around that monster. No way."

"Bullshit!" I heard Teddy say. "I don't think dicks that big exist."

"I actually have a pic of it," Zoe said, sounding embarrassed. "I paid five dollars extra for him to let me take a picture. For, umm, research purposes."

"And by research you mean diddling your bean?" Kat asked.

"No!" Zoe shrieked, at a glass-shattering pitch and volume.

"Admit it!" Autumn said. "You use it to jill off. You know it, I know it, we all know it."

"More to the point, show us the photo!" This was Teddy again.

"No! It's private," Zoe said, sounding prim. "He made me promise I wouldn't spread it around."

"Zoe, shut the hell up and show us the photo. You're not posting it on the internet, you dumb bitch, you're showing your sister and best friends." This was Autumn.

"Fine!" Zoe sighed.

I ripped off the blindfold and saw my girls around me, the seats black leather, the Pacific on our right which meant we were heading south. Everyone was gathered around Zoe, who was searching through her photo library.

"Ha, here it is." She tapped the thumbnail and we all clustered closer.

"Ho-lee sheeeeyit," Kat drawled. "You weren't kidding, girl."

She certainly had not been exaggerating. The photo showed a chest, groin area, cutting off at the knees. The dick in question was colossal. Truly, insanely colossal.

"How is that real?" I asked, dumbfounded. "And how the hell is it supposed to fit inside a normal female vagina?"

"Right?" Zoe was giggling. "In person, it's even bigger. The photo doesn't do it justice. It would have taken both hands to get all the way around it. It would be like giving a handjob to a salami, like the big ones you see hanging from the ceiling at a butcher's."

"I wonder if he's done porn," Kat asked. "That's what I would have asked."

"I did ask," Zoe said, giggling even more breathlessly. "He said he's trying to get into it, which is why he's in LA in the first place. Apparently just having a six-pack and a monster cock doesn't make you a shoo-in at high-dollar porn studios."

"Weird. What else would you need?" Autumn said. "It's not like porn stars can actually act."

"I don't know," Kat said, "I've seen some with decent acting."

Zoe eyed Kat. "And how much porn are you watching, there, babe?"

"Enough," Kat said, her voice arch. "A girl has needs, and let me tell you, the dating pool is slim pickings, these days."

"Dating pool?" I said with a frustrated sigh. "It's not even a pool, it's a damn puddle. I swear I've dated every halfway attractive male between the ages of twenty-five and fifty in a hundred-and-fifty-mile radius." I looked around as we approached the outskirts of LA. "Where the hell are we going, anyway?"

"We are going to my favorite dive bar," Kat said. "I know the owner, and I had him call all his single buddies and offer them dollar beer night, so we'll have a lot of hot eye candy to party with." She wiggled her eyebrows at me. "And, you never know. We might even get you lucky tonight."

I took another sip, stifling a laugh. "No no no, when I sleep with a man, *he's* the one getting lucky. I happen to be damn good in the sack, I'll have you know."

"Nobody calls it the sack anymore," Teddy said, laughing. "Showing your age, babe." She took the bottle from me. "And I think you better hold off until we get some food in you. You're already getting tipsy."

"I told you!" I shrieked. "Tequila, beer, and no food. You guys are in trouble." I pointed around at my friends. "Do NOT let me get naked tonight, and for *sure* no drunk hookups. I'm *so* tired of drunk hookups."

Kat smirked. "I make no promises."

At that moment, we pulled up in front of a dive bar on the outskirts of LA—a true dive. A tattoo parlor was on one side, still open, and a pawn shop on the other. The door was propped open with a big silver keg, and bodies moved inside, lights flashed, music pumped.

I eyed Kat. "Are you sure this place is…safe? It looks kinda sketchy."

She cackled. "Hell no it's not safe! But I'm buddies with the owner, Hector, and nobody fucks with Hector." She danced in her seat as the driver of the party bus parked a few spots down from the bar. "Hector makes the most bomb margaritas I've ever had in my life. He promised me he'd make us a legit bucketful, and also, tacos. There's a tiny little kitchen in the back, and if he likes you, Hector will get his wife to make tacos for you, and that woman makes tacos I would do a murder for."

"Do a murder for?" I slowly reached out and took the bottle of Patron away from her. "I think you've had enough." I swirled the clear liquor—it was almost gone. "Holy shit! The six of us killed a fifth of Patron in less than an hour."

"You haven't had Hector's wife's tacos, or Hector's margaritas. They make you forget how to grammar."

She stood up. "Ladies, it's time to celebrate our best friend and our beloved boss as she turns forty." She took the bottle and finished it off. "We sure did kill this son of a bitch, didn't we? Well, we're just getting started. Let's get naked wasted and make bad decisions."

"No!" I stood up and tugged my skirt down. "I'm *not* getting naked wasted. I almost got a ticket for public indecency last time I got tequila wasted."

Kat gestured out the bus windows. "Does this look like the kind of area where you'd get arrested for taking your shirt off? Knowing Hector and his buddies, they'll cheer you on and then beat up anyone who tries to take a photo. They'll absolutely enjoy the show, but they won't be assholes about it." She sashayed toward the front of the bus. "Trust me, old lady. Have I ever let you down?"

I cackled, following her. "You're a terrible influence and you're going to get me in trouble. Lead the way!"

There was laughter and clapping and cheering from my friends as we exited the bus. We had pre-partied pretty hard, and I had a feeling tonight was going to be a night to remember.

Or, knowing how we all got on tequila…a night to forget.

CHAPTER TWO

"OH GOD, IF I EAT ANOTHER TACO I'M GONNA BARF," I said, pushing back from the table. "So good. So full."

"Quitter," Teddy said, stuffing the last of a taco into her mouth. Seven? Eight? I don't even know. These were not small tacos, either. "Best tacos I've ever had. I'm gonna gain ten pounds to my ass and thighs from eating so many, but *fuck*, so good. Worth it."

"I'll just drag you to Zumba and we can dance our asses off, literally," Kat said, polishing off another taco herself.

Teddy made the sign of the cross. "Begone, Satan. Exercise is from El Diablo and I categorically refuse to do it."

"Wanna know my secret? Lots and lots of very athletic sex," Laurel quipped. Or at least, I figured it was a quip. With Laurel, you never knew. "And walking. I walk every night. I put in my earbuds and I turn on an audiobook and I walk. And squeeze my butt cheeks a lot. Firms 'em up."

"That's exercise," Kat said, droll.

"No, it's just walking. I don't even get warm," Laurel answers, dead serious. "I don't like to get sweaty and out of breath unless there's a dick inside me."

"Just asking for a friend here," I said, tracing my finger through salt on the rim of my margarita glass, which had not been empty at any point in the evening, which was beginning to wane into night, "but what counts as athletic sex? I mean, I like to think I get it on like Donkey Kong, but I'm not sure what constitutes as athletic."

"Ever try the wheelbarrow?" Laurel smirked at me. "That'll get ya sweaty real fast."

I blinked. "The...*wheelbarrow*."

"Yeah. Just what it sounds like." Laurel took a long drink from her margarita. "He's standing up, holding your legs, you're face down with your hands braced on the floor, and he's drilling you while you hold yourself up. Takes a lot of upper body strength." She snorted, giggled. "Unless you just do like a headstand sort of move, but the angle's better if you hold yourself up."

"Sounds hard," I said. "Why would you do that? How is it any better than prone bone on a bed?"

"Be*cause*," Laurel answered, pointing a finger at me, and I wasn't sure if it was her finger wavering or my eyesight, or both. "Because of geometry. He can hold your legs wider apart, for one thing, and for another, it's just a different angle. The dick feels different. I dunno. You just have to try it to understand."

"Wow," I snickered. "Just wow."

"What?" Laurel shrugged, her expression demure and arch. "I like fun fucking."

Zoe spluttered around a mouthful of margarita, caught it with a napkin, shaking with laughter. "Fun fucking?"

"Also known as adventure sex." Laurel handed Zoe another napkin. "Although the two are slightly different. Fun fucking is weird positions. Like pretty much ninety percent of the Kama Sutra."

"And what, pray tell, is adventure sex?" Autumn asked. "Inquiring minds would like to know."

"Anything risky," Laurel answered. "In the bathroom of a bullet train in Japan, or under the bleachers at your nephew's football game, or...or handjobs under a table at a black-tie gala."

I set my glass down slowly. "You have not."

"Let's make that a game of two truths and a lie," Laurel said. "I've done two of those."

Teddy stabbed a finger at Laurel. "I know for a fact you don't have a nephew. And also that's gotta be, like, illegal."

"How in the *hell* did you manage it in the bathroom of a bullet train?" Zoe asked. "Those things are *not* large."

"That was both risky *and* athletic." She smirked, bit her lip with a lecherous gleam in her eye. "It required careful timing to get both of us in there at the same time without anyone noticing. And then he leaned back against the wall and I squatted on his knees and basically twerked myself to an O on him. Tricky, but worth it."

"I had no idea you were so kinky," Autumn said.

Laurel held up a finger. "It's not kinky. Kink is, like, bondage and S and M, and foot fetishes and furries. I just like fun positions in fun places."

"'Like the back of a Volkswagen?'" I quoted.

"'It's not a schooner, it's a SAILBOAT!'" Kat answered.

Everyone else was just staring at us.

"*Mall Rats*?" Kat said. "No? None of you have seen it?"

"How can we be friends with them now?" I asked. "It should be mandatory viewing at Six Chicks Realty."

"Along with *Chasing Amy* and *Clerks*," Kat added.

"I've seen *Clerks*," Zoe said. "It was funny."

"Didn't that same guy do…what's the one with Alanis Morrisette and Professor Snape?" This was Autumn.

"*Dogma*," I answered.

"Why are we talking about this?" Teddy asked. "I'm confused."

"Because Laurel was talking about sex in fun

places, and in *Mall Rats*, there's a running joke about having sex in a very uncomfortable place, like the back of a Volkswagen." I sighed. "It's only funny if you've seen the movie."

"Still, the point of all this," I said, "is that I had no idea Laurel was so adventurous sexually."

"Neither did I," Kat said. "You're so buttoned up and posh and proper."

"Haven't you ever heard the saying, 'queen on the streets, freak in the sheets?'" Laurel said.

I threw a blue corn chip at her. "Girl, you nasty."

"I'm single, I'm at the peak of my sexual powers, I'm beautiful, I've got money...why not enjoy myself?" She preened, patting her chignon and stroking back pretend wayward strands—which there never were, because she would never allow anything so pedestrian as flyaways.

"Do you ever..." Teddy trailed off, sighed, took a long pull off of her margarita. "Do any of you girls ever want, like, something...long term?"

There was a moment of silence as we took in the enormity and seriousness of Teddy's question.

"What, like a...*boyfriend*?" Zoe asked.

"Or...the 'M' word?" Autumn hissing "M" in a stage whisper.

Teddy shrugged. "I dunno. Either one."

"I'm good with hooking up," Laurel said. "Keeps it neat. No breakups, no hurt feelings, no cheaters pissing me off and making me do things I then regret. Like breaking irreplaceable antique pottery over his dumb skull."

"No assholes breaking your nose in two places because you're sick of his shit and finally summon the courage to say so," Teddy said, lifting her now-empty glass in a toast of one.

"No assholes mooching off of you, thinking you're gonna be his sugar mama and wanting you to drop everything every afternoon for mediocre sex in his cheap West Hollywood loft." Kat picked up the pitcher of margaritas, poured the last of it into our glasses, and then turned around in her seat and half lifted to catch Hector's eye for more.

"No endless parade of same-faced douche canoes slutting their shitty screenplays around Hollywood pretending to be producers and writers when all they really are is bartenders and baristas and CPAs," I said. "No lawyers and hoity-toity execs wearing overpriced suits thinking you're looking for a Tiffany ring and a place on his shelf as a trophy wife with no career and no goals and no identity. No dead-end quasi-relationships predicated on lackluster half-drunk sex and zero emotional connection." Suddenly, it was a flood rushing out of me, a rant, and I couldn't stop it. "No more sitting in a booth alone for two hours waiting for him to no-show, and getting slowly wasted on hundred-dollar bottles of wine. No more thinking finally, *maybe* this guy is it, maybe *this* guy actually has a soul that goes deeper than his ball sac and a mind that can function beyond his own career. No more wondering if you're going to wake up one day and be sixty and still pimping overpriced houses in Malibu, living alone, still trolling Tinder for the next mindless fuck at one in the morning after a night of shouted conversations in a bar full of putzy, over-cologned children."

When my diatribe finally ran out of gas, everyone was staring at me.

"What?" I asked, stuffing a chip into my mouth.

"Tell us how you really feel, why don't you," Kat said.

"I just did." I took a sip, eyeing them. "What? You're all staring at me."

"What brought that on?" Teddy asked.

"I dunno. You and Laurel started it, and you can't tell me you were joking. Teddy, you came to *my* house after Thomas hit you. You and I watched as my former friends-with-benefits ex-policeman PI worked him over and dragged him out of your house. We got drunk on gin and Lacroix afterward and watched *Practical Magic*. So don't tell me it was a joke. And you, Kat—your history of getting suckered into being a sugar mama for douchebags way too young for you simply because they have nice abs and a short refractory period is a well-known thing, and not just to me.

Zoe, Autumn, neither of you are any better. We're all hookup artists and serial daters and cougars and sugar mamas."

Hector came by with two more pitchers and a fresh bowl of salsa and a new basket of chips, efficiently gathering our empty pitchers and plates and dirty napkins. When he was gone, I continued.

"So yeah, my little rant just now was something that's been building up inside me for a while." I sighed. "I'm forty and still single, never been married, never even been engaged. Shit, I've never been in a relationship that's lasted more than a year and a half, and that was only because he traveled for work three weeks out of every month. It's bugging me. I think Teddy's question just unearthed a whole bag of shit I've been ignoring for a long time."

"So…what?" Kat said. "You're suddenly going to…what? Join Match dot-com? Troll Tinder and tell prospective dates you're looking for something serious, not just a hookup?"

"I don't know, *Kat*," I snarked, "I'm not saying I have any answers. I'm just saying, I'm wondering the same thing as Teddy. Have any of you ever thought, even like in the back of your head at two in the morning as you fall asleep, about wanting a relationship that means something? Or…or kids?"

Teddy was shredding a paper napkin and feeding the pieces into a sweating glass of melted ice water.

"I have—thought about having kids, at least. After Thomas, I'm not sure if I'll ever be able to trust a man again. I thought I loved him, the fuckhead. I did things with him that I'd normally *never* do—"

"Like what?" Laurel asked—the perennial horn-dog of the group. "Do tell, darling," she drawled in a fake-posh British accent.

Teddy blushed furiously—she was the more intro-verted of us, the least likely to share salacious details. "You know, just…stuff."

"Like what?" Laurel grabbed her arm and shook her back and forth playfully. "I NEED TO KNOW YOUR KINK."

"It's not kink, you weird-ass woman," Teddy half snapped, half laughed. "Until Thomas, I was a va-nilla sex sort of chick. The craziest thing I ever did in bed was doggy style and the occasional cowgirl ride. Thomas was…more adventurous. He wanted…anal. And…um, other stuff."

"Anal isn't that weird," Laurel said. "You just have to be smart about it. Ease into it."

"Okay you know what, Laurel? I really don't need or want to know about your exploits in anal sex." Teddy shuddered. "We tried it once, just a little explor-atory thing, and it was…nope. Nope nope nope, that's output only for this chica." She laughed. "He asked me to peg him once, and that was fun. He wanted me to suck him off, like, all the damn time. It got tiring.

Like, I don't mind doing that, truly. It's not my favorite thing, but if it makes him happy and he'll return the favor, hey, I'm down. Like, hey buddy, I'm not gonna gag myself on your dick—I'll let you my fuck my face for a minute or two, but you just damn well better be ready to go downtown and eat me out afterward, or we're gonna be saying goodbye *real* fast."

There was a concentrated silence, and then we all cracked up, shrieking half-drunk laughter. Teddy was baffled.

"What?" she demanded. "What's so funny?"

"You're just normally so quiet and reserved about that stuff," Kat said. "It's amazing to hear you talk like that. I honestly had always imagined you being kind of a starfish."

Teddy blinked, confused. "A starfish?" She tilted her head. "What the hell does that mean?"

Laurel slumped in her chair, flung her arms out, splayed her legs apart, closed her eyes and opened her mouth, and let out a monotone, robotic groan—kind of a polar opposite version of the Meg Ryan fake orgasm scene. "Oh yeah, oh yeah, right there, yeah."

Teddy's jaw dropped open, and then her expression contorted into a glare. "Excuse me, but that's insulting. I happen to fantastic in bed. Just because I don't generally want to do stupid shit like the Butter Churner and like, the Flying Dutchman with an Upside Down Half Twist or whatever the fuck doesn't mean I don't like sex and don't passionately and energetically get into it." She huffed. "I like sex. I *love* sex. I want lots and lots of really good sex. I just…I want it…to *mean* something." She ducked her head as if preparing for a barrage of castigation from us. "I don't mind a hookup now and then to take care of my needs, but…I want more, I guess. I do. And it's hard, because after Thomas I'm scared of men, of relationships, of trusting like, anyone. But I *want* to."

I continued munching on chips and salsa, because although I was pretty full, it was still only ten and something told me I'd need food in my belly to absorb the berserk amount of booze we were going to consume before the night was over.

"Can we go back to how you've thought about kids?" I said.

Teddy shrugged. "I just…you're the first of us to the big four-oh, but none of us are far behind. And yeah, I think about it sometimes. You know, the whole stereotypical late thirties middle of the night panic about whether I should freeze my eggs in case I meet the perfect guy, wondering if my reproductive clock is ticking down and if I'm cut out to be a mother and if I want to be a mother in the first place, and…you know. That whole schtick."

"Yeah," I said, my voice faint, "that whole schtick."

Kat eyed me. "You too?"

I rolled a shoulder. "I've had thoughts." I frowned

at her. "You can't tell me the thought has *never* crossed your mind. You've *never*, not once, looked a new mom with a baby in a sling as you show them around a house and talk about nurseries and baby gates, and had even the briefest, faintest tingling of wishing you could have that too." I chewed on my own admission a moment. "Especially when her husband is so sweet and fawning, carrying around flowery diaper bags and wearing a spit-up stained shirt and looking at that woman like she hung the damn moon and stars."

Laurel pretended to choke, and then gag. "Oh god, I think I'm gonna be sick. I can't stand that shit."

Zoe blew a raspberry at Laurel. "Oh please, Laur. You have too thought about it. I *know* you have. You can play ice queen sex goddess all you want, but I know you've got a soft little nougaty center in there that's looked at a sweet little baby with rosy cheeks and those little crazy giggles they get when you tickle their widdle bellies and wanted one of your own."

Laurel narrowed her eyes, leaned over the table toward Zoe. "Soft...little...nougaty center? How *dare* you?"

Zoe was unmoved. "Put the façade aside for a moment, Laurel. It's just us, honey. You can be honest with us. We won't think less of you."

Laurel sat back. Considered her glass of margarita as if it held the answers. Her voice was quiet, and we all had to sit forward. "Fine. Yes, okay? I've

thought about it. For, like, ten seconds. And then I remember, oh yeah, I'm the least nurturing, least maternal, least considerate and least selfless bitch you've
ever met in your whole life and I'd be a fucking *terrible* mother."

"I disagree," Kat said. "Remember when I got
strep throat and the flu at the same time? Who took
care of me?"

Laurel sighed. "I did. But you're my friend. And
all I did was bring you soup and medicine."

"And sat with me on the couch for three days,
watching eighties movies and making me a bazillion
smoothies and cleaning up my snot rags because I
couldn't even get up." She touched Laurel's hand.
"You're not *her*, Laurel."

All of us knew what Kat meant—we'd all met
Laurel's mother. Take Cruella de Ville, cross her with
Miranda Priestly, toss in a dash of the evil stepmother
from Cinderella, and top it all off with a liberal sprin-
kling of Lisa Vanderpump, and you've got an idea
what Elise Crane-McGillis was like.

"I was raised by that woman," Laurel said. "And
we all know you become your mother no matter
what you do."

"Bullshit," Kat spat. "I will *never* be my mother.
I refuse." She patted Laurel's hand. "You're *not* her,
Laurel. You play the part well because it serves you
socially and professionally, but we all know you're

really a sweet, thoughtful, caring, wonderful woman underneath."

Laurel blinked rapidly, tipped her head back and let out a gusting sigh. "I'm not drunk enough to get maudlin, goddammit."

I was sitting beside her, and I wrapped an arm around her. "It's not maudlin, babe, it's emotion. And it *is* allowed, you know. We won't tell anyone you have feelings."

"You better not," she whispered, laughing. "I have a reputation to uphold." She eyed me. "Of all people, Lizzy, *you* have had thoughts of wanting a child?"

I shrugged. "Yeah, I have. Like you, I squash it immediately, and usually go have wild and irresponsible sex with a man way too young for me simply to prove a point to myself. But I've had the thoughts." I sighed. "It's hard not to."

"Okay, but can I just point out something that may or may not be obvious but relevant?" Autumn, the peacemaker, the logical one. "Unless you do in vitro with a sperm donor, it's kind of impossible to have a kid without a man. And most men don't like leaving kids just, lying around. They try to avoid that, I think. The good ones, at least. The shitty ones leave kids lying around and don't give a shit, and that's how you end up with Zoe and me."

"I think that's as much about Mom as it is the men, though," Zoe pointed out. "She was the one who got knocked up by a literal transient hobo under a bridge at seventeen, and then went and got knocked up less than six weeks after giving birth…by an orderly at the hospital, no less."

Autumn shrugged and nodded. "True. Mom was a ho." She held up a finger. "But, one could argue that she was a ho because her own dad ran away like a sissy when she was two, and Grandma was left to raise four girls alone at twenty-one with no income and no job skills. Kind of set a tone for our family history. Mom ran away at fourteen because Grandma literally couldn't afford to feed them all and keep the lights on."

We're all rapt, as Zoe and Autumn have always been pretty reticent to spill their family history, which we knew was tough, but not to the degree.

"Let's go back to the original topic," Laurel said, pointing at me. "You, and babies. How *do* you figure to have a baby without first figuring out a relationship? I mean, after your rant, it sounds like you're pretty well dead set against trying to fall in love."

"Love is bullshit," I said, flinging a hand dismissively. "Men aren't capable of it. All they care about is getting their dick wet. Once they're tired of your pussy, they're off to find something younger, tighter, and wetter." I looked away, then down at the table. "Relationships are doomed to fail from day one, and I do *not* fail."

Teddy sighed, an almost pained sound. "I don't

want to agree with you, Lizzy, but it's hard not to. I *want* to believe in love; I *want* to believe that there are good men out there, men who do actually care and are actually capable of real emotion and real depth. And I want to believe I can find him—that we all can."

"And *yet*—who among us has ever found such a specimen?" Kat asked, her sharp dark gaze sweeping us all. "I haven't. Lizzy hasn't. Laurel hasn't. Zoe? Autumn?"

Zoe was quiet. "I…I mean. No?"

"But that doesn't mean they don't exist," Autumn said. "I think they do."

"So do I," Teddy said.

"Good men are like parking spaces," Laurel said. "The best ones are always taken."

"Good men are like bras," Kat said, "the ones that look good are uncomfortable, and the ones that are comfortable are boring and plain and don't flatter you at all."

"Weird comparison," I said, laughing, "but I see what you mean."

"So, what's the answer?" Teddy asked. "How do you get a baby without the expense and hassle of sperm donors and in vitro, if you won't do relationships?"

"The problem is not that men aren't willing to knock a girl up," Kat said. "The problem is either they don't want the responsibility and thus aren't willing to take the chance of a girl trying to tie him down with a baby, or they *do* want to knock you up, but they also want you barefoot and pregnant in the kitchen, making them sandwiches and fetching them beer and slippers."

"That's sexist and untrue," Autumn said.

"Sort of," Zoe said. "I think it's more that they want a trophy wife. They want the respectable appearance of a wife and two-point-five kids without having to give up boinking their secretary and playing golf with their idiot buddies."

"We are a cynical bunch of biddies," Teddy said, cackling. "This is a shitty and cynical conversation."

"Yes, yes it is," I agreed. "But I can't say I don't agree with Zoe and Kat." I apparently have finished yet another margarita, and Laurel is pouring me more. I feel it loosening my tongue even further, but it's my fortieth birthday and fuck it, right? "You know what we need? A billionaire."

Teddy snorts a laugh into her glass. "A billionaire?"

"Yeah, we need a billionaire. Not one to share, we each need one." I dip another chip into salsa. "Jesus, someone take the chips and salsa away from me. I'm pathologically incapable of not eating them if they're in front of me, no matter how full I am."

"Explain," Kat said, taking me at my word and moving the chips and salsa to the other end of the table.

I dip my finger in the salt on my glass rim, lick it off

my finger. "Okay, so...I'm wasted, so this may be the dumbest thing I've ever said. But—but! Think about it: if you give him a contract saying you're not interested in locking him down with a baby, a billionaire is perfect. A young one, mind you, not one of those crusty old guys who made his billions the slow hard way. I'm talking the hot young ones who got rich suddenly. He wouldn't be intimidated by the fact that we're successful and have a shitload of our own money, right? That's point number one—young guys are usually either gold diggers or scared of us because we're more successful than them, and the older ones are usually boring and can't keep up with our flabbergasting sexual prowess, and just want us to settle down and be arm candy or baby machines. I'm not looking for either, right? I want a sexy guy with a big dick and a nice body who can make conversation and doesn't want my money and doesn't want to settle down with me; he doesn't have to be, like, *actually* a billionaire, just someone better off than me so I know he's not looking for a sugar mama. And I want said unicorn man to put a baby inside me the fun way and then get the fuck out of my life. I mean, you read these romance books, and they make it seem like hot young billionaires are a dime a dozen. Throw a stick and you hit six of 'em. So how hard can it be? You just have to find one. They're out there, dammit."

We're all laughing, and none louder than me.

"We could put an ad in the paper!" Laurel said, gesturing with her hand to place imaginary blocks of words in the air. "Beautiful successful single woman, forty, seeks attractive male billionaire to knock her up. No strings. Financial validation required. Serious inquiries only."

"YES!" Kat shouted. "Let's do it! Oh my god, it's so great. You know how many men would line up to answer that ad? We could spend a calendar year on our backs getting plowed by sexy rich guys before we ever even go off birth control! Laurel, you're a motherfucking genius!"

"That's not exactly what I meant," I said. "But… the idea does have merit. It wouldn't be a scam if you're not trying to get money out of them. It's just a way to weed out the too old and too young."

"And plus, you can vet their genes," Autumn said, getting into the spirit of things. "You can select the perfect father that way—it doesn't have to be just financial validation. You could request medical history to make sure they don't have, like heart disease or club feet in their family."

"Clubfeet?" Zoe turned on her sister. "What the hell is wrong with you? Jesus, woman."

"If he's hot, that's all the vetting I need," I said. "I mean, unless you're talking someone adopted, how frequently do you have just one person in the family who's all hot and sexy and everyone else is hit up with the ugly stick? Not often, I'd say. If he's hot, chances are he's got good genes."

"It just goes to my point," I said. "It's a foolproof plan. Billionaires, I'm telling you. Have hot sex, get a baby, and then shoo the guy away with a signed contract saying I don't want a dime from him."

"What if he doesn't want to leave his offspring just wandering around?" Zoe asked.

"Then he wouldn't answer the ad," Kat responded for me. "If you don't want to leave a baby lying around somewhere, you don't go knocking up desperate forty-year-old single women."

"I'm *not* desperate," I said, turning on her. "Are *you* desperate?"

"No, but I'm not the one talking about putting an ad in the newspaper so I get knocked up without risking getting into a relationship."

"I'm not scared of getting into a relationship," I protested, "I just don't want one."

"You are too scared of relationships," Teddy said.

"No, I'm not," I insisted, a little too vehemently. "I just want—"

"What you want is a baby," Kat said. "You just can't admit it."

"Why the hell would I want a baby?" I snapped. "Responsibility. Time away from work. A whole human dependent on me. A human who is helpless and can't eat or sleep or shit without me. I'm not ready for that! Why would I want that?"

"I don't know," Kat said, "why would you? You

bought it up. You just suggested an ad for a billionaire to impregnate you."

"I didn't bring it up, Teddy did!" I pointed at Teddy.

"I did not bring this up! It was her!" Teddy in turn pointed at Laurel. "She started it with her fun fucking and adventure sex bullshit."

Laurel rolled her eyes. "And what does the fact that I enjoy a good vigorous pounding in challenging positions have to do with you biddies suddenly wanting to be mothers? Or having a quote-unquote *meaningful relationship*?" She shook her head. "I just want to be fucked into oblivion, not saddled with a barfing, screaming shit-machine that never sleeps and needs me literally every ten seconds for the next eighteen years. *Or* a baby."

"I mean, we *all* want to be fucked into oblivion," Zoe said. "Who doesn't? Waking up with a sore hoo-ha, walking into work bowlegged, having to think really hard to remember if you had four or *five* orgasms...yes please. Having to fend off the hot but dumb ass-bag who did said vigorous pounding because he thinks you suddenly want him to fuck you like that every day and wants you to call him daddy and is already shopping for a ring because he's never had a pussy like this? Yeah, no."

Laurel shrugged. "I dunno, if I found a guy who could fuck me into oblivion, give me five orgasms a day, *and* can spell his own name without referring to his driver's license? I'd call him daddy and wear his ring. I don't know that I'd marry him, and I certainly wouldn't let his ass knock me up, but shit girl, I'd ride that train for all it's worth."

We all cackled, but it was more that we knew she wasn't kidding. And that most of us felt similarly, to varying degrees.

"And what we're all agreeing is that we could make this a club," I said. "Billionaires to give us all babies."

"The Billionaire Baby Club," Kat said. "Like the Babysitter's Club, but with wild fucking instead of babysitting."

"The Billionaire Baby Club," I repeated. "It does have a certain ring to it."

Laurel looked around the table. "We *are* just talking shit because we're drunk, right?"

There was a chorus of agreement, because of *course* we were all just bullshitting. We were on our, like, the tenth pitcher of strong-ass margaritas, plus the pregame on the bus, and while all of us could hold our liquor like damned professionals, make no mistake, we were hammered.

It was all in good fun.

I didn't want a baby.

I would *not* be putting an ad in the paper for a billionaire to knock me up.

I would go back to finding casual dick the

old-fashioned way—trolling bars and the occasional Tinder date.

Casual Dick.

That's the name of the game for someone like me. No meaning, no responsibility, no future. Just good sex with a decent guy. And great sex every once in a while, with a good guy. And more frequently, meh sex with sub-average ass-bags who couldn't find my clit with both hands and a flashlight even if I gave him turn-by-turn directions *and* drew him a map.

Just jokes, all this.

Babies, clubs, ads…it's all just stupid jokes be-tween a group of drunk and horny friends.

CHAPTER THREE

"AND HERE WE HAVE A BEAUTIFUL OUTDOOR DINING space, complete with a brick pizza oven. The infinity pool, of course, and the built-in hot tub. It all overlooks the city, and I mean come on, can you beat that view?" I stepped to the side so they could admire the view. "I could show you the master suite and tell you all about the acres of handpicked marble and the shower with a rainfall head and no less than eight directional nozzles, and the his-and-hers walk-in closets, but really, do you even need to see it?"

The buyers didn't respond—they were standing at the edge of the yard, where the fence rimmed the abrupt drop-off.

"This view is what you're paying for," I said. "And at an asking price of under ten million, it's a steal. For this square footage, this location, and this view?"

The silent conversation again, their eyes meeting, thoughts exchanged without words. Ugh.

"Why don't I head inside and let you all talk about it?" I suited action to words, heels clicking across the stone.

I fiddled with the folders on the kitchen island, which contained disclosures and glossy pamphlets and my business card. It wasn't long before they came back in, hand in hand, grinning at each other, their agent trailing behind them.

"We'd like to make an offer." He squeezed his husband's hand.

"We'll go in at nine-three," their agent said.

I suppressed a wince. "My clients are seeing a lot of movement on this, and with inventory being what it is right now, there's just not a lot of room for negotiation. I'll bring them whatever you decide, but I'm not sure they're willing to go that low, and I wouldn't want to waste anyone's time." I glanced at their buyer's agent, whom I knew was notorious for underbidding.

The couple stepped away to confer with their agent and came back. "Nine-point-five," the agent said. "And my clients and I feel strongly that that's a very fair offer."

I nodded. "I agree, it is fair. Let's get the paperwork drawn up and I'll send it over to my clients ASAP."

My phone rang at that moment. I held up a finger to the buyers and their agent and headed outside. "This is Lizzy Stephenson," I said.

"Good afternoon," a deep male voice returned. "My name is Walter Alwyn. I am calling in response to the ad you placed last week?"

I stumbled, shocked into imbalance. "The...the ad?"

"Yes. In the LA Times. I was wondering if you'd like to meet for drinks and to discuss...possible terms."

"I...um..."

The ad? They didn't. They did fucking *not*.

"Purely preliminary discussions, you understand. I'm sure we both have questions and concerns to iron out, considering the nature of your ad."

"To be honest, Mr. Alwyn, you've caught me at a bad time. Could I perhaps call you back later?"

"Certainly. This is my direct number, so just call me at your leisure."

"Thank you for calling, Mr. Alwyn, I'll get back to you."

I managed to put it out of my head enough to focus on the offer, which I received and passed along to my clients, who countered with nine-point-seven; I sent that over to the buyer's agent and knew it would take a few hours at least for the buyers and their agent to discuss the counter. All the girls were out when I got back to the office, and I had a slew of emails to answer, paperwork for the pending sale of Gerry's property to work on. I had an ability to tune out almost everything while I was working, so I heard the sounds of my girls coming back and settling in to do their own office work, but I kept my focus on my work.

Finally, I'd chipped away at my mountain of emails and paperwork, at which point it was closing in on five o'clock. The girls were mostly chattering, which meant they were wrapping up their day as well.

I stood up and perched on the edge of my desk. "Ladies, your attention please."

Voices hushed and they all turned to face me; I rarely used my "boss" voice with them, and when I did, they paid attention.

"I received a rather interesting phone call today." I watched some exchanges of nervous glances. "I see you know what I'm talking about."

I waited.

Silence.

"Well?" I tapped my shoe on the floor. "Who placed the ad?"

Laurel raised her hand. "I mean *technically*, I put the actual ad in the actual paper. But it was a group effort. And it was Kat's idea to do actually do it."

"Oh sure, bitch, throw me under the bus why don't you," Kat said, flipping an unsharpened pencil at Laurel, who batted it away.

"Well, it *was*," Autumn said. "But I admit, we all agreed it would be funny."

"Funny?" I glared at them each in turn. "You

know what's *not* funny? Getting a very real phone call from a very real man named Walter Alwyn who seems absolutely serious about meeting with me to discuss 'possible terms.'" I did finger quotes to emphasize the phrase he'd used. "What's not funny is receiving that call while I'm on the verge of selling a ten-million-dollar property that I've been working on for a year and a fucking half."

Embarrassed silence.

I held out my hand. "Let me see it."

Laurel reached under her desk and pulled out her purse—a vintage Louis Vuitton—dug into it, pulled out a folded section of newspaper. She brought it to me, and the ad in question was circled.

Beautiful, successful single woman, 40, seeks attractive male billionaire to impregnate her the old-fashioned way. No strings. NOT seeking sugar daddy. Validation required. Serious inquiries only, please.

I read it through several times. "Impregnate her the old-fashioned way? Not seeking sugar daddy?" I palmed my face. "I can't believe you actually put an ad in the paper. It was a fucking joke! We were *drunk*!"

"This was a joke, too!" Kat yelled.

"It's a real ad in a real newspaper!" I shouted back. "Real people are going to answer. You put my actual personal phone number in it!"

"Laurel!" Kat whirled on her. "You were

supposed to put a fake number in it, you dumb hooker!"

Laurel covered her mouth with her hand. "Oops. My bad."

"What the fuck, Laurel?" Kat glared in turn at Laurel. "Why would you do that?"

"I meant to mix up a few numbers, but then I got a call while I was putting it in, and I guess I must've just put your real number down by accident." She made an *oops* face. "It really was an oversight, honey. I'm sorry."

"I have a question," Teddy said, taking her long brown hair out of the bun and combing her fingers through it. "Who is Walter Alwyn?"

I blinked at her. "Why does it matter?"

She twisted a pencil in her fingers, and then pinched it between her nose and upper lip, eyeing me speculatively, thoughtfully. She shrugged, and the pencil dropped from her nose to the desk. "I dunno. It maybe doesn't. But I'm also thinking…what if our deepest truths come out when we're drunk and we just disguise them as jokes?"

I pressed my fingertips against my temples. "It's too early for this bullshit, Theodora."

"It's five twenty-two in the afternoon, *Elizabeth*." She brushed her fingers across the trackpad of her laptop to wake it up, typed in her password, and then her fingers flew across the keyboard in a flurry of clickety-clacks. "Walter Alwyn…I'll have to guess on the spelling of his last name…oh, here we go. Wait, no, he's in a retirement home in Palm Springs. Oh! Here we are! Walter Alwyn, founder, president, and CEO of Alwyn Medical Supply. He invented…something to do with catheters? Ew. Okay, um, let's see if we can find a recent photo."

"Teddy, why are you looking him up?" I asked. "It was a joke."

She glanced at me over her computer. "Was it, though?"

That gave me a moment's pause.

Was it? I mean, yes.

Maybe.

It was, right?

"Oh come on," I groaned. "Like I'd really let some random guy just…impregnate me? I don't even want a baby!"

Kat walked over to me. Held my shoulders. "Lizzy, honey. Sweetheart. Darling."

I rolled my eyes. "Kat, snookums, sugar dump-ling. What?"

"Remember that party we went to?" She arched an eyebrow, and I knew what she was referring to, but I played dumb. "The Baby Incident? At that big swanky party for that gargantuan mega-estate. Don't tell me you don't remember."

Of course I remembered.

Every realtor and agent and broker in a

two-hundred-mile radius had been invited, because it was a high eight-figure list price, nudging up to nine figures. Massive place, dripping in ostentatious luxury, owned by a revolving door of A-list actors, musicians, and athletes. I hadn't expected to get the listing, but hell, I'd go to a good party just for the fun of it, and because you can never network too much. I'd decked myself out in a little red number that flirted heavily with the Venn diagram overlap of classy, sexy, and slutty. We'd networked, and I'd actually gotten some work out of that party, a couple good mid-price listings. But what she was referencing was the Baby Incident. Deserving of the capital letters, it had been a bizarre experience.

One of the brokers in attendance had brought his wife and infant daughter, which was…acceptable, but a bit passé at best. He'd gotten promptly wasted, and his poor wife had spent most of the evening chasing him around babysitting his drunk ass while also trying to care for her baby, who was cranky and difficult—which I suppose was understandable since the party had gone late into the night, well past what I imagine is a normal hour for an infant.

I know nothing about babies, as has been established—but the poor woman had been at her wit's end and no one seemed inclined to help. So I, tipsy enough to do stupid things but sober enough to do them responsibly, had offered to help. I'd figured she'd

have me call a cab for her drunk-as-a-skunk idiot husband, or…or something innocuous. Instead, she'd
dumped her screaming, squalling infant child into my
arms with a tearful sigh of relief, and had immediately hauled her husband out the door, literally dragging him. And left me there with a screaming baby.

So I started singing to it. What else was I supposed to do? Wonder of wonders, however, the little
creature had stopped screaming and stared at me with
something like puzzled interest. The crowd around
me had burst into hopeful applause, since the baby
had been squalling without bothering to even breathe
for at least an hour, and so I kept singing. I sang every
song I knew, awkwardly holding a baby whose name
I didn't even know. It, she, whatever—the baby—had
gone drowsy, and then her head had lolled onto my
bare shoulder, and then I'd been stuck holding a sleeping infant, which had felt like holding a live grenade.

At the time it had been raw panic, like what the
fuck now? Why am I holding a baby? Somebody take
it! No one dared, though, mainly I think because no
one else in attendance had children, or if they had it
was years past, but also because no one dared rouse
the little terror.

If I was being honest with myself, the panic had
also come from how weirdly *not* weird it had felt to
hold the sleeping child.

Half an hour later, the mother had come back,

looking furious but alone, and retrieved her baby from me. She'd thanked me profusely, apologized to everyone for her husband, and had unceremoniously toted her lolling, floppy-limbed daughter out of the party.

I'd dragged Kat back to my house and refused to talk about it, decisively not laughing at any of her jokes or insinuations about ovaries and babies and calling me mama and mommy and mommy dearest for days and days.

Since then, I've resolutely and fanatically avoided holding any more babies.

That soft squishy feeling I'd gotten somewhere in my chest had been scary and I hadn't liked it at all.

"Nope," I said to Kat. "Not recalling."

Kat cackled. "Liar, liar pants on fire."

"I'm wearing a skirt," I said. "Not pants. And nope, no fire."

"What'd you tell Walter Alwyn?" Teddy asked.

"That it was a bad time and I'd call him later." I shrugged.

She pivoted her laptop on the desk to show me a photograph she'd found online. "A silver fox, for sure."

That was generous. He was good-looking, sure, if you liked sixty-five-year-old men who sold pee tubes. It was a shoulders-up photo, but he looked trim and lean, with clean-cut hair that was silvery-white and a clean-shaven jaw. He gave off pretty decent Anderson Cooper vibes.

I shook my head at Teddy. "I'm going to call him and tell him it was all a misunderstanding."

"Okay, but he's hot for an older guy!" Kat said.

"Just talk to him," Zoe urged.

"No!" I stood up, paced away. "For one thing, even if I was serious about any of this, which I'm not…what makes you think I want to bang Grandpa? I'm into younger men, remember? No offense to Mr. Alwyn, but I'm not about to get knocked up by a man twenty-five years my senior. Also, I'm forty and he's sixty-five…that's just asking for fertility issues. Again, *if* I had been serious about the billionaire baby club idea, I'd pick a hot younger guy shooting lots of hot young spermies with a higher chance of latching onto my aging ova."

There was a lot of laughter at that, and Autumn spluttered. "Hot young spermies?" She gestured at the photograph of Walter Alwyn. "I dunno, Lizzy, he looks pretty spry. I bet he could fill you with you some hot spermies, just maybe not hot *young* spermies. Beggars can't be choosers, you know."

"Well then good thing I'm not a beggar. And also, worth noting here—I'm *not* going along with this."

"Hear me out," Zoe said. "But what if you did?"

"I'm not. Take the ad down." I turned away from the room to shut down my laptop and gather my things, more as an emphasis of finality than out of a need or desire to actually do it.

"Lizzy," Kat murmured, still standing close to me. "Think about it. Maybe not this Walter guy, but if you got another response from someone more in your age bracket, maybe it's worth thinking about going along with it, even if just one step at a time."

I resolutely shook my head. "No."

"Why not?" Kat moved to stand directly in front of me. "You said at your party that you didn't want any more drunk hookups, that you were tired of them. Maybe this is the chance to find…something else."

"Like love," Teddy muttered, but low, as if she didn't want the rest of us to hear it.

I heard it. "Teddy, I'm *not* husband hunting."

"I'm not saying you are," she said. "You can want a man who cares about you and not be looking for a ring and a house in the suburbs with a white picket fence."

"You're always on the run, Lizzy," Autumn said. "You never slow down. You work more than any of us. You never let yourself have anything but the quick and easy stuff. We just…like Kat said, and you said yourself, you're tired of hookups. Shit, I think we all are. It was a drunk joke, yes, but Teddy put it best— sometimes your deepest secrets come out when you're drunk. And I think you want something else. I'm not saying, like, a *meaningful relationship*, necessarily, but something different. And you'd never slow down long enough to find it yourself."

I collected my purse turned away. "I'm going home."

Kat grabbed my arm. "We were trying to do something for you that you wouldn't do for yourself."

"You take care of us," Laurel said, in a rare serious moment. "You sent us all on all-inclusive vacations last year. You closed the whole brokerage down for a week so we could all go. But you didn't go. You stayed and kept working. You took all of our appointments for us."

"You called in that favor to get me my condo," Teddy said.

"You took a serious chance on hiring Autumn and me," Zoe said. "We were new to the business, you didn't know us all that well, yet you still hired us. And you showed us the ropes, gave us good listings."

I huffed. "What does any of this have to do with anything?" I headed for the door again. "So, I'm not a shitty person. You're my friends—of course I take care of you."

"The point is," Laurel said. "This was us doing something for you."

"By putting my real phone number in a newspaper want ad?"

"Yes!" Kat snapped. "Because you'd never bust out of your little work-hookup bubble on your own. You said yourself you want something different. But *do* you, like *actually*? Or was that just drunken nonsense?

Because I think you do want something different, you just don't know how to make yourself get out of your own way to try and get it."

"A baby," I whispered. "It was about babies. Not men."

"So you *do* want a baby," Teddy said.

I groaned in frustration. "I don't *know!*" I yelled. "I don't know! Do I? It sounds stupid. Why would I want a baby? A baby would mess up my life. But Teddy, you fucking…you got my brain going and now I can't stop thinking about it. It's not like I'm super upset about turning forty, you know? Yeah, it's a milestone, but I don't, like, feel *old*. I just don't *know*. I don't know. I'm confused. I don't know what I want. I just want…*more*. Something more in my life." I pushed past Kat, marching for the back door. "Now I'm *actually* going home."

I heard a flurry of whispers, including an exchange that sounded as if they were discussing whether I'd actually meant the order to take down the ad, but I couldn't be sure and coming back to demand to know would ruin the efficacy of my dramatic departure.

I'd decided to hold off on the new car for a while longer, so when I climbed into my car it was the same midnight blue Miata convertible I'd been driving for nearly twenty-five years. Even if and when I did get a new car, I wouldn't get rid of my Miata—driving it was comforting to me, like putting on a favorite cardigan. I put the top back, tied my hair into a bun and plopped my custom-made, Swarovski-blinged Six Chicks Realty ball cap onto my head; I whipped out into traffic and decided to take the longer scenic route home.

My home was a penthouse condo in a little boutique building overlooking the ocean. It had cost a hell of a pretty penny, but it was worth every single one. Two bedrooms, two bathrooms, and a little over three thousand square feet, it was comprised of at least sixty percent master suite. The actual bedroom itself was fairly small, big enough for a king bed, a bureau, a bookshelf, and a little seating area in the corner near the door to my balcony, the rest of the space was a colossal walk-in closet with God's own organizational system, and a marble paradise of a bathroom. The closet featured a wall dedicated entirely to purses, another wall for shoes, an island for jewelry and accessories with a small built-in bench seat, and rack after rack for my clothes. The bathroom had a soaking tub and a walk-in shower and a makeup vanity…

My home was my haven. I'd gotten it before it was even done being built, so my personal taste and design aesthetic had informed the final build.

I poured myself a glass of wine and took it out onto my balcony, put my feet up on the railing and watched the rollerbladers and the runners and the power walkers and the moms in pairs with fancy strollers and designer leggings even though they would barely work up to breathing hard. Beyond, the surf crashed and surfers rode the waves, and swimmers bobbed and laughed.

The Billionaire Baby Club. I couldn't believe they'd actually done it—those crazy-ass bitches had actually put the ad in.

I didn't believe for a second that Laurel had mistakenly used my actual number. I'd seen the woman talk on the phone closing a multi-million-dollar sale, type on her computer, and shoot off a text all at the same time; multitasking was her thing. So, nothing as pedestrian as getting a phone call would be enough to make the unflappable Laurel McGillis commit a mistake like that.

She'd done it on purpose.

A thought niggled at the back of my head, though. One I couldn't quite dislodge.

What if...?

Yeah, I know—it's stupid. Ridiculous. Idiotic. Nonsensical.

I didn't want a *baby*.

I discovered I'd finished my glass of wine but decided against pouring a second—despite the over-the-top amount of alcohol consumed at my party, I didn't drink much more than a glass or two for the most part. Instead, I held my empty glass and watched the sun turn the ocean orange.

And wondered—*did* I want a baby? Was it just my biological clock going bonkers because I'd turned forty? Or was it something more? Something deeper?

Either way, Walter Alwyn deserved to be let off the hook gently, so I called him back.

He answered on the third ring. "Hello?"

"Good evening, Mr. Alwyn. We spoke earlier—you called me about the ad."

"Ah, yes. I admit you have me at an advantage—you know my name, but I don't know yours."

I swallowed. "My name is Elizabeth. Um. The truth is, that ad was…"

"Too good to be true?" He sounded like he was laughing, a little. "I figured. But hey, it was worth a shot. And for what it's worth, you sound like you're a beautiful woman."

"I just figured I owed you at least a call—"

"It's all right. No need to explain, Elizabeth. Have a good evening."

I hesitated. "Mr. Alwyn…I have a question, if you don't mind."

A brief pause. "Shoot."

"Would you have gone through with it?"

"I'd have taken it one step at a time. I'd need an NDA, probably, and some kind of a contract stipulating my money was not any part of the deal. If you're beautiful and successful and you just want a baby but don't want to go the…clinical route? I understand that. And to be perfectly honest with you, Elizabeth, a large part of the reason I answered the ad was because I'm not getting any younger and I've never married and honestly probably never will, but something inside me still wants to see my family line continue, to some degree. Perhaps not my name, but… some part of me, to pass on into the world. Crazy, maybe, but there's the truth." A chuckle. "And hey, making babies the old-fashioned way is my second favorite pastime."

"Second favorite," I said, laughing. "What's your first?"

"Making money, of course."

"Well, thank you for your candor, Mr. Alwyn."

"Of course." Another pause. "If you ever change your mind, or if you happen to find yourself in need of the company of an older unmarried man with more money than he knows what to do with, just give me a call."

"I'll keep that in mind," I said. "Goodbye, Mr. Alwyn."

"Goodbye, Elizabeth."

The call ended, I set the phone on my thigh and considered some more.

Making babies the old-fashioned way.

Be honest with yourself, Lizzy. I heard Kat's voice in my head, because she was always somehow my better angel on one shoulder and the devil on the other, at the same time.

Did I want a baby?

A real baby that was mine. A baby that had

grown in my personal uterus for nine months, which was then all mine to raise alone, which was dependent on me.

My life would change, totally.

I'd need time off of work after I'd had it. I'd need a sitter, or the baby would have to go to work with me and go to showings…

The building my office was in had an available unit above mine which was used mainly for storage by the owner. I'd looked into it before, in case I wanted to expand and needed more floor space for new agents. But, in an alternative universe where I had a baby, I *could* feasibly, rent it and turn it into a nursery, so there would be somewhere on site for him or her to take naps and such, away from the bustle of the office itself, which saw a decent amount of traffic in the form of clients coming in to sign paperwork, and god knows the girls are never exactly quiet.

Wait…

I was actually considering it?

I think I was.

Advertising for a hot young rich guy to bang me, knock me up, and go away.

Was I really that crazy?

Yes. Yes, I was.

CHAPTER FOUR

NINE THIRTY THE NEXT MORNING. I WAS JUST BACK FROM an early showing of a penthouse in a condo building not far from mine. It hadn't netted an offer, but they'd said it was in the top three, but they had to see a few more before they made a final decision.

The girls were all in the office at the same time, a rarity for this time of day.

"Do hot young billionaires even read the actual newspaper?" I asked, apropos of seemingly nothing.

There was a moment of silence, and then Zoe snickered. "Someone was up late thinking."

"I was just thinking…*if,* and it's still a big if, I was to play along with this stupid joke of an idea…would we even get the right kind of audience engagement in a newspaper?" I flipped a pen around my middle finger. "Newspapers are more of an older audience, I think."

"So what, then, an Instagram ad?" Autumn suggested.

I laughed. "Yeah, a sexy photo of me in a bikini, asking for rich guys to come fuck me. That's the perfect idea."

"I mean, that *is* the general gist," Laurel said.

I frowned and held up a finger. "No, the idea is for *one* guy, the *right* guy, to fuck me. Not, like, an open casting call for a gang bang."

Autumn eyed me. "So, Lizzy." She put her chin in both hands, elbows braced on her desk. "You're thinking about it."

I shrugged. "I'm not ruling it out. It could be fun."

"It's looney," Zoe said, grinning. "I love it."

"I just…" I sighed again. "Am I completely nuts for even considering a baby at all, regardless of the manner of conception? Like, where is this even coming from? I'm a single girl, a career woman, bachelorette for life. Why am I all of a sudden contemplating the utter absurdity of the responsibility of a *child*?"

Teddy smiled at me. "It's crazy, yes, but also…it's not. Not entirely. I know you don't think so, but you *are* a nurturing person, Lizzy. You've enjoyed your life as a single woman focused on her career, but a lot of that focus, especially over the last few years, has been on the five of us. It's time to do something for yourself, Lizzy. I think this could be a process you could enjoy. And I mean finding the right one, the right guy to, um, help you have a baby."

I blew a raspberry. "You might be right. It still

sounds like a ridiculous way to go about it, but hell, normal is boring, right? So I may as well try this the crazy way." I pointed a finger at Laurel. "I know you put my personal number in there on purpose. Fix it. I'll give it a shot, but there's got to be a better way to go about this than random men calling my personal phone number while I'm trying to sell houses."

Laurel smirked. "I admit nothing. But I *do* have some ideas." She used an elegant finger to nudge a twisting tendril of sun-colored hair away from her eye. "You trust me, Lizzy?"

I snorted. "Not a bit, darling, not a bit. But I'll play along."

She rolled her eyes at me. "You do too. I house-sat for you while you were in Barbados. And you don't trust just anyone to take care of your condo. That's your first baby."

"No, my first baby is my Miata." I laughed. "My condo is my second."

Autumn tapped her chin, eyeing me thoughtfully. "You know, Lizzy, I know you've gone to look at that Porsche a few times now, but if you're looking at having a baby, you might need to reconsider a two-seat sports car."

I groaned. "I know, I know. I drove past the dealership the other day and almost stopped in to buy it, and something made me hold off." I smirked. "I *do* like the Panamera. Four full seats, but it's still got all the sexiness of a Porsche. And I'll still have my Miata for the top-down, wind-in-my-hair experience."

Autumn rolled her eyes and shook her head; my penchant for very nice things was a well-known weakness.

Kat had clients come in then to go over paperwork, so our conversation was put on hold, and then I had another showing, this one a place a good forty minutes north. That showing went well but didn't net an offer; they said it was too small and they wanted something with acreage. I was on the drive back down to the office with the top back and my favorite playlist slamming on the fuzzy speakers via my aux cord to my phone. My phone rang, a number I didn't recognize. Not unusual by any stretch of the imagination, but a frisson down my spine made me wonder if maybe this was another call in response to the ad.

I let it ring four times, thinking I'd just let it go to voicemail, but then some idiot curiosity had me sticking my AirPods into my ears and answering.

"Hello, this is Lizzy."

"Hi, um. I'm calling about the ad."

Fuck. I knew it.

"Uh, hi." What do I say? What do I say? "About that, I—"

"I'm not exactly a billionaire, not yet, but I'm valued pretty damn close to it and I'm only thirty-seven, and I saw the ad and I figured it was a joke, but hey, you never know so I'm just calling to see if it was real, and if you maybe wanted to meet for coffee." He sounded…nervous. "We could talk. If you're for real about it."

"How about…" Shit, was I really going to do this? It was pure craziness. "Can you put a little portfolio together for me and text it to this number? Some current photographs. Like, um, so I know you're you and it's not a catfish or some shit. How about a photograph of yourself where you're holding a, um…a rutabaga."

A deafening pause.

God, I'm an idiot.

He cleared his throat. "I don't even know what a rutabaga is."

"Me either!"

"So…"

"I'll look it up when I'm not driving."

"Weird flex, but okay." He laughed. "Fine. A selfie with a rutabaga, whatever the hell that is. Anything else?"

"A basic bio. Who you are, what you do. Any relevant medical issues. Stuff like that."

"Okay." Another pause. "So…this is real? Like actually?"

I laughed. "Maybe? Honestly it's a bit complicated."

"Complicated." He laughed again—he had a nice laugh, smooth and mellow and genuine. "Maybe I should ask for the same from you? Photo with a kumquat, and a short bio." Another laugh. "This feels oddly like meeting someone from Tinder, you know?"

"Except it's the old school version."

"Classified Ads: the O-G Tinder."

Were we…flirting?

"What's your name?" I asked. "First only, for now."

"Braun."

"Like brains over brawn?" I asked.

"Well, it's spelled differently, but yeah, sort of. B-R-A-U-N."

"Braun. Well, Braun, I'm Lizzy. Nice to meet you, sort of."

"Nice to meet you too, sort of." He laughed yet again, and I was already starting to like his laugh. "This is a bit weird, you know."

"It's *really* weird." I sighed. "But hey. Just wait till you meet me."

"Are you weird, Lizzy?"

"I mean." I cackled. "Define weird. I don't wear shoes on my head, and I don't speak Klingon."

"If that's your parameters for weirdness, I think we'll be fine. I don't do either of those myself, but I should probably admit now that I'm a computer nerd."

"A computer nerd, huh?" I found myself grinning ear to ear. "Like, with a pocket protector and dental headgear and pressed khakis with a button-down and loafers?"

"I said computer nerd, not utterly hopeless." One of his laughs. "But. I *did* have headgear from seventh grade through freshman year. And there *was* a time where I dressed like a forty-year-old accountant. But those phases have passed. I wear jeans and a T-shirt most of the time, don't wear braces anymore, and have never had a pocket protector."

"I see. I can probably work with that."

"How benevolent of you to accept my mortal foibles." His end of the line was muffled for a moment, and I heard him speaking to someone else, and then it clarified again. "Sorry about that. So, what do you do?"

"I'm a luxury real estate broker."

"Ooh, fancy."

"Oh yeah, I'm super bougie."

"Do you have any single item that can fit inside your house that costs more than, say, three thousand dollars?"

"Um." I had several. "Yes?"

"Bougie."

"I *did* admit to it. I am bougie, but I'd say I'm not high-maintenance."

"I can probably work with that."

"How benevolent of you to accept my mortal foibles," I said, laughing.

"Hey, so I have to go," Braun said. "I'll text you the photo with the rutabaga later tonight."

"And you asked for…what was it?"

"A kumquat. It's a fruit, I think."

"Rutabagas are vegetables, I believe, but I could be mistaken."

"I think you're right. But I guess we'll find out."

"Goodbye for now, Braun," I said. "Talk to you later."

"See ya."

Would I? See him, I mean. I hadn't expected to have an actual conversation with him, a perfect stranger who'd replied to an ad about knocking up someone up.

So crazy. Possibly idiotic. But also…kind of genius.

I stopped by a market on the way home and found some kumquats. They were small orange fruit, about the size of a large olive. I bought a few, along with some fresh chicken and asparagus to make for dinner; I liked to cook and tried to make fresh whole food for myself a few times a week at least, rather than living off of carryout and dine-in all the time.

When I got home, I left the kumquats on the counter while I preheated the oven and seasoned the chicken and asparagus. Once they were in the oven, I poured a glass of wine, took the kumquats out onto my deck and considered this whole nutty idea once more.

I could just use this as a weird way to meet a guy. Like, meet, have dinner and drinks a few times, see if we click, and if we did, screw him. If not, screw him in the other sense. But the ad had been about knocking me up. As in, with a stated goal of getting me pregnant. Which, considering I wasn't on the hunt for a boyfriend—I hated that term, but calling someone a lover was even weirder, and saying partner made it sound like I was gay which I had no problem with, but it just gave off the wrong impression, so it was a conundrum I could never figure out and always ended up avoiding it altogether by just not dating anyone longer than a week or two…

Wait, where was I?

Oh. Considering I wasn't on the hunt for a *relationship*, meant whatever this was would be more like a friends-with-benefits situation, minus the condoms and with the addition of a built-in escape clause.

So, all it really was, was sex.

Until I got pregnant, and then it was my issue to figure out.

Weird. I'd spent my entire adult life frantically avoiding pregnancy—I'd gotten on birth control at sixteen, after my mother had caught me in a heavy petting situation with my boyfriend in his car—and here I was about to consciously engage in sex with a stranger with the stated intent of ending up pregnant.

I'm such a dumbass.

I couldn't tell my parents, that's for sure. Dad would have a heart attack, and Mom would disown me.

But…I was sick of doing things the way I'd been doing it, in terms of relationships and sex. This may be, on the face of it, just another way of hooking up, but at the end of it, I'd be in a whole new phase of life and hookups and all that nonsense would be over.

I set my wine down, cupped a handful of the kumquats, and snapped a few selfies from different angles, and then flipped through them. A few I deleted, a couple I saved and went back and forth, debating. In one, the angle was flattering, but in the other, I liked my smile better.

Screw it, send both.

So, I did, with a short message: *Lizzy Stephenson. 40. Single, never married or engaged, never been pregnant. Real estate broker based in Malibu. I own my own brokerage and employ my five closest friends—our firm is Six Chicks Real Estate.*

I sent it, along with the photos, and then sat down with my feet up, sipping my wine and waiting for my food to be done.

I wondered what kumquats tasted like. I googled it, and it said to eat them whole, peel and all, so I popped one in my mouth—and was pleasantly surprised, I ate another. Inspiration struck, and I snapped a selfie of myself with a kumquat in my mouth and sent it before I could reconsider. It didn't come across sexual, fortunately, more just silly and kinda funny.

My timer went off, so I headed in and checked on

my chicken—it needed a few more minutes—and my asparagus—pretty much perfect. So I plated the asparagus and put the chicken back in.

DING: my phone jangled with a text message alert.

Braun Bennet, 37. Tech start-up owner. I invented an app that tracks and compiles data into graphs and charts for business owners. Essentially, say you have a presentation to make with a business proposal and you need all sorts of graphs and charts, my app is an easier way to input the data and get a spiffy graphic. There's widgets for movement and animation and all sorts of technical stuff like that. I sold it to a big-time investor for a nice chunk of change, and now I'm working on my next app.

The message came through first, and I read it, and while I was reading, my phone *blooped*, and a photo came through.

Oh.

Oh my.

What a snack. Sharp cheekbones, that's the first thing I noticed. Heavy five-o'clock shadow, dark. Big deep dark eyes framed by thick-rimmed round glasses. Messy wild hair a shade that wasn't quite black and wasn't quite brown. It wasn't long, and it looked like it had been recently cut, but either he ran his hands through it regularly or he just didn't bother combing it. Either way, it was sexy as fuck.

Nerd-sexual. OMG yes. There was a silver strand or two near his temples, and smile lines around his eyes that gave him a more mature look, but overall he looked boyish and attractive. Three years younger than me, well within acceptable hookup range, according to my normal standards.

He was holding a handful of root vegetables that looked like turnips, bulbous and reddish-brown and hanging from his fist by long green leaves. He had a big goofy grin on his face, and I could hear his laugh in my head, and I bet that laugh and that grin would be goofy and charming and contagious.

I wondered if he was rocking a dad bod, or that sexy skinny not quite ripped look. Hard to tell from the photo, but he seemed pretty lean. I wasn't super picky about body type—I didn't love the bulgy muscle WWF look, but neither did I have a thing for dad bods. Anything in between was fine by me, as long as you presented yourself well. Clean clothes, nice clothes. You didn't have to be decked out in the latest men's haute couture, but don't come at me in sweatpants and a dirty T-shirt. I liked abs, and strong legs were a must.

I wondered what Braun's type was. Blonde and busty? Supermodel skinny? Or maybe he liked a big booty Judy?

I was two out of those three, and not skinny, so you do the deduction.

Braun: *So. What's next?*

Me: *Not sure, TBH. Never done anything like this before. This isn't a Tinder hookup, or I'd suggest we meet for drinks. Are you in Silicon Valley?*

Braun: *Actually, no. I invented my app with some help from friends while working at a bar in LA and attending Caltech. Once I sold it, I saw no real reason to move all the way down there, since I could work on another app just as easily here, so I stayed.*

Me: *Did you finish your degree?*

Braun: *Yeah. I figured why not? I had the money, suddenly, so I paid off my debt and finished faster than I would've since I didn't have to work at the bar anymore.*

Me: *What's your next app?*

Braun: *it's a secret. LOL. No, really. I was contracted by a non-public corporation to develop an exclusive, in-house app. It's in the IT world, and it's super specific and super technical, so even if I could talk about it, unless you're into information technology and cloud networking, you're not going to find it interesting anyway.*

Me: *Wow, that's kinda cool, actually. Can I pretend you just admitted to being a spy?*

Braun: *LOL sure. It's sexier than talking about data transfer rates and server farms.*

Me: *So, Mr. Spy. This whole thing is kinda weird, right? I'm not sure what I'm doing or how to go about it, so I'm honestly just winging it. Why don't we meet for drinks?*

Braun: *Sounds good. I'm not much for drinking, though, so how about we do coffee instead? Tomorrow, 98am? I can pop up to Malibu if it's easier.*

Me: *98am? Is that some kind of new techie way of telling time?*

Braun: *LOL yeah, absolutely. I just have big thumbs and suck at typing on cell phones. So you'll have to forgive the occasional egregious typo. What I meant was, NINE O'CLOCK ANTEMERIDIAN. You name the place.*

I named my favorite local coffeehouse. *See you at NINE O'CLOCK ANTEMERIDIAN.*

Braun: *A real ballbuster, huh?*

Me: *Yep.*

Braun: *I can probably work with that.*

Me: *LOL. See you tomorrow.*

He sent a waving hand emoji, and I laughed, because I had a feeling he liked having the last word. Which would be fun, since I also enjoyed having the last word. So, I sent a GIF of Tom Hanks from *Forrest Gump*, where he's waving goofily.

Braun: *I have a top-secret spy app to work on. If you don't stop texting me, this conversation will never be over and I'll never get anything done and I'll get fired and it will be your fault. Do you really want that on your conscience?*

I waited a good five minutes, at which point my chicken was done. I dished myself up, and realized I'd eaten almost all the asparagus while I was messaging with Braun, so I just ate the chicken standing up. I was grinning.

I sent him a GIF of Shirley Temple looking bored.

Half an hour later, he sent me a GIF of Will Smith in a suit rubbing his middle finger against his forehead.

My phone rang, then, the burbling ringtone that signified a FaceTime call.

I answered it, and it was the whole gang, in a six-way video call. I sighed. "Ohmygod. What? What do you all want?"

"We just wanted to inform you that we took the ad out of the paper," Laurel said. "We're working on alternatives as we speak, and we wanted to know if you were totally opposed to an Instagram ad, just not, like, actually you in a bikini."

"Actually…" I bit my forefinger knuckle. "I may have already arranged to meet someone for coffee tomorrow morning."

Silence.

"Like, someone who called about the ad before we took it down?" Autumn asked.

"Yeah."

"WHO IS IT?" Came a chorus of shouts.

"His name is Braun Bennet. He developed and sold an app, and he's super cute."

"You looked him up?" Kat asked, around a mouthful of something.

"We, um, we've been texting. He sent me a selfie, and I sent him one."

Laurel looked dumbfounded. "You sent him a selfie." Her voice was flat, disbelieving. "You *never* send selfies."

It was true—I didn't. I thought they were typically tacky and self-aggrandizing. My social media feed featured real estate photography, food, and links to my latest listings. Never a selfie of me, ever.

"Well, this was a special occasion."

"How do you know it was him?" Teddy asked.

"Because we stipulated weird things to make sure. He sent me a photo of himself holding rutabaga, and I sent him one holding kumquats. Which are actually pretty tasty." I held up the remaining fruit for the camera to pick up.

"What the shit is a rutabaga?" Kat asked. "And whose idea was *that*?"

"It's a root vegetable like a turnip, apparently, and mine."

Autumn's video went grainy for a moment, and then glitched, froze, and resumed. "And you're meeting him tomorrow?"

I pinch the bridge of my nose. "Yeah, I guess so."

"You're really doing this," Zoe said.

I inhaled deeply, let it out slowly. "I'm just meeting him, to start with. We'll see how it goes from there."

"But you're really considering it," Zoe pressed.

I shrugged. "I mean, yeah. You idiots talked me into it, and now I can't get the idea out of my head. I've been doing life in a routine for years now, with no variation. And unless I make a significant alteration to my routine, things will just stay the same in an endless loop of showings and casual sex and hanging out with you biddies. And...I guess I want something different. This, as crazy as it is, seems like it could be a fun way of shaking things up."

"By having unprotected sex with a complete stranger." Autumn arched an eyebrow.

"Wait, so now that I'm actually taking steps to doing this cockamamie plan, you're rethinking it?" I asked, incredulous. "*You* put the ad in the paper with my *real phone number*."

"That was Laurel," Zoe said.

"I didn't honestly think any real, viable billionaires would respond," Laurel said, sounding chagrined, a complicated expression on her face, a mixture of humor and embarrassment. "I figured you'd get a few dozen funny prank calls and then we'd take the ad down. Like, you'd have to screen your calls for a while, but it was supposed to be funny. I also didn't think you were serious about this when I did it."

"But still, Laurel, you ought to know better," I said.

She sighed. "You're right, I did and I do, and I apologize."

"Apology accepted," I said.

"I have a question, though: how is what Lizzy is doing any different than sleeping once with some random dude you met on Tinder? The only difference is the end goal. And obviously you'd both have to get clean bills of sexual health." Kat chomped noisily on a pretzel stick. "And you'd have to have a contract for him saying you're not after his money, and something about how you're not interested in having him in the child's life." A frown. "Would you prevent him from knowing the child, if he wanted to?"

I blinked. "I hadn't even considered that. What if he does? I don't know. I guess it would depend on…if I like him or not. Like, as a person, after the sex is over. Because we all know that once you've fucked a guy, you find out either you continue to like who they are, or more frequently, they're douchebags and you can't fathom what made you go home with them."

"What if you sleep with this guy one time and he goes full asshole afterward?" Teddy asked.

I shrugged. "Back to the drawing board? You guys could go ahead with whatever plan you were concocting."

"Lizzy…" Kat trailed off, sighed. "What if you end up actually *liking* this guy?"

"I won't. I'm forty years old and I've never met, slept with, dated, or even spoken to a man who made me want to spend more than twenty-four hours in his presence. The lone exception is Ahmed, and the only reason I kept seeing him as long as I did is because he was overseas ninety percent of the time, and we had an agreement that our relationship was nonexclusive. So I slept around while he was gone, and he did too. We just hooked up while he was in town. It was convenient, and the sex was fantastic. But he was boring to talk to. Like, whoa. All he wanted to talk about was business, this vineyard, that distillery, blah fucking blah. And honestly, I rarely spent more than, like, a handful of hours with Ahmed at any one time. We'd meet for dinner, drink wildly expensive wine, and then we'd go back to his place to fuck. Once we were done, I'd go home. There was no pillow talk, no real intimacy. And that's the way I like it. Thus, the brilliance of this arrangement."

"What will you do about sex after you've had a baby?" Laurel asked.

I shrugged. "I figured you guys would babysit for me. If it's a hookup for sex purposes only, I don't see any reason to even have to mention the baby, right?" I shook my head and waved my hands. "I'm getting ahead of myself. First things first, and that's to have coffee with Braun Bennet."

"It's a cool name, at least," Teddy said.

I bit my lip, considering. "Hold on." I pulled up our group text thread and sent over his selfie. "That's him."

"Holy hot nerd," Kat said. "Yum. I'd fuck him."

"So would I," Teddy said.

"You are all so crass," Laurel said, playing the arch, elegant lady with impeccable manners.

"You would chew him up and spit him out in seconds," Kat said, with a snorting laugh. "Don't play like you're any less crass than we are, Laurel McGillis."

"Whatever," Laurel said, inspecting her fingernails in a show of insouciance.

"We expect a full sitrep the moment your meeting is over," Zoe said.

"Sitrep?" Teddy asked. "Is that, like, a new exercise?"

"Situation report," Zoe clarified. "It's government slash military slang for 'give us the details.'" She smirked. "The last guy I dated was military, and I got him to teach me some fun lingo."

"I'll be into the office once it's over, so of course you'll get a full report."

"And if you sleep with him, we expect all the dirty details," Kat said, wiggling her eyebrows in a silly but suggestive manner.

I rolled my eyes. "I'm not going to have sex with the guy after a nine a.m. coffee date."

"You might," Kat said. "If you like him enough."

"There's a lot of logistics we'd have to work out first," I said. "This isn't a sex-only hump-and-dump date."

"Yeah, you're choosing a man to inseminate you," Laurel said. "Kind of a big deal, actually."

"Isn't the term 'inseminate' only for having semen put in you artificially?" Teddy asked. "I think it is. I think the term here is 'impregnate.'"

"Inseminate makes it sound like I'm a prize mare," I said. I rubbed my face. "This is stressing me out. Let me just get through coffee with him first, okay? I need to go—I have to choose my outfit."

"You should wear the red dress," Kat said, smirking and then biting her lip.

"If she wore that, I'm not sure the poor man would let her leave the coffeehouse without impregnating her," Laurel said. "No straight male stands a snowball's chance in hell against Lizzy in the red dress."

"I'm *not* wearing the red dress," I said. "No way. It's coffee, not a black-tie dinner party."

The red dress was my secret weapon. The single most expensive thing I owned after my condo—and even that was nearly a tie—the dress was a one-off, custom piece by a now-deceased boutique designer who'd only done a handful of pieces and a handful of shows, but he'd made a serious splash in the fashion world before his untimely death. I'd sold him his house on the Malibu coast, and he'd paid my commission with that dress, which he'd designed and made specifically for me. When I put it on, I was walking sex appeal. Jaws dropped. Heads turned. Heart rates went into the red zone. Dicks went hard.

Thus, I only wore it on the most special of occasions, and it never failed to produce at least three marriage proposals per event.

"I'll wear my best jeans and a tank top," I suggested, just to rile up Laurel.

"*Hell* to the no, you won't," Laurel snapped. "This is serious. It's not a jeans-and-tank-top thing." A heavy sigh. "I'll be right there."

I laughed as her square went black. "It's damn near Pavlovian, at this point," I said.

Kat was cackling. "It really is. You know she's going to show up with the back of her Range Rover stuffed with dresses, skirts, blouses, and shoes."

"Obviously," I said. "Why do you think I said it? She's got the most amazing clothes."

"I'll see you ladies in the morning," Teddy said. "I'm gonna take a bath."

The rest of the group signed off, and I tossed the phone on my bed and went into my closet. Despite my taunting of Laurel, I really wasn't sure what to wear. It was coffee at 9 a.m., so it had to be casual, but I wanted to make a good impression. Laurel was my best weapon in this situation, because if she hadn't gotten into the real estate business with me, she'd probably have ended up stylist to the stars or something. Her taste in fashion was impeccable, and we were nearly the same size.

I had a few options laid out on my bed when Laurel texted: *Let me up. I have options.*

I let her up, and she blitzed into my bedroom, both arms laden with clothing.

"Okay, here we go," she said, tossing the piles of clothing onto my bed. "Option one, an adorable miniskirt that absolutely screams schoolgirl, with this super cute boyfriend button-down. Casual, but sexy. He won't be able to take his eyes off your legs, and let's be honest, you have killer legs."

She pulled the items out of the pile as she spoke and held them up, tossing them aside.

"Option two, a tight white pencil skirt. It'll do fabulous things to your ass. With it, a nice casual V-neck sleeveless top, I have several colors to choose from. Wear your best pushup bra under it, and you'll spend the entire meeting reminding him where your eyes are." This option joined the first on the bed, up near my pillows. "Option three, my favorite sundress. It's casual but sexy. Put a nice wide belt on, some wedge heels for added height and butt lift, and bam, he's your man."

I tapped my chin. "I'm gonna nix the pencil skirt. Too formal. No heels, I have to give a tour of the Murray estate later, and you know how much walking there is." I held up the sundress. "I like this."

Laurel rifled through the pile of clothes. "Ah, the belt." She handed it to me. "With the right bra, your tits will look amazing in this."

"My tits will look amazing no matter which bra I wear," I countered. "I have amazing tits."

"You do." She eyed me. "You could free-tit it." A smirk. "That'd really get his attention."

"I haven't gone braless in public in my entire adult life," I said, "I'm not about to start now. And especially not for this."

She grinned. "That's my favorite way to wear that dress. The looks you get? It's fun."

"Fun?" I cupped myself, shook them. "Have you seen these? No way. I'd knock someone out."

She snorted. "Like I'm that much smaller? Try it. I dare you."

"No!"

"Chicken." She clucked like a chicken, bobbing her head and tucking her hands into her armpits, dancing around.

I cackled—get Laurel alone, and she was downright hysterical. "Oh my god, Laurel, you're such a dork. I'm *not* free-titting it."

"You've seriously never once gone out in public without a bra?"

I frowned at her. "I'm shocked you have. You're all miss fashion all the time."

She bit her lip, grinning. "Actually, I do it a lot, on hookup dates especially. Sometimes, depending on the outfit, I'll put on pasties so my nips don't show."

I shook my head. "You never cease to surprise me, Laurel."

"It makes guys crazy," she says. "It's a whole different way of teasing them. The trick is to wear something that shows either a lot of side boob or inner boob. They go nuts."

"I'm not going braless," I repeated.

She arched an eyebrow. "Try it on, right now, just me and you, no bra. Just to see."

I sighed. "Fine."

None of the six of us were particularly prudish about nudity, especially around each other, so I stripped out of my clothes right there, tossed my bra onto the bed, and slipped the sundress on. It felt weird, but as I faced my full-length mirror, I could see why Laurel was pushing the issue.

I looked...hot. *Really* hot. It was a flattering cut as it was, but no bra just made it...different. I couldn't quite define why, but I liked it. I turned this way and that, and I knew if he, or anyone, looked closely enough it would be obvious I wasn't wearing a bra.

Laurel was watching me carefully and laughed triumphantly. "See what I mean?"

I sighed. "Fine. You win—it's a good look, with this dress at least."

She grabbed my arm and leaned close to me. "Now, you really want to feel crazy? Wear the dress and not a damn thing else. No bra, no panties. Just the dress."

I bit my lip. "Hell no." I turned to look at her. "You've done it?"

"Of course. It's extremely liberating. You just have to own it."

"I can't believe I'm even considering it."

"You're meeting a man who answered an ad in the newspaper," she pointed out, "for the express purpose of determining if you want to let him intentionally impregnate you. And you're feeling squeamish about not wearing underwear?"

I snorted. "I mean, when you put it that way…"

"You're doing something crazy," she said. "You may as well go all the way in, get a little daring with your wardrobe for the first date."

I shimmied out of my underwear and kicked them aside, twisted this way and that, turned to see myself from the rear. "I mean, you can't quite tell."

"If a wind blows the dress against you, you can. Otherwise, no, not really. *You* know, and it *feels* like everyone else will know too, but they don't. It's a fun experience."

"I'll think about it." I hugged her. "Thanks for coming over."

She hugged me back awkwardly, stiffly—she wasn't much for affection. "Yeah, well, you have boring taste in fashion, so I had to come rescue you from your business casual skirts and blouses, and—shudder—*jeans*."

She wouldn't be caught dead in jeans. I didn't think she owned a single pair, while that's pretty much all I wore when I wasn't working, which was pretty much never.

Her eyes drilled into mine. "Are you really going to try to get pregnant, Lizzy?"

"I kind of think so." I bit my lip. "It's crazy. But it's been in the back of my mind for a long time. I want someone to share my life with, but all the men I've ever met are dumb and impossible. The logical answer, therefore, is a baby."

She frowned. "I'm not so sure about that logic, babe. But, if you're sure it's what you want, then I'm with you." She glanced away. "My mom never wanted children. She was always very open about the fact that I was an unwanted accident. She and Dad had too much champagne at a party one time, got busy in a laundry room, and bam, nine months later she was saddled with a human she didn't know what to do with."

"A laundry room?" I was stunned. "Elise Crane-McGillis got pregnant in a laundry room at a party?"

Laurel nodded. "Yep. The one and only time my parents had unplanned sex, I'm pretty sure. Possibly the only time they ever had sex with each other at all, actually." She shrugged. "Theirs is a marriage of finances and convenience. Mom has her pool boys, literally, and Dad has his personal assistants."

"Pool boys? Like actually, she keeps hot young pool boys to sleep with?"

Laurel rolls her eyes. "Most of them are younger than me, and she makes them wear these trunks that are basically a male thong, and they're all ripped and shredded and straight out an Abercrombie ad. They pretend to skim the pool and bring her drinks, and when she wants one, she points at him and goes into the pool house."

I made a grossed-out face. "Really? You've watched this happen?"

"Oh yeah. Mom is shameless."

"Where does she get them?"

"I don't know, honestly." Laurel finally snickered. "I asked her one time, and she told me a magician never reveals her secrets." She bit her lip, and the snicker turned into a full-on cackle. "I slept with one of them myself. And where she gets them, I don't know, but I'm damned determined to find out because *damn*."

I faked a gag. "You've shared men with your *mother*?"

"No." She preened, pretending to be arch and prim. "I made sure Mom hadn't done anything with him first. And then made him swear he wouldn't tell her I'd gotten to him first."

"Oh...my...*god*." I couldn't help a disbelieving laugh. "You gave your mom your sloppy seconds."

"She doesn't need to know," Laurel said. "It was

one time. And I was at the end of my four-week hiatus from sex."

"I still find that strange."

She shrugged. "It just...shakes things up. It makes going back to sex that much better. Like doing Sober October makes wine taste that much better."

I shook my head. "You are one strange person, Laurel. But I love you."

She scooped her clothes up, leaving me the schoolgirl skirt and top as well as the sundress I was still wearing. "So you have options." She kissed me on each cheek, because did I mention she'd been raised half her life in France, and still did a lot of weird European things, like double cheek kissing. "Have fun. And don't wear anything under the dress! You'll thank me later!" she called, as the penthouse elevator doors closed between us.

I studied myself in the dress, sans bra and sans underwear, and tried to picture myself having coffee, in public, with a guy I was considering having bare sex with, on purpose.

The whole thing was crazy, so why not?

CHAPTER FIVE

I T WAS WINDY, TODAY. OF COURSE.

It kept pressing the thin cotton of the dress flat against my body, molding the material to my curves. I'd had to park a couple blocks away from the coffee shop, and on the walk there I'd already made one guy walk into a streetlamp post, and another guy had gotten into a fight with his girlfriend, and another guy had almost rear-ended someone in his Ferrari.

Perhaps free-titting it had been a mistake, in retrospect. Free-titty...free-kitty, too. Not a scrap under the cotton. And holy shit, what a feeling. I didn't mind showing a little skin, and was fine wearing slightly slutty dresses to cocktail parties and trolling for hookups at bars. But this was different. Why, I couldn't have told you, but it was.

A slutty dress still actually covered the important bits. Left them *almost* out, but not actually. This was the opposite—everything was decently covered, but it *felt* like they were bare for the whole world to see.

Jury was still out on whether I'd have the guts to do this again.

The coffee shop was busy at this time of the morning, but I'd seen a table available outside, and they had additional seating upstairs on the roof.

I got in line to order coffee and stood slightly turned so I could keep an eye on the door—I was early, because I was the obnoxious type that was five minutes early to everything. I had ordered and was waiting when I saw him.

Oh.

Oh…*wow*.

My skin tingled and my lungs tightened and my belly flipped.

His selfie hadn't done him anything like justice.

Six-feet-something, lean. His arms filled out the sleeves of his plain white V-neck T-shirt, which was tucked behind a black leather belt, faded blue jeans with rips here and there that seemed from age rather than design. Black boots, scuffed, loved. Classic black Ray-Bans, which he pushed up into his hair as he entered, his intense dark gaze sweeping the cafe.

He was more than a yummy snack, the man was…fine—as—*hell*.

Those cheekbones were to die for, and his stubble was approaching nearly a beard, thick enough to be attractive but not so unkempt as to look scruffy.

I could work with this.

He saw me, recognized me, and faltered a step. Stopped mid-stride, blinked rapidly, and his hand lifted to scratch his jaw and pass across his mouth, a gesture of something like disbelief. He shook his head, grinning as if laughing at himself, and then lifted that same hand in a wave. I waved back, accepted my latte from the barista. The line was short as he entered, and he reached the register quickly, ordered a plain black coffee, and received it immediately. I was waiting off to the side for him, and as soon as he'd paid with cash and waved off the change, he turned to me.

"Hi," he said, his gaze raking over me. He extended his hand. "Braun."

"Hi, Braun, I'm Lizzy." His hand was warm and gentle, and *huge*. "Nice to meet you."

"Great to meet you too." He went to pass his hand through his hair, caught on his sunglasses, which he tucked into the V of his T-shirt; his eyes flicked over me from head to toe again, slowly, as if he couldn't quite help himself from taking another long look. "You are *beautiful*."

I couldn't help a grin. "Thank you." I glanced at him, let myself look him over. "You're looking pretty fine yourself, Mr. Bennet."

He sipped his coffee, winced, coughed. "Hot."

He cleared his throat. "So, you want to sit outside, up-stairs, take a walk?"

I shrugged. "Which do you prefer?"

"I'm gonna be in a chair checking code all day, so if it's all the same to you, I wouldn't mind taking a walk."

I kicked a foot, showing my sandals. "I'm wearing comfortable shoes, so why not?"

We headed outside, and I followed Braun across the street to the sidewalk along the beach. The wind was still strong, molding the dress against me inde-cently. His eyes missed nothing, and my core tightened.

He blinked, and tore his eyes away, sliding his sunglasses on. "So, Lizzy. I have to admit, I'm curious about the ad."

I laughed. "Right into it, huh?"

He shrugged. "I'm not much for small talk."

"Fine by me, I tend to be the same way." I sipped, and tried to decide what to say, and how much. "Fuck it." I laughed again. "It started as a joke and ended up serious."

He glanced down at me, then away. "Explain?"

"Well, I just had my fortieth birthday last week—"

"Happy birthday," he said.

"Thanks. And my friends and I were joking around about putting an ad in the paper, except my friends ac-tually went and did it, and here we are."

He glanced at me again, one eyebrow lifting.

"'Beautiful, successful single woman, forty, seeks attractive male billionaire to impregnate her the old-fashioned way. No strings. NOT seeking sugar daddy. Validation required. Serious inquiries only, please.'" A direct, exact quote; either he'd memorized it or he had an eidetic memory. "How does that go from a joke between friends to actually…going along with it?" He ran his hand through his hair. "You actually…um—intend to end up…pregnant?"

I hesitated. "Yes?"

He laughed. "You don't sound certain."

I sighed. "I mean, yes. Yeah."

We walked a few steps in silence, and then glanced at me again, sipping his coffee carefully. "I don't want to sound like I'm perpetuating stereotypes here, but is it one of those your-biological-clock-is-running-out sort of things?"

I let out a bark of laughter. "Wow, that's direct."

"Sorry. I'm not good with filtering myself." He stopped, facing me. "I hope I didn't offend you, but I want to know what this is, what I'd be getting myself into."

"No offense taken," I assured him. "I don't know, honestly. Or, I'm still working through my own reasons for this, if you want the truth. I'm kind of…going on instinct. It's not desperation, I assure you that. I'm not, like, baby crazy." I looked up at him. "It's complicated, Braun, that's what it is."

"I just wouldn't want you to end up pregnant and suddenly going, 'oh shit, it was just a phase.'"

"I appreciate your concern." I spied a bench out in the sand a ways, off the sidewalk. "Want to sit?"

He nodded and headed for it. I made it a few steps into the sand and kicked off my shoes, held them in one hand. We reached the bench, and Braun immediately toed off his boots, peeled his socks off, and shoved his jeans up just under his knees to reveal strong, hairy calves and large feet. He dug his toes into the sand, stuffing his socks into the boots and setting them under the bench.

"Why wear the jeans and boots, in that case?" I asked, laughing.

"I'm letting my buddy borrow my car for the day, so I rode my motorcycle. I have a leather jacket, but I left it with my helmet on the bike." A shrug. "Jeans and a leather jacket are essential safety items for riding a bike."

"What kind of motorcycle?" I asked.

"Indian Scout. It's vintage, from 1960."

"And what kind of car?"

He grinned. "My baby. It's a '64 Shelby Cobra."

"A genuine Shelby Cobra?"

"You're a car girl?"

I nodded. "I love cars. Got it from my dad."

"Hot," he murmured to himself. "Yeah," he said, more to me this time, "it's a genuine Shelby. Original, numbers matching."

"No shit." I frowned at him. "And you loaned it to a friend?"

"He wanted to impress a girl," he said with a shrug.

"Must be a good friend."

"Him, or me?" he asked with a laugh.

"Well, you for sure, if you're loaning out a genuine Shelby Cobra. But him, if you're willing to."

"Yeah, he is. Plus, I told him I'd put out a hit on him if anything happened to my car."

"Ah," I said, laughing, "there's the truth."

He stretched out, legs angling away, crossed at the ankle, one arm casually across the bench behind me. Weirdly, I was okay with it.

"So, Braun." I sipped. "Why answer the ad?"

"Curiosity." He shrugged. "If nothing else, it sounded like a fun new way to meet someone, regardless of how things go. We could just end up having coffee, and that's it. Maybe we don't click. Maybe you change your mind. I dunno. I'm a bit of a wild hair, for a computer nerd."

"Meaning?"

"Meaning, I've been bungee jumping and skydiving, I surf, I'm a certified scuba diver. I like fast cars. I have a Porsche 911 GT3 RS that I race at a track." He smirked at me. "And, apparently, I answer ads asking for someone to impregnate them."

"Down to business, then," I said, grinning. "What

would it take for you to let me drive your GT3 at the track?"

He threw his head back and laughed. "Not where I thought you were going with that."

I liked his laugh. Just hearing him laugh made me smile. Made me want to keep coming up with funny things to do and say just to make him laugh again. And he laughed easily, which just threw fuel on that particular fire.

He regarded me through his Ray-Bans. "I guess my question is, where we go from here, in terms of the content of the ad."

I swallowed hard. "Meaning, sex." I tried to make it sound flippant, casual. I wasn't sure if I succeeded or not.

He nodded, and things seemed serious, suddenly. "Yeah. The old-fashioned way. That's what the ad said. Meaning, sex. Instead of in vitro or whatever."

"Right." I tugged at the top of my dress, as the scoop neck was drifting lower and lower and my bits were beginning to show a bit too much; the movement only served to draw Braun's eyes to my chest, however, and even behind the opaque lenses of his sunglasses I could feel his gaze lingering. "So, the thinking is that I'm happy being single, okay? I for real am. Yeah, it's true I've never had much luck in the dating department, but it's also true I've never really tried all that hard, either. I like my freedom. But the maternal part of me which I freely admit I've neglected in favor of my career, has been getting louder the last couple years. Maybe being a man, you can't even begin to understand—I don't know. You mentioned the biological clock, like the biological imperative to have a baby. It could be that. I know not all women feel that, and I sort of figured I was one of those. But then suddenly I'm realizing I'm not."

"So why not go the clinical route?" he asked. "It's none of my business, I realize, but I am curious. You don't have to answer."

I shrugged. "I dunno. I like sex?" I grinned at him, letting my eyes take in his shoulders and arms and chest—he didn't have a Hollywood superhero body, but he was fit. I liked it. A lot. "I figure, I like sex, and sex is the natural, normal way of conceiving, right? And as far as I know, I'm perfectly capable of conception. So why bother with the expense and clinical sterility of going in and getting artificially fertilized, or whatever, when I can go about it the good old-fashioned way of lots and lots of sex? The catch is, I don't have a husband or boyfriend. And I honestly don't want one. I've trolled bars and Tinder and all the usual suspects for enough years to know that I'm not quickly or easily going to find a…um…partner, I guess, for what I have in mind. I'm not looking for a friend with benefits. I'm not looking for a romantic relationship. I'm not looking for a hookup, like some quick and dirty banging in some struggling actor's shitty West Hollywood apartment. I'm not looking for a sugar daddy either—nor do I want to be a sugar mama. I've got my own money, and plenty of it—I'm very successful, very comfortable. I don't want anyone else's money and I don't want a sponge with a cock."

Braun nodded, his expression neutral. "I'm with you so far." His arm was slung across the back of the bench just inches from me; not quite touching in an intimate way, but nearly. "So that's all what you're *not* looking for. Can you elucidate what it is you *are* looking for?"

"Oooh, you get points for using 'elucidate' in a sentence."

"How many points do I have so far?" he asked.

"Oh, at least…like, five. A point for being tall, dark, and handsome, a point for having great taste in cars, a point for being direct and real without being…a horndog bastard, I guess, considering the nature of this whole deal; that's three points. Another point for using elucidate in a sentence, and if I'm being honest, I'd award you a whole 'nother point because I'm super attracted to your laugh."

"My laugh?" He seemed genuinely surprised by that. "Really?"

I shrugged. "Yeah. Is that weird? I like the way you laugh. I don't mean attracted like, oh my god I'm going to spontaneously orgasm every time you laugh. I just mean, you laugh easily and it's one of those infectious laughs. I noticed it first when we talked on the phone."

"Hmmm. A whole point for my laugh. I'll take it. And no, not weird. Unexpected, I guess, because I've always been a little self-conscious about it, to be honest."

"Well, don't be."

He watched the waves, and a surfer riding a cresting barrel. "I had to grow into it. Like I had to grow into my ears. I was a gawky, awkward, nerdy, goofy kid with big ears and a laugh too deep and too honking for my body."

"Well, I'd say you did a serious Longbottom."

He blinked at me. "Harry Potter references will get you points with me. Or *Lord of the Rings*, or *Star Wars*, or any of the usual nerd fare."

I nodded. "I'll keep that in mind. Will I lose points if I admit I haven't read any of the *Lord of the Rings* books?"

"Have you seen any of the movies, at least?"

I bit my lower lip, wincing. "Um, sort of?"

"What does that mean?"

I shrugged, hoping it came across as coy. "It just means the movies were on, but I wasn't exactly paying the closest attention."

He laughed. "I think I take your meaning." He

arched an eyebrow at me. "If you can sit through at the very least the first three, I will take you to the track and you can spend as many hours driving my GT3 as you did watching *Lord of the Rings*."

"Isn't that, like, nine hours of film time?"

He snickered. "If you watch the theatrical versions, maybe as *little* as nine hours. If you watch the director's cuts? Way more. *Way* more."

"Oh." I tapped my chin. "And something tells me we'd be watching the director's cut."

"Absolutely." He waved a hand. "Something to think about, at least. You never answered my question, though."

"About what it is I'm looking for with this whole thing?" I asked, and he nodded. "I can try. Probably would be good to put it out there even for myself. Good-looking, because let's be honest, our relationship such as it is, would be almost entirely physical. But not a boring dolt or a vapid douchebag because being forty, I doubt I'll get pregnant the very first time so it will have to be an ongoing thing and conversation will be necessary, and if I was to want any one thing in a man outside of looks and sexual ability, it's good conversation. But, this wouldn't be a romantic thing, as I said. Once I'm pregnant, he'd be cut loose. With a contract saying so, I think. For both of us. So I know he won't come demanding to know what I've done with his offspring in five or ten years or something, with some weird midlife crisis regrets. And for him, to know I'm not going to be coming knocking on his door looking for child support or a father figure."

"No father figure?"

"I'm close to my dad. My mom is probably going to shit puppies about this whole thing, but my dad will take it in stride, the way he does everything. And he'll be a good father figure."

He nodded, musing. "I see. And why the ad?"

"Honestly, like I said, it started as a joke. Me and my girlfriends—who also are my employees—all like to read steamy romance novels. And if you read those, they make it seem like hot billionaires are just lurking around every corner waiting for you to fall onto their big throbbing cocks, if not into swoony, hearts-and-stars and happily-ever-after love. And I was like how hard could it be, and my friend proposed an ad in the paper. I thought that was it, a joke, ha ha, okay let's move on. Then, a week later, I get a call from a guy about the ad. Color me confused, right? Turns out they thought it would be funny to actually run the ad for real, and my one friend thought it would be additionally hysterical to put my actual phone number in there, too. And now, here we are."

"Because you do actually want a baby, and you do actually want to conceive it through good old-fashioned sex, and you want it to have a built-in end date, of the moment you know you're pregnant."

I thought about it, searched myself for the answer, but at this point I knew it: "Correct."

He nodded, thinking. "I'm assuming there would be an exchange of sexual health reports."

"Absolutely."

"And the aforementioned contract regarding finances and parental rights."

"As far as the parental rights thing, one way of going about it is removing…the father, whomever it may end up being—you possibly—from the birth certificate, or just not listing a father at all, or a legal affidavit saying I absolve you of all parent responsibilities… or just you going about your life and I go about mine and it's just an agreement saying we're going about our lives after the terms of the agreement are fulfilled. There's more than one way to go about it. You could still sue for rights later, of course, if you at some point suddenly decide that you're not okay with a kid you don't know."

"And I'm assuming sexual monogamy would be a given for the duration."

"Well, yeah. Considering we're both taking the risk of unprotected sex, that would have to be an absolute mandate for both of us."

He nodded. "So, do you have other…candidates… to vet?" A glance at me.

"Eager to get started, are you?" I grinned at him wryly.

He tipped his head to one side. "I mean, you're the goddamn sexiest woman I've ever met in my life, and you're killing me in that dress, so…yeah, honestly, I am. But this is your thing, and we'll do it your way."

I felt a funny little flip low in my belly. "You're just saying that because you can tell I'm not wearing a damn thing under this dress."

He closed his eyes, tipped his head back, and groaned. "Shiiiiiiit," he murmured, a drawn-out sound; he brought his head forward and looked turned back to me. "No, Lizzy, I did not realize that."

I frowned at him. "Braun, you've been staring at my tits since the moment you saw me in the coffee shop. This whole thing is about sex, and it's flattering, so it's not like I'm mad about it, but you can't honestly tell me you didn't realize at very least that I'm not wearing a bra."

He removed his sunglasses, and his eyes met mine. "I did surmise that much, yes." His gaze slid slowly down my body, and I felt his desire like liquid warmth coating my very flesh; his eyes fixed on my thighs, the apex, where my dress draped against me. "I did not, however, realize you weren't wearing underwear."

"Well. I'm not." I laughed. "Not a stitch."

"Is that normal for you? Just curious."

"Not at all."

"Why do it for this meeting, then? Surely you know you're beautiful enough to attract any heterosexual male on the planet without having to taunt him this way as well."

"I certainly didn't intend to *taunt* anyone."

"Now that I know, it's literally the only thing my mind is capable of thinking about."

"That I'm not wearing *any* undergarments at all, or a specific kind in particular?"

"I don't even know." He put his sunglasses back on. "The no underwear thing does throw me for a bit of loop, I guess. Thinking about you being bare...I mean, it's not like that dress is short enough I'm thinking I'd get a look if you moved just right, like if it was a miniskirt or something. But still. I have a hell of an imagination, and if nothing else, Lizzy, I feel a very powerful lust for you growing exponentially by the moment."

"A very powerful lust, you say?" I licked my lips and pressed my thighs together.

"Growing exponentially." He groaned. "And it's taking every bit of my will and self-control to not let that physically manifest in a way which would be... problematic at best, in such a public setting."

"Do you wear underwear, Braun?" I asked.

He smirked. "I do." He lifted his T-shirt, baring a tan belly and dark curls of hair; he reached under the waistband of his jeans and pulled up the elastic of a pair of underwear: Armani, black, and probably briefs, unless I missed my guess.

Thoughts of Braun naked but for a tiny pair of tight black briefs danced in my head, and I got all tingly. My thighs pressed tighter together, and I felt my mouth go dry and I had to clench my hands together to keep them from doing anything rash—like getting us arrested for public indecency.

The man was hot, had a good body, and big hands. And in my experience, big hands generally equated to big other things, and I was becoming very eager to get started with the baby making.

"Ever free-ball?" I asked, because I liked the mental image of unzipping his jeans and having something thick and delicious popping out into my hands.

God, something had to be wrong with me. I'm horny, sure, but Braun was making me feel things beyond the usual.

He smirked. "Free-ball. No, I can't say I have. Not in proper clothing. In a bathing suit, of course. But jeans, or slacks? No."

"You ought to try it, sometime," I said. "It's quite an experience."

"I see. I might, at that."

I felt my purse buzz as my phone rang. "Excuse me a moment." I fished it out and glanced at the screen: *Laurel*. I smiled apologetically at Braun, who shrugged good-naturedly and withdrew his own phone from his pocket. "Laurel, I assume you're calling for a very good reason."

"I need to know what you think the lowest possible fair price is for the Dolman property."

"Now? You need to know this *now*?"

"Why, are you...*busy*?"

I sighed. "Laurel."

"What? I have clients who want a second opinion on an offer. The buyers feel their offer of three-point-three is more than fair given the comps, but the sellers feel it's worth closer to four given the updates they've done. I told the sellers to counter at three-five, but they're stuck at three-eight and the buyers won't go any higher and I'm *this* close to clinching a really sweet three-way deal."

"Laurel, you don't need me for this."

"It's tricky because I'm representing both buyer and seller for different transactions. So they all feel they need a third party to weigh in."

"So, you're representing the Dolmans as their seller's agent, and the buyers for the sale of their property as well as their purchase of a new place?"

"Well, no. Kat is representing the purchase, I'm just representing the listing of their current home."

"I see. Because that would be stretching the ethical limit quite a bit, I think."

"What do the comps indicate?" I glanced at Braun, who was answering an email; he smiled at me distractedly, went back to reading and typing—he did indeed have big thumbs, and had to constantly backspace to fix errors from mistyping.

"Three-five at most. Three-three is fair, but on the low end. The Dolmans would shit bricks if I suggested they accept three-three, since they think they should get four. But they don't have the square footage or the lot size for that price point."

"Then you have to show them the comps and try to get them to take three-five, or you have to get the buyers to go higher. If you say three-five is fair, then I'll back you on that. I'm still at my…meeting, so I can't go over the comps right this moment. If you really need my direct input, it'll have to wait till I'm at the office."

"I can tell everyone involved that you agree three-five is a fair price both ways, then."

"Yep. I trust your judgment. It's your listing, your sale. But my memory of the Dolman property is that you're right, it's worth three-five for sure, but not quite a full four."

"Okay. Thanks." A hesitation. "So, how's it going?"

"We can talk when I get back."

"Can't I even get a hint?"

"No. We'll talk later."

"Fine. Lame, but, fine."

I laughed. "Good*bye*, Laurel."

"Bye."

I tucked the phone back into my purse, and a moment later I heard the swoosh of an outgoing email, and then Braun was facing me.

He leveled a long look at me. "So, Lizzy. Final

verdict on my end is, I'm in. As if there was any doubt, I'm sure. A woman like you, I'd wager any amount of money you have your pick of men begging for the honor of doing this with you."

"Flattering, but if you want the truth, you're the second respondent. The first was sixty-five. Not bad looking, and probably a great guy, but I'm looking for someone within at least ten years of my age, closer to five if possible. Just for…compatibility purposes."

"I understand that." He slid his arm across the bench back again, this time more around my shoulders than merely behind me. "Any questions you'd like to ask me?"

"Are there any pertinent medical issues in your family history which I should be aware of?"

"Nope. Mom and Dad are both healthy, living, and married for forty years. Grandparents are both alive on both sides, both between eighty and ninety. Uncles, aunts, all that, no genetic issues."

"You're not, like, an anomaly in your family? In terms of looks, I mean."

He frowned. "Not sure what you mean."

"I mean, you're a hell of a good-looking man, Braun."

"Thanks." He didn't preen or puff up. Just smiled. "So am I, like, the swan in a family of ugly ducklings, you mean?"

"Basically."

"No. I look a lot like my dad. I've got my mom's personality and my dad's physical characteristics. Mom is a research physician in a think tank, and super cerebral, supersmart. So I get my inclination for academia and nerd-dom from her. Dad is...well, complicated. Former college athlete, soccer and hockey. Still plays hockey in a pickup league, actually. But he's also a physics research professor at Caltech, looking into super obscure stuff even I'm not sure I understand much less could explain."

I nodded. "I see. Good to know." I turned into him, angling to face him, and settled a hand on his thigh. "I've always believed in waiting twenty-four hours before making a big decision or purchase."

"Me too." His arm dropped more onto my shoulders than the bench.

"So, I'm not going to let myself act on my immediate impulse." I bit my lip, smiled, feeling coy and provocative and playful. "But. I will offer you a recommendation."

"And what would that be, Lizzy?"

"Bring a clean bill of health with you next time we meet."

His lips quirked up in a grin. "I see."

"What I mean is, Braun, you are the leading candidate at this time, so while I'm not prepared to formally offer you the position just yet, I can say your chances look good."

"I await your final decision eagerly, in that case." I could feel his gaze lingering yet again on my breasts. "Very eagerly."

"I don't like to assume anything goes without saying, generally speaking, so what I would like to point out, for the record, is that the exclusivity clause begins now. For both of us. Just so we're clear."

"I don't believe I could even think of another woman at this point, Lizzy." His chest lifted in a deep breath, which he let out heavily. "And I can guarantee I'll be thinking about *you* a lot between now and our next meeting."

My breath caught. "That's mutual, I assure you."

He stood, extended a hand down to me. "Shall we walk back to where we parked?"

I took his hand and let him pull me to my feet; his hand engulfed mine. He towered over me, and for a moment he just looked down at me and I up at him, and I felt his eyes on mine rather than anywhere else. I was tempted to push the sunglasses up away from his eyes so I could read his gaze. So I could feel the push of his desire.

Being the object of lust, in the right circumstances, is intoxicating.

I was, currently, drunk on it.

And awash with my own lust. Which I wondered if he felt. If he felt my eyes on his broad shoulders, his trim waist. On the cut of his jeans around his thighs, the way his zipper bulged.

The wind, which had, while we were sitting, died down a bit. But now that we were walking again, it was whipping against us stronger than ever. And again, it molded my dress to my curves, pressing the thin cotton against my pebbled nipples and the round weight of my breasts, against the bell of my hips and into the apex of my thighs. If he hadn't noticed before, in that moment there was absolutely not a single shred of doubt that I was bare under the dress—the cotton against my flesh molded to the crease of my thighs against my sex and pressed into the seam, outlining me so clearly I may as well have been standing in front of him totally nude.

His eyes floated down my body. Lingered on my nipples, and then on my sex.

"Damn, Lizzy." He sucked in a breath through his teeth. "I believed you, but *damn*. Not a stitch on you down there."

"Nope."

He grimaced. "Good lord." He turned away from me, started walking.

I laughed. "Okay, then." He was power walking and I had to trot to catch up. "You all right there, big guy?"

"Nope."

"You're walking kinda funny," I said.

"Yep."

"Having a…*hard* time, are you?"

He turned his Ray-Ban gaze onto me. "Yes, Lizzy, I am. If you want to make sure this arrangement doesn't start in the nearest public bathroom right the hell now, then you'd better...I don't know. I don't know what you'd better. I can't even think straight right now." He stalked forward again.

"The nearest public bathroom, huh?" I kept up with him, which took all my power walking ability. "I've had some wild times in my life, but I can't say I've ever done that."

"Me either. Pretty far outside my usual comfort zone, but right now, the way I'm feeling..." he trailed off, shaking his head.

"The way you're feeling, what? How are you feeling, Braun?"

"Not in control."

"Is that so?" I followed him across the street. "And that's unusual for you, is it?"

"Very."

"And what would you losing control look like, Braun?"

We were passing a narrow space between two large buildings, and he abruptly whirled, pushed me into the narrow alley, and flattened me against the wall with his body. His chest was hard against mine, and his hands gripped my hips, fingers digging into my flesh. Even through the dark lenses of his sunglasses, his gaze burned, pierced like lasers. I felt his desire between us, a thick hard ridge against my belly.

"Like this." He growled, a low grumble of desire. "You're all but fucking naked, with curves any sane man would kill to possess, wearing a dress that does more to highlight than conceal. And you're talking about you and me having raw, bare sex, and a lot of it by the sounds of what you're saying. Teasing me. Flirting with me." He flattened his hands around my hips, pulled me harder against him. "I'm a nice guy, Lizzy. I really am. But I'm not *that* nice."

"Just the right balance between nice and not nice, is what you're saying," I whispered.

"I'm saying I'm so fucking *attracted* to you, it's making me crazy." He ground against me as he hissed the word "attracted." "And by attracted, I mean—"

"I can feel exactly what you mean," I murmured. "I can feel it very clearly."

"Lizzy…"

"Braun."

"This isn't the place for this." His actions ran counterpoint to his words: he rested his forehead against mine and I smelled him, coffee and deodorant and man, familiar yet foreign, and one of his hands slid around from my hip to cup my ass cheek, and his other hand drifted the other way, around front, between us, to the apex of my thighs and touched me gently, searching.

"No," I agreed, "It certainly isn't."

"We haven't exchanged tests."

"No, we have not."

His touch found something he liked, and pressed cotton against flesh; I whimpered, because what he'd discovered was a delicate little spot of my anatomy which I very much wanted him to keep touching, to the point that I was losing the capacity to remember why exactly we couldn't do this here, now.

"We haven't signed any agreements," he continued, whispering as if his finger wasn't gliding in circles over the cotton which covered my delicate little pleasure center.

I gasped, licked my lips. "Nope. Not a one."

"All of which adds up to this not being a very rational or responsible thing, what we're doing right now."

"Once again you are correct, Mr. Bennet." I flexed my hips against his touch. "But yet, I don't seem to find myself telling you to stop." I bit my lip to keep from crying out; Braun had angled his body so he was blocking the view of me from the sidewalk mere feet away; even so it would be obvious to any passerby something inappropriate was happening.

I. Didn't. Care.

Shit, it made it all the hotter.

Braun's touch had my knees shaking, threatening to drop out from under me. Lightning sizzled where he touched me, and his other hand now drifted up from my butt to my ribs, to cup my heavy, tingling breast. I arched against him. His circling finger was everything, making me lose all awareness of propriety. I just wanted—needed—him to keep doing what he was doing…just for a little longer, another moment. Just enough so I could…

Oh god.

"Sshhh," he murmured.

I guess I'd said that out loud.

I quaked, and he touched, and I exploded, and he caught my cry with his mouth, a kiss to swallow my nascent scream, a kiss from a man I knew not at all. But god, could he kiss. And god, did he know his way around an orgasm, because this one was wrenching me into pieces, shaking me apart like a dog with a squeaky toy.

I came down from the wild frothing high of orgasm very, very slowly. He was leaning against the wall, blocking the sight of me still. His finger drifted away from my sex, but his other hand remained at my chest, toying possessively with my breast, which at some point he'd tugged free of its cotton prison.

"Fucking beautiful," he murmured.

"I thought you were a computer nerd," I breathed.

"I am."

"My impression of computer nerds was that they were not supposed to be gods of the female orgasm."

He grinned. "I Longbottomed between junior and senior year."

"And found yourself the subject of female attention."

"A lot of it, and for the first time in my life."

"Which I assume you took full advantage of."

"Yes, but mainly in the form of a girlfriend whom I dated through sophomore year of college."

"You should find her and thank her for teaching you so well."

"I think it's more the subsequent experiences." He tugged the top of my dress back up, covering me.

I rested my head against the rough brick. "I feel like I should thank you for that," I said.

"I couldn't help myself." He grinned, a feral baring of teeth.

"Does it seem like I wanted you to?" I glanced down at his zipper, which was bulging to what seemed like had to be its bursting point. "That looks uncomfortable. I could help you out with that."

"Hard to hide that in public," he murmured. "Tempting, however."

"Mommy, what are they doing in there?" a tiny voice said.

"Just, um…talking," came the mother's voice.

I tugged my dress into a more decent approximation of in place. Braun pulled away, smirking down at me.

"Like when you and Daddy drank all that adult juice and then went into the pool house? I saw you and Daddy talking like that."

I choked on a laugh.

"Except I think you were talking to Daddy's bathing suit area. Because you were kneeling down."

"OKAY," the mother said, loudly, insistently. "Let's go, Cecily. We're going to be late for your dance class."

The voices faded, and I finally let out the bark of laughter I'd been holding in. I met Braun's eyes. "Is there anything you'd like me to say to *your* bathing suit area, Mr. Bennet?"

He swallowed hard. "As a matter of fact, I can think of a few things, yes." He took my hand and pulled me out of the alley and into a slow walk down the sidewalk. "But not here, not now. As much as certain parts of me may think otherwise."

We reached the coffee shop, and I gestured in the direction of my car. "I'm parked down there."

He indicated a motorcycle parked across the street and down a few feet. "I'm right there."

He walked me to my car, and I hesitated with my door open, keys in hand. "We could…go for a drive… if you know what I mean."

He closed his eyes, sighed heavily. "I'll be okay. Mostly."

I laughed. "Well. It was…*lovely* to meet you, Braun. I'll be in touch."

He snorted. "You'll be in *touch*, will you?"

I patted him on the chest. "Yes, I will. And soon."

He frowned down at me. "I don't know if I can wait that long."

"Call me later tonight, then. We talk about whatever…pops up."

He cackled. "You're just full of bad puns, aren't you?"

"Full of bad puns right now, full of something else the next time we're together."

He groaned. "You're mean."

"Is it weird to you how quickly this escalated?"

"Yeah."

"Me too."

He took a step backward. "Go."

"Yeah."

But I didn't. Finally, he let out a laugh and turned around. "Goodbye for now, Lizzy." He waved without turning around, a lift and a flap of his hand.

Strolled casually away, as if he hadn't just fingered me into the most blinding orgasm I'd had in a very long time…in an alley. Mere blocks from my office. In broad daylight…shit, before ten in the morning.

Within an hour of first laying eyes on him.

Luckily he had more prudence than I did, or I'd have done something very, very rash to him right then and there.

Involving my mouth and his bathing suit area, except it wouldn't involve talking.

Although, if I wanted to get pregnant, I should probably make sure every last drop of that stuff goes in my hoo-ha, rather than my mouth.

But then...

Who's to say we couldn't enjoy the process, a bit?

He'd certainly seemed to enjoy himself in the alley...

I looked down at my lap, and there was a wet spot where the dress had been pressed into me, soaked from my desire very literally.

Wow. And here I thought that was just a hyperbolic trope from steamy romance novels. Guess not.

I pulled out of the parking spot and into traffic, gunning it a bit recklessly.

Hooooo boy, did I have something to share with the girls.

CHAPTER SIX

A LL THE GIRLS EXCEPT TEDDY WERE OUT OF THE OFFICE when I arrived, thankfully, and Teddy was on an intense-sounding phone call, her Bluetooth earpiece in her ear, one hand navigating her laptop's trackpad and the other jotting notes furiously. She barely noticed me enough to glance at me, smile a tight, distracted hello, and return to her work.

I settled at my desk and dove in, hoping to distract myself from the morning's…activities. Laurel had emailed details on the Dolman property and the comps she'd used; I sent her an email back affirming that I concurred with her assessment and offering to speak with either party if need be.

Really, she'd just used that as an excuse to try and get a scoop from me.

I only had a few minutes before I had to leave for my showing, but I had a handful of things I needed to get done first.

Including changing. I couldn't very well show a house *sans culottes*. Fortunately, I kept a garment bag here with two full outfits, including a spare bra, panties, shoes. You never knew when you'd need a sudden change of clothing, although this wasn't the circumstance I'd envisioned.

I changed in the bathroom, and felt more… composed, wearing proper undergarments and a less provocative outfit. I finished the other items on my to-do list, and then headed out for the showing, dropping Laurel's dress off at my dry cleaners on the way.

I managed to maintain my professional bearing and composure the rest of the day, and while my showing didn't net an offer, I had a feeling they'd be requesting a second showing soon. I had an appointment right after the showing to view a potential client's home, a beautiful stucco hacienda-style outside LA. I was going to give the listing to Zoe, I decided, once the clients had signed a one-year listing agreement.

I only thought about Braun a few times, alone in the car.

Go me.

Finally, after most of a day in the car between Malibu and LA, I arrived back at the office in time to tidy up the day's work and throw off a few last emails before calling it a day.

The girls were all in attendance, and of course they all pretended to remain studiously at work as I called the new clients to confirm a few details, and then I put together the listing.

"Zoe." I waved her over. "New listing."

She pulled it up on her laptop and sat on the other side of my desk as we went over it, discussing list price and reasoning as compared to the client's ideal price and market conditions.

Finally, Kat stood up. "Fuck this," she snapped. "I'm not gonna sit here and pretend anymore. Spill the beans!"

"Yeah, what happened with Braun Bennet?" Teddy asked. "And why weren't you wearing a bra when you came back? Don't think I didn't notice."

Laurel just smirked at me triumphantly.

"I met with Braun, yes." I kept my voice neutral, pretending to be absorbed with photos of a recent listing on my computer. "He's great, actually. Superhot, but in a nerdy sort of way."

Laurel wriggled in her seat. "Ooh, nerds are *so* fun. I've had some shockingly, unexpectedly great sex with nerds."

"Of course you have, Laurel," I said.

"Explain the no-bra thing," Kat said. "You always wear a bra. You slept in a bra the last time we shared a hotel room."

"It was a sports bra, and I was jet-lagged," I argued. "And don't worry about it."

Laurel sat back in her chair, twisting a tendril of

hair around her finger. "Inquiring minds would like to know, Lizzy. You can tell us."

"I was talked into it," I deadpanned.

"And how did it go?"

I sighed, shut my laptop lid, and pivoted in my chair to face the group. "A little too well, maybe."

"Meaning?" Kat demanded. "Details, woman. Details."

"Well, let's just say I won't be needing to run any more ads." I bit my lip, unable to hold back the grin anymore.

"Spill!" Kat said, gliding across the floor on her chair's casters. "Spill, spill, spill—something happened, I can tell."

I glanced at Laurel. "It's your fault."

"What is? What happened?"

"The, um, outfit…you picked worked a little too well." I closed my eyes, remembering the heat of his gaze on me the entire time we'd been talking. "I'm not sure he was able to make direct eye contact with me more than two or three times in the whole hour we spent together."

Autumn frowned at me. "I mean, if you went out with those monsters unleashed, it's a shock you're not already pregnant."

Laurel was barely able to contain herself. "Was it just the monsters you left unleashed or was something else…left free to roam, shall we say?"

All eyes focused on me, very intently, then.

"Well…"

Teddy clapped a hand over a gasp. "No!" Both hands, then. "You didn't."

"What?" Zoe demanded.

"You weren't wearing any underwear, either!" Teddy yelled. "You went out, in public, in *that* dress, without bra *or* panties. To meet a man. In *public*!"

"Yes, Teddy, in public." I rolled my eyes at her.

"You were all but naked!"

"I was perfectly covered."

Laurel was cackling. "I win, I win! Did he have to roll his jaw up off the floor?"

Kat was eying me. "Something happened. You're still not telling everything."

She knew me too well.

I shrugged, glancing up and away, picking at a blemish on my fingernail. "I mean…a little something, maybe."

Kat grabbed the armrests of my chair and braced herself on them, glaring at me from inches away. "Elizabeth Stephenson. Tell me what happened right now."

I booped her nose. "I will, if you unhand me, Katja Spears."

She sat down. "Fine. I'm sitting. Now spill!"

"So angry," I muttered. "You must be a South Pole elf."

She flipped me off. "Quit stalling and tell us what happened. You look like the cat who ate the canary."

"Thufferin' Thuccotash," I said, in a shitty but funny impression of Sylvester the cat from Looney Toons.

"LIZZY!" they all yelled in unison.

"Fine." I drew the suspense out a bit longer. "You know the space between the camera store and the little boutique? He couldn't contain his desire any longer, and I found myself rather intimately acquainted with that little space."

Silence.

Kat burst out laughing. "You did *not* fuck him in an alley in broad daylight. No way. I refuse to believe it."

"No, we didn't have sex in the alley in broad daylight." I doodled on my notepad rather than look at any of them. "He finger-banged me in the alley in broad daylight. Well…through the dress. There was some titty grabbing."

Laurel frowned. "And where *is* the dress, by the way?"

"Dry cleaners."

Zoe shook her head. "I would never have pictured you letting anything like that happen."

"Me either," I said. "It was weird. I've never in my life felt such intense physical chemistry. It was crazy. I lost my mind a little bit."

"A little bit?" Kat snorted. "You've never done anything even remotely like that, that I'm aware of. If you've ever even had sex outside a bedroom, you haven't shared it with me."

I blinked, thinking. "Actually, come think of it, I don't know that I have. I mean, I've had kitchen counter sex and couch sex and car sex. But never out in public, or anything like it." I tapped my chin. "Except that one time in high school when I let Ricky McKellan feel me up under the bleachers. But we got caught before it could go any farther than over-the-clothes groping." I laughed. "Which, technically, is all this was with Braun, except insofar that I got a hell of an orgasm out of it."

"From an over-the-clothes fingering?" Laurel asked, dubious.

"I think I was super primed for it," I said. "I don't know. It all happened really fast. I wasn't expecting it, honestly. I let it happen, and I don't regret it." I grinned at them. "I think I'm really going to enjoy this process with him."

"Yeah, I bet you are, if this morning's events are anything to go on," Kat said.

"Did you return the favor?" Teddy asked.

"I would've," I said. "But as he pointed out in the moment, that's a bit harder to pull off in public in broad daylight, in an alley just off the sidewalk. We'd have gotten busted for sure. So no, I didn't. I even offered to go for a drive with him." I smirked. "I think he's saving it up."

"I wonder if he has any idea the hellcat he's latched onto," Kat mused.

I frowned at her. "Hellcat?"

She snickered. "I shared a room with you in college, bitch, I've heard you have sex."

"You should hear yourself," I answered, laughing. "If I'm a hellcat, what does that make you? A succubus?"

"If any of us is a succubus, it's Laurel," Kat said. "And I mean that with love."

"Isn't a succubus a demon who preys on sleeping men?" Teddy asked.

Laurel straightened, lifted her chin. "That was one time, and he enjoyed it."

Kat spluttered. "It was a joke, but now I'm curious."

"Me and my big mouth," Laurel sighed. "It was in college. There was a big house party and I ended up passing out in a guest room. I woke up with this super-hot guy in the bed beside me, wearing nothing but a pair of gym shorts and sporting some serious morning wood. I'm always horny first thing after I wake up, and…I…took advantage of him. I'm not proud of it. But he woke up partway through, and I stopped, and apologized. He said I'd only have to apologize if I didn't keep going."

"By take advantage, you mean…what?" Autumn asked. "Oral? Or, like, you were riding him?"

She shrugged. "His shorts were super baggy, so I pulled the leg up over his thing, and…yeah, I totally went down on him."

"You're crazy," Teddy said. "While he was *sleeping*?"

"Yup." She shrugged. "It was hot. He offered to return the favor, but I didn't let him."

"Why the hell not?" Kat asked.

"Honestly, because I had to pee really bad," she said, laughing. "And also I liked the mystique of it for him. It would be a great story for him to tell." She dropped her voice into an impression of a douchey guy. "'Dude, I passed out at this party, and I woke up getting my dick sucked by this superhot blond chick. She sucked me off and then just left, man. Crazy shit, man, for real.'"

I laughed. "You are one of a kind, Laurel, for real."

"I know," she said, tossing her hair and smirking. She pointed at me with a pencil. "Back to you, missy. What are you going to do about this guy, now that he's given you an orgasm within an hour of meeting you?"

I held out my hands palms up in an "I don't know" gesture. "Get tested so I know I'm clean, draw up a contract, and start fucking him six ways to Sunday until I'm knocked up."

"What if you end up *liking* him?" Teddy asked.

"I won't," I said, my voice firm. "Not a chance."

"If you're attracted enough to him to let him finger you in an alley the first hour you've known him, it *does* seem possible." She held both hands up, palms out, in a gesture of surrender. "Just saying."

"No just saying," I said, stabbing a finger at her. "You take that back right this instant, Theodora Pike."

"Ooooh, you got the full name, Teddy," Zoe said. "Now you done it."

Teddy crossed her arms over her ample bosom, unapologetic. "I'm simply raising a possibility, so you have a plan in case things go sideways—for example, if you were to fall for him."

"I'm *not* going to fall for him," I insisted. "The only emotion I feel for him, or will ever feel for any man, is pure animal lust for his big ol' cock and balls."

"Speaking of big ol' cock and balls," Kat said. "What do we know about how he's hanging? Packing anything good?"

I shrugged and shook my head. "I don't know for sure, because I didn't get to unveil anything. I mean, despite the fact that I got off, the only part of either of us that got naked at all was one of my boobs. But...he had a pretty sizable bulge going on behind his zipper, and his hands are nice and large."

"I read somewhere that if you measure from the tip of his middle finger to the base of his hand, you'll have a pretty exact length of his erect penis," Autumn said. "I've never verified this, though."

Zoe snorted. "There's a bunch of stuff like that—measuring the distance between thumb and tip of the index finger, shoe size—it's all bullshit. The only way to know for sure how big a guy's erect dick is, is to find out the fun way."

"I read about a study done by actual researchers in, like, um…Korea, I think it was, where they found a solid correlation between the ratio of the length of the index finger and ring finger. Like, the more discrepancy in length between the ring finger and index finger, the larger the penis," Laurel said. "But, that's confusing, and not very helpful when trying to determine in a crowded bar whether the guy you're checking out is packing a python or a micro-peen. In my admittedly extensive personal research, I'm with Zoe. The only way to know for sure is to stick your hand down his pants and find out…the *hard* way."

We all groaned at her pun, and Autumn threw a paperclip at her.

"Would it be out of the question to request a sneak pic of his dong?" Kat asked. "Inquiring minds would like to know."

I sighed. "Inquiring minds are very demanding around here," I said. "And no, I'm not going to sneak a picture of his penis."

"What if you sext him?" Laurel said. "Then you could just accidentally let us see what he sends."

"I don't even like taking fully clothed selfies," I

said, "what the name of all that's holy makes you think I'm going to take a naked selfie? Hell no."

"That's what you said about going commando under the dress," Laurel pointed out. "And look how that turned out for you."

"Not happening," I insisted. "No way. No sexting, no nudes."

"Why the hell not? What if he sends you one?" Kat asked. "You're telling me you wouldn't respond in kind? Especially after he got you off and didn't demand compensation in kind?"

"The orgasm count *is* in his favor," Teddy said.

"I don't keep a running tally of orgasms," I said.

"Horse shit. You do too," Kat said. "We all do. And it's not so much a running tally as it is keeping track of the ratio—one for him, two for me is the optimal ratio. One to one is acceptable. If the ratio is in his favor, the chances of a repeat performance with me goes to zero."

I held up one hand, palm out, to stop the discussion. "This isn't about repeat performances or anything else. It's about having some good sex with a decent guy with the singular goal of getting pregnant. That's it. That's all I care about. So far, all signs point to I'm going to have a good time. And I'll make sure he does too, you all know I take my partner's pleasure seriously, as you all do. But in the end, it's a limited engagement. Once I get pregnant, see ya. Buh-bye now."

"I'm not concerned about my partner's pleasure," Laurel said. "As long as he's focused on making me come, he'll have the time of his life. Guaranteed."

"Well, you certainly don't lack from confidence in your sexual prowess," Kat said, snickering.

"No, I don't, and with good reason. Every man I've ever *allowed* to fuck me goes away saying I'm the best fuck of his life." She shrugged, an elegant, not quite but almost arrogant move.

"Allowed to fuck you," Kat repeated, with a snort. "One of these days, Laurel, you're going to meet a guy who's going to rock your world and you're not going to know what to do with him."

"Not likely." She examined her fingernails. "Possible, I admit, but highly unlikely. Especially considering my track record of scoring overnights with A-list hotties."

"Yes, Laurel, we know," I deadpanned. "And I think Kat's absolutely right. Someday, a guy is going blow into your life and take you down to size."

She sat forward, leveling a glare at Kat and me. "If there's a man out there who could take me down to size, as you put it, I swear on a stack of Bibles that I'd get down on one knee and propose to *him,* and then lay down on my back and beg him to put a baby in me. I'd settle down and be a wifey, if there's a guy out there who could not only keep up with me but take me to task sexually."

"You swear?" Kat said. "For real? Because I'll hold you that. I think you're overdue. It's happening, babe, and soon. I can feel it in my nuggets."

I cackled—Kat and I spoke a shared language of random movie quotes—this one was a reference to *Surf's Up*, an animated movie about surfing penguins featuring Shia LaBeouf and Jeff Bridges, an underrated film, in our shared opinion.

"Yes," Laurel answered, ignoring the reference. "It's not going to happen. And if it does, I'll propose to him and let him make an honest woman out of me."

"Marriage *and* babies?" Kat said, holding out her hand.

"Marriage *and* babies," Laurel said, shaking Kat's hand. "But if it doesn't happen in the next calendar year, you owe me."

"Owe you what?"

She considered. "A Chanel purse, or the monetary equivalent."

Kat nodded. "And if it does happen with a calendar year, you owe me the same."

"No, because if it does, your part of the bet is seeing me waddling around pregnant, answering to 'wifey.'"

"No, that's not the bet. The result of finding a man who can dominate you in bed is you getting married and pregnant," Kat said, stabbing the top of her desk with a finger. "My end of being right is you buy me a Chanel purse or the monetary equivalent—that's the wager."

I was laughing. "You two are ridiculous." I put my hand on top of theirs, which they were still shaking. "But I'm with Kat, and I'll share the cost if we're wrong. If we're right, Kat can have the purse." I gathered my things and headed for the door. "Well, after this fascinating conversation, I'm ready to go home. I have to make a doctor's appointment."

"Send him a nude!" Kat called after me. "Just do it and thank me later."

"Not happening!" I singsonged over my shoulder.

CHAPTER SEVEN

B EFORE I COULD SECOND GUESS THIS ABSOLUTELY, monstrously, absurdly, roundly and soundly idiotic idea, I hit the Shutter button on my phone's camera.

Kat had ended up swinging by late in the evening, after a miserably failed Tinder date, and we'd had a few too many glasses of wine, and Kat had spent the majority of the night trying to talk me into sending Braun a topless selfie.

For funsies, she claimed. After all, this whole thing was an experiment in doing things I'd normally never do. Going out in public wearing a dress commando, for example. Letting a man I'd known less than an hour finger me in public, in an alley, as another example. Getting pregnant at all, most significantly. So, she argued, why not just throw all caution and sensibility to the wind? Why not send him a nude? What did I have to lose? Nothing ventured, nothing gained, right? And if I did this, I might just get an early glimpse at his goods, and I *was* curious, wasn't I?

Thus, I found myself buzzed enough to listen to her: in my closet, bedroom door closed, facing my full-length mirror, phone held out to one side of my body. I was wearing cream tailored silk slacks, black wedge heels, and had my pale blue button-down sleeveless blouse unbuttoned. I'd removed my bra and put the top back on, for effect. My large, cream-and-ivory breasts were pinned between my arms, pressing them together so they squished to look even bigger than they already did, with half-dollar size light brown areolae, plump pink nipples. My left elbow was pressed against my ribs, hand casually draped up against my jawline and ear, right arm in a similar position, only holding my phone.

I clicked another, adjusted my smile, the angle of my head, the curl of my fingers, and snapped one more.

"Let me see before you send it!" Kat called, on the other side of the door. "And let me in, dum-dum. It's not like I haven't seen you buck-ass naked a thousand times."

My condition of doing this was that Kat couldn't watch me take the selfies—I'd be too self-conscious. I had to work up to the courage to do it, using the buzz of the wine and the memory of his touch, the hard bulge of his zipper against my thigh as he circled my throbbing sex with his finger.

Damn, damn, damn; I was tingly in my down-under bits just remembering how he'd made me feel.

Yeah, after the orgasm he'd given me, he'd earned this.

I buttoned a few of the buttons on the way out of my closet and shoved my bedroom door open for Kat. We sat side by side on my bed as I pulled up the photos I'd snapped.

Kat blinked, eyebrows arched. "Damn, girl, you're looking so hot *I'd* do you, and I'm straight."

I rolled my eyes. "Oh, stop."

She swiped through the four snaps I'd taken, and then back the second one. "This one. Best smile, best angle."

I added the photo in question to my thread with Braun, but hesitated. "This is crazy, Kat. I have a professional reputation to maintain. He could send it to all his friends or post it online, or…or…"

"Or none of the above," Kat said, reaching over me to tap the Send button before I could stop her. "He'll be appreciative and respectful, and hopefully send you a dick pic."

"I need to say something, though," I said, left them and right forefinger poised to type. "I can't just send him a topless selfie without any kind of explanation."

"Sure you can." She tapped her chin. "But, I am curious as to what you'd say."

I typed: *I was feeling grateful for our crazy little... experience...earlier, and figured maybe this would be a nice way to pay you back, since I couldn't exactly reciprocate at that exact moment.*

Kat nodded vigorously, grinning. "Send it, send it. That's good. Let's see how fast he responds, and what he says."

Three little dots appeared, jiggling and dancing.

Bloop.

Braun: *would you believe I was thinking about taking matters into my own hands at the very moment you sent that? I've been having trouble concentrating all damn day, thinking about you.*

Me: *Thinking what?*

Me: *And if you did take matters into your own hands...I wouldn't mind a pic back.*

Me: *or better yet, a video.*

Braun: *Serious?*

Me: *I sent you a topless pic. Yes, I'm serious.*

Braun: *Just so we're absolutely clear, here...you are asking me to send you either a photograph or a video of me...jerking off to your photo. Which, I have to say, is the hottest fucking thing I've ever seen in my life. You have the most amazing breasts, truly. You didn't need to thank me—getting to touch you and make you come was a privilege.*

"He calls them breasts?" Kat asked, reading over my shoulder. "That's so cute."

"I think maybe he's just being...extra polite. What grown man calls them breasts?" I laughed. "It is cute, though."

"Ask him."

"Ask him what?" I glanced at Kat, frowning. "What he calls them for real?"

"Yeah. I'm curious."

Me: *Photo AND/or video, yes. That is exactly what I'm asking you to do, just so we're clear. Also, inquiring minds would like to know...do you call them 'breasts' normally? Like, is that your everyday term for the female mammary gland?*

Dots bounced.

Braun: *I mean, to the extent that I refer to them in average conversation, like with my guy friends...? I guess I usually call them boobs. Why?*

Me: *Just curious. Between my friends and I, we usually call them titties.*

Braun: *That kind of feels...juvenile, to me, idk. Breasts seem like the...mature, and respectful term. Boobs is like when you're being crass and vulgar with your buddies. Although I guess in that situation, tits is the de rigueur term. Like, did you see the tits on that girl over there?*

Me: *Or, you should see the tits on this girl I met—she sent me a nude, you want to see it?*

"Ah, testing him," Kat said. "Smart move."

His reply was immediate: *I would never, ever. I know we don't know each other for shit, and this whole thing is weird and not a relationship nor is it going to be, but...you CAN trust me, Lizzy. I'm a private person by nature, and I would never disrespect a gift like the one you gave me in sending me that photo by showing it to ANYONE.*

Kat clapped a hand over her breastbone. "Awww, that's actually really sweet." She bit her lip and shook her head.

I sighed. "Yeah, it is."

Kat snickered. "Breasts seems like the mature and respectful term. God, he *is* a dork. It's so hot! How have you not called him over here and fucked him already?"

"It's not dorky to be respectful," I shot back. "And we have to set down some...parameters before we have sex. We need to exchange sexual health reports and I need some kind of contract or agreement."

"You want me to write one up real quick?" she asked. "I have my laptop. I can have something drafted in a couple minutes."

"Sure." I eyed her. "Yeah, please. That would be good."

Kat was way better at writing in technical-sounding legalese than I was—probably because she'd gradu- ated with a prelaw degree, and still occasionally talked about finishing her law degree once she was tired of real estate.

I wandered into my kitchen as Kat slid her laptop out of her purse. I slid onto a stool and wondered at the long pause in the conversation with Braun; was he looking at my picture right then, in his bathroom, his big fist sliding up and down his cock?

I tried to imagine it, and only served to work myself up even more.

Bloop.

A still frame of Braun in front of a bathroom mirror, with a little white triangle in the middle indicating it was a video. Over on my couch, Kat was tap-tap-tapping away. I tucked my AirPods into my ears and pressed play.

"So, uh, I've never done this before. It's probably going to be stupid, but hey, I'm up for trying new things with you. I've never done anything like what I did with you earlier today either, so that's a first. This is another first."

His deep smooth voice reflected his nerves; he was wearing the same jeans and T-shirt as earlier. His bathroom looked super nice, marble counter, big mirror, a fancy walk-in shower behind him.

He picked a tablet up off of the counter, recording the whole time, and set it to sit upright, unlocked it with the code, brought up our text message thread. Tapped on the photo I'd sent him.

"Shit, look at those tits," he growled. "So big, so juicy. I can't wait to get my hands on them…squeeze 'em, play with them. I don't know if you'd be down for it, but I'd fuck 'em if you'd let me."

I swallowed hard, bit my lip until it twinged in pain. As he spoke, he unzipped his jeans, shoved them down to reveal black briefs, tight, straining to contain a massive bulge. God, this was hot. I pressed my thighs together and gnawed on my lip, watching with literally bated breath as he let his jeans sag down around past his knees. Hooked one thumb into the waist of his briefs, thrust them down around his thighs. I gulped; he was *huge*. Fucking enormous. Almost as thick as my wrist, veiny, sticking straight up against his body, tip wavering just beneath his belly button. He growled, put two fingers on the photo and spread them apart to zoom in so the screen was filled with just my face and tits. His hand circled himself and he slid his grip down, slowly. Up. Down again. Faster then, and I heard him grunt.

"So fucking hot," he murmured. "I'm picturing you in the alley, remembering how that tit felt in my hand. How good your ass felt as I grabbed it." Faster, and faster his fist flew, blurring. "You want to know what's really making me crazy? How you sounded when you came. Like you could barely contain a scream. Shit, shit. You a screamer, Lizzy? I bet you are. I bet you get super loud."

Oh, you'll find out, Braun. Don't you worry. You'll find out.

Very, very soon.

His fist blurred, and I watched a droplet of precum bead on his tip. He slowed, growling. His jaw clenched, and the picture wavered.

"Here you go, Lizzy. This is what you do to me."

With a long low growl, he released, spurting a thick stream of cum all over the marble counter, gripping himself tight and slowly grinding his fist up and down, and then he spurted again, and again.

"Maybe next time, it'll be your hand making me do that," he gasped.

And then the video ended.

Holy…

shit.

Wow. Just…wow.

Me: *Maybe next time it'll be my mouth making you do that.*

Braun: *maybe next time I'll do that inside you*

Me: *that was hot AF. In case you were feeling as nervous about it as I was.*

Braun: *thanks. I was crazy nervous. Could you see my hand shaking in the beginning? Once I started getting into thinking about you, I stopped being nervous.*

Me: *So far, every aspect of this thing with you is comprised of firsts. I have never, ever done anything like the things I've done with you. I honestly don't know what's gotten into me.*

Braun: *Same.*

"You're texting him?" Came Kat's voice behind me.

"Yeah."

"Did he send anything?"

I considered my answer without turning around to look at her. "Kat…"

I heard her close her laptop lid and felt her move to sit at the island beside me. "He did, but you're not sure if you want to show me."

"After what he said about not disrespecting a gift, I just…"

"It would be hypocritical to know you'd be pissed off royally if he were to show any of his buddies your selfie, and then turn around and show me what he sent you."

"Pretty much."

She regarded me. "You know, I'm starting to wonder if maybe Teddy had a point."

"No." I shook my head resolutely. "It's not like that. I've just never been a hypocrite and I'm not about to start now." I bit my lip around a grin at her. "Also, what he sent was…kind of private."

She twisted on the stool to stare at me. "Well at least tell me about it. Something, anything."

I turned my phone face down on the counter,

traced the oval outline of the cameras on the backside. "He sent a video, and let's just say…sex with Braun is *definitely* going to be very, *very* enjoyable."

She squealed. "He's packing?"

I mouthed the word *huge*. Held my hands several inches apart, and then made a wide circle with the fingers of both hands to indicate my perception of his girth. "So big."

She groaned, head tipped back, and rubbed her face with both hands. "And you won't show me."

"Kat, no. I can't. In pretty much any other situation, you know I would."

"Not fair. But I get it. I'm not going to encourage you to be hypocritical." She eyed me. "What if you told him he could show his friends if you could show yours?"

"No!" I shoved at her shoulder. "I don't want him showing my tits to a bunch of coders and programmers. For one thing, he's based in LA, so it's entirely possible I either already have or will end up selling houses to some of them. I'd lose all credibility if that were to happen. No one would hire me if they knew I was letting nudie pics get spread all over LA."

"Nudie pics," she echoed. "You're as much of a dork as he is." She patted my hand. "I know, I know. I wasn't serious."

"You just have to go find your own."

"I'm trying!" she said, voice raised. "But for real,

I'm about to run that ad we worked up for you but about me. I'm that desperate to find good dick."

I frowned. "It's not about finding good dick."

"Yes it is. That's absolutely what it's about. Good dick, and the yummy stuff that comes out of it."

I made a face. "Eww, Kat. Spunk is *not* yummy."

"Spunk? You did *not* just call it that, woman."

"Fine, cum. Sperm. Seed. Jizz. What other term would you find acceptable?"

She eyed me. "You don't like it?"

"*Like* it? Not really. I don't mind it, I don't find it, like, disgusting, mainly because most guys go so adorably idiotic when you blow 'em. But I wouldn't say it's something I find yummy."

She bit her lip and nudged me with a shoulder. "I do."

I made an incredulous face at her. "You do. For real?"

"Yeah. When I'm done, I like to lick away every last drop." She shrugged. "But you know I'm weird like that."

"Guys must love you."

"I *have* received more than one marriage proposal by the time I'm done with a man." She did a Laurel impression, preening and tossing her hair. "I get on my knees and bring them to theirs."

"God, Kat."

"That's exactly what they say!" She glanced up at

the ceiling. "Only, they tend to be considerably more breathless."

"I bet."

She eyed me. "Are you planning on going down on him? Or are you thinking you should save all his *spunk* for trying to get pregnant?"

"Don't make fun of me, it's not nice." I sighed, shrugging. "I don't know. I wondered the same thing."

"I think you could probably have some fun and still make sure you get enough inside you to make a baby."

I bit my lip, thinking how, in the video he'd sent me, the amount of cum that he'd shot out had been…a veritable river.

"Yeah, I'm not thinking that's going to be a problem," I said, deadpan.

She giggled. "Stop, stop, or I'm going to try to convince you to show me the video, and I'm trying to be a good influence."

"If you were trying to be a good influence, you wouldn't have gotten me tipsy and convinced me to send him a topless selfie."

She shrugged. "Different definitions of good influence, then."

I sighed. "Did you draft an agreement?"

"Yep." She slid me her laptop, open to a short document:

This constitutes a written, binding agreement between Elizabeth Stephenson and Braun Bennet, wherein the following terms are hereby agreed to between both parties. Elizabeth Stephenson and Braun Bennet, the undersigned, hereby agree to a temporary sexual relationship for such a period of time as is necessary to verify conception of a child on the part of Elizabeth Stephenson; this relationship is to be considered sexual in nature, and for the duration of the period necessary to verify conception, both parties must abstain from any sexual contact with any persons other than the individuals named herein, and previous to any sexual encounters, both parties shall provide medical documentation of freedom from any sexually transmitted diseases.

The terms which the undersigned hereby agree to consist of the following four (4) items:

1) The liaisons between the parties as well as the terms contained in this agreement shall be kept private and shall not be discussed or disseminated in any public way or on any social media platform, for any reason;

2) the liaisons between the parties shall constitute conversational, interpersonal, and sexual interactions only; no monies shall be exchanged or requested by either party, at any time into perpetuity, for any reason, neither requested directly nor implied; any monies spent by either party for the duration of the liaisons shall be considered voluntary and based on the discretion of the individual and shall not be tabulated nor accounted as part of the agreement;

3) there shall not be any demand or expectation of

parental rights for any progeny or issue which might result from the liaisons; in the event of a birth of a child as a natural result of this agreement and liaisons, it shall fall to a subsequent agreement between the parties whether there shall be further contact between either parties and the resultant child, based upon the mutual wishes of everyone involved;

4) once conception is verified, this agreement is considered fulfilled in all terms, and contact, whether personal or sexual, is considered at an end. Any further contact between the parties subsequent to conception shall be outside the terms of this agreement and not subject to any terms, conditions, or agreements, and shall be conducted as both parties see fit, in a normal personal, relational, financial, and sexual manner.

By signing this document I, the undersigned, agree to the terms of this document.

I read it over carefully several times, and then connected her laptop to my personal printer and printed two copies. "This is great, Kat. You're a marvel."

"I try."

I went and got the documents. "That last section...you're providing an in-case clause, for after this is over. In case...there's something."

"I mean, yeah. I know you're all like, no, no way, not happening." She leaned into me. "But you never know. That's all I'm saying—you never know. So we're just covering every eventuality."

"It's a nonstarter. It's not what this is. I don't want that."

"I know. I'm not arguing with you. I'm just covering your bases." Kat checked her phone. "Shit, it's after midnight. I should get home. I was all revved up for a hookup, which obviously was not in the cards, and now I'm all revved up but no one to work my transmission, if you know what I mean."

I snorted. "That was the worst analogy I've ever heard."

"You'd rather I came right out and said I'm going home to watch porn and flick my bean?"

I faked a gag. "Nope. Bad analogies are better."

She laughed, patting me on the back. "Well, it's been a fun night." She kissed my temple. "Have fun watching that video…again and again…and again. And again."

"And revving my transmission, or whatever you said."

"Right." She whispered in my ear. "You could always dial him up for a late-night booty call. Pre-agreement fun. Know what I'm saying?" She floated out of my condo, waving at me as she exited, not waiting for my response. "Just a thought."

"Bye, Kat. Thanks for all the bad ideas."

"It was a great idea and you know it."

The elevator closed, and I flipped my phone back over.

I had one text from Braun: *You still there?*

Me: *Yeah. My friend Kat was over. In the spirit of full*

accountability, she was the one who convinced me to send that. I may or may not have been slightly tipsy at the time. Not anymore, and I was in full capacity to make sound decisions. Just...a little liquid courage. Anyway, she left. And no, I didn't show her the video. I wouldn't do that anymore than you would.

Braun: *I wouldn't have known.*

Me: *I know. But I would have. I couldn't expect one thing of you and another from myself. Not how I operate.*

Braun: *I do appreciate that. And, in any event, I have to say I'm thankful for Kat's encouragement. I have that photo saved to my hidden folder. I may or may not have it open even now.*

Me: *I have to say, now that I'm alone, I'm all kinds of worked up from watching that video. I kinda wish you were here to help me out, like you did earlier.*

Braun: *I could be.*

Me: *It's after midnight, you're in LA, I'm in Malibu, and I have a showing at 8 tomorrow morning. Also, I have a better idea. Well, not better, but different, considering it's not realistic for us to see each other tonight.*

Braun: *and that idea would be...what? Inquiring minds would like to know.*

Me: *You have no way of knowing, but the inquiring minds thing is becoming an ongoing inside joke between me and my girls. And now you too. SO MANY INQUIRING MINDS.*

Braun: *horny minds, then.*

Me: *Horny? You just jerked off a few minutes ago. You're still horny?*

Braun: *so, so, so horny. That was like...an appetizer. Just enough to make me realize how fucking ravenous I am.*

Me: *So you could come again, right now?*

A brief delay, and then a picture came through. Braun was on a bed, the photo a top-down angle, him lying on his back and holding his phone above himself. He was shirtless, wearing a pair of loose basketball shorts. He was tenting the front of them like crazy.

Braun: *That answer your question?*

Me: *I don't know...I can't quite tell. I'd have to see more to say for sure.*

I took my phone into my bedroom, shut the door. Lay on the bed, heart pounding. What the hell was I doing? This wasn't part of the deal. This was supposed to be sex and nothing but sex. Instead, I was sexting him. FLIRTING. Dirty, dirty flirting. It was hot, and fun, and so far outside how I normally operated that I had no clue what I was doing, except operating on pure libidinal instinct.

I unbuttoned the shirt again, hesitated, and then just took it off, threw it across the room. I undid the front of my slacks and slipped my hand inside, touching myself, and held the camera up overhead, snapped a photo. Before I could overthink it, I sent it.

Braun: *Holy shit. God, you're fucking gorgeous, Lizzy.*

Me: *You don't have to flatter me.*

Braun: *It's not flattery. It's just my honest reaction.*

He sent a photo, then: the shorts, shoved down. His thick member exposed, flat against his belly. He had gorgeous abs, absolutely delicious. Shadows of definition but not shredded. Hard muscle over his chest, thick arms, broad shoulders. He had that V of delineation pointing from his hips to his groin, high-lighting his thick, long, hard sex.

Me: *goddamn, Braun.*

Braun: *What*

Me: *just you. You're freaking sexy as hell.*

Braun: *You don't have to flatter me.*

I brought up the picture, stared at it, imagined it in my hands, sliding against me, thick and solid, warm, the veins stuttering through my fingers. It'd be heavy, and so, so hard. It'd taste like salt and flesh, it'd slide into my wetness and fill me…

I flicked on my video camera and hit the red Record button, closed my eyes and held the camera overhead, facing down, as I let my imagination wander, let my tongue run words freely as they flowed out of me, let my fingers circle. A few swipes with my hand inside my pants, and then I awkwardly shimmied them down one-handed, kicked out of them.

I panned the camera to show him all of me, toes to scalp, naked, on my bed.

"I'm thinking about you," I whispered, as I touched myself again. "I'm thinking about your cock. I'm thinking about how it would feel. God, it'd feel so good I bet. I'd put my mouth on you, stroke you with my hands. I'd put you inside me. I'd do so many things to you, Braun. You're handsome, so hot. So sexy. Your cock is so, so big, so beautiful, and I want it. I want it so bad." I was crazy, now, barely aware of what I was saying. Fingers flying, swirling, circling. Hips flexing, pumping, staring up at the camera as if it was him, but in my mind seeing only him, above me, staring down at me. "Shit, oh god, oh shit, I'm gonna come. You thought I was a screamer, and you were right—I...oh, oh...oh god *BRAUN!*" I screamed his name as I came, seeing stars behind my tight-shut eyelids, coming so hard I couldn't breathe for a moment.

I peered cross-eyed and panting at my phone, tapped the Record button to stop it, and then the blue button with the white arrow to send it. No hesitation, this time.

Holy shit.

I'd just taken a video of myself masturbating and sent it to him.

WHAT THE HELL WAS HAPPENING TO ME?

CHAPTER EIGHT

"C LEAN AS A WHISTLE, LIZZY," MY DOCTOR pronounced, bringing me the folder with my results into the room. "Not that I expected any different. You've always been careful."

"It's a…formality," I said.

She quirked an eyebrow up at me. "Considering unprotected sex with someone?"

I ducked my head. "Yeah."

"Well, just be sure you know what you're doing. It's not just the diseases that happen when you have unprotected sex, you know."

I stared at her, droll. "Yes, Dr. Washburn, I am aware."

"Just putting it out there. Sometimes people are aware of the facts but have a way of convincing themselves that it won't happen to them." She shrugged. "Unprotected sex leads to pregnancy. It's inevitable. You're perfectly fertile, Lizzy. I know women look at forty as some kind of cutoff for fertility, but it's not. You're not even premenopausal. You may not get pregnant the first time, or the second, but if you keep having sex without a condom, you *will* get pregnant. It's just a matter of time."

I smiled at her. "Thank you, Doctor. I mean that—thank you. I really needed to hear that." I tucked the folder into my purse and stood up—I'd gotten dressed again long since, following my exam. I'd gotten the tests at a facility a few days ago, and had the results sent to my doctor; I'd been in need of a yearly physical anyway. "You see, that's the whole purpose."

"Getting pregnant?"

I nodded. "Yes."

"I didn't know you were in a relationship."

"I'm not."

She blinked. "Oh. Well. I'm sure you know what you're doing. Just be careful. Not just physically. Raising a child alone is challenging—I should know, I raised three by myself."

"Thank you again, Dr. Washburn."

"Of course. You're all set."

I checked out with the receptionist and headed out to the parking garage. I'd been in communication with Braun the past few days, mostly innocuous stuff—he'd said he was going to be pretty busy these next couple days, cramming code, whatever that meant. I'd been busy, too—several showings each day, plus four appointments for new clients, plus a party for a hundred-million-dollar listing in Beverly Hills last night, which I'd wanted of course but hadn't gotten. I hadn't expected to—my biggest competition for the stratospheric-amount listings simply had me edged out in experience, personnel, and budget. I was closing in on him, though, and I knew I'd nail my first hundred-million-dollar listing at some point soon. There were only so many of them, obviously, and I really, really wanted one.

I got into my car and texted Braun: *I have my tests.*

Braun: *Me too. Just got them earlier this morning.*

Me: *So. Want to meet?*

Braun: *Today?*

Me: *Now.*

A short pause. Then bouncing dots. *When and where?*

Me: *Idk. Your place or mine?*

Braun: *How about, for our first time we meet somewhere neutral. I'll get us a suite at the Viceroy L'Ermitage.*

Wow. High end.

Me: *Lol, I'm not sure I'm dressed for that.*

Braun: *It doesn't matter. You won't be dressed at all, soon enough.*

Me: *I like the way you think.*

Braun: *See you soon. Not soon enough, but soon.*

Me: *Eager to begin, are you, Mr. Bennet?*

Braun: *After the other night, you're all I think about. Literally. I've watched your video more times than I care to admit. Yes, Ms. Stephenson, I am very eager to begin.*

Me: *Driving now.*

He thumbs-upped the message, and I focused on driving.

Or, as well as I could with images and fantasies of Braun and his cock and everything I was planning on doing to and with him dancing through my libido-ravaged brain.

I navigated with my brain on autopilot, and then I was sliding to a stop in front of the hotel and a valet was taking my car and I was checking the only other message Braun had sent: *Penthouse. I've asked the concierge to meet you with a key.*

My guy was not fucking around, booking the penthouse at the L'Ermitage.

I approached the concierge, a sleek, refined, black man. "Hi, I'm Lizzy Stephenson. There should be a key for me?"

"Yes, ma'am," he intoned, smiling brightly at me as he handed me a keycard in a cream envelope made from hideously expensive card stock. "Here you are. Is there anything else at all I can do to make your stay more pleasurable?"

I think it's about to get as pleasurable as it can be, I thought, but didn't say. "No, I think I'm all set. Thank you."

"Of course, ma'am. Please do not hesitate to call down should you need anything."

I waved and headed for the elevator bank. I swiped the card, and it automatically chose the penthouse, rising smoothly and swiftly.

When the doors opened, I knew if I was uncertain as to his financial status before, I had no reason to be any longer. You don't book a suite like this without serious, serious money…and he did it last second, on a whim.

Clean, modern, sleek and elegant, with chandeliers dripping crystals, textured walls, a muted palette with pops of bright colors via throw pillows and lampshades and vases. Expansive, open, but with no wasted space; a breathtaking view of Los Angeles from every window, which were floor to ceiling and plentiful, letting it absolute buckets of natural light. The furniture was expensive and comfortable but tasteful, the decor neutral and attractive. The whole effect purely screamed understated wealth, the kind of wealth which doesn't need to be ostentatious or obvious.

I didn't see him immediately upon entering the suite, but I could smell his presence, sense his presence. I set my purse on the side table which sat near the entrance, along with the keycard, stepped out of my shoes.

If I'd known I was meeting him today, I'd have dressed differently, but fortunately I had a weird obsession with my bra and panties needing to match at all times. I never, ever wore a mismatched set. And I also didn't go in for cheap granny panties and blah white underwire Sears Catalog bras. Oh no. I was *bougie*, as Kat would say—I splurged on the good stuff. Purses, shoes, and lingerie, those were my kink, monetarily speaking. And honestly, it wasn't lingerie I bought for myself so much as just expensive, custom-fitted, and comfortable bra and underwear sets.

All that to say, I was rocking a deep plum set today: my skirt was a tight pencil skirt that cupped my ass and hips tightly enough that I had to wear a thong to prevent panty lines, and the bra that went with it was a half-cup push-up to emphasize my cleavage in the top, which featured a plunging neckline. My clients this morning had been a group of middle-aged men considering a retail space, so I'd dressed to kill, because I'd take any edge I could get, especially when it came to clinching a sale with a bunch of tight-fisted investment capitalist types.

I was pretty confident Braun would enjoy undressing me.

A sliding door opened somewhere, likely in the bedroom. Braun emerged from the bedroom, and my breath caught.

He was wearing a pale blue suit, bespoke judging by the cut of it, with a blindingly white dress shirt under it, no tie, the top two buttons undone. French cuffs, understated silver cufflinks. Barefoot. I'd always had a thing for hot guys barefoot and shirtless in jeans, because come on, it's just a sexy look. But this? Barefoot in a custom suit? A hint of chest peeking through the open V of his shirt. He had a glass of red wine in his hand, a cell phone pressed to his ear.

"Yes, yes, absolutely. Rollout should happen immediately—yes, I know there are still a few bugs to work out, but none of them are major. We need this to go to market *now*, Craig, while there's nothing else out there like it. We're poised to corner the market on this, if we go now. It's a killer app, with features no one else has even thought of, but word is spreading already and it's only a matter of time before someone beats us to the punch—shit, shit, yeah, that's true, we can't roll it out with that happening. Okay, so how long to work that out? Two more weeks is not acceptable, someone will have something out by then." He grinned at me, held up his index finger on the hand gripping the wineglass, which he took a sip from and then handed it to me. "Dammit, fine, okay. Tomorrow I'll come in myself and go over the code. I can't really spare the time, but if it's what we have to do to get it out ASAP, then that's what I'll do. It's my baby, dude. Okay, I'll see you tomorrow. I don't know what time. I have code to go through on my other project, but that's not as time-sensitive as this, and I'm paid by billable hours, whereas I've got royalties on the line with this. Okay, anything else? Because I have something *far* more... pressing, at hand."

I sipped the wine while he listened, but as he listened, his eyes raked over me, head to toe. His gaze was frankly appreciative, taking in the plunge of my neckline, the plump swell of my cleavage spilling up out of my blouse, the round bell curve of my hips. He circled around me, um-humming now and then—I could tell he was splitting his focus between listening and understanding, and...me.

I stood, sipped, and waited. He stepped slowly around behind me, taking in the view from behind. I felt his eyes on my ass, outlined and highlighted by the tightness of my skirt. Then, I felt his hands where his eyes had been, a palm pressing against my lower back, sliding down to cup the swell, pausing to squeeze and appreciate before passing across to pay the same attention to the other side. I held the wineglass with both hands, eyes closed as I soaked up the feel of his big strong hand circling and squeezing my ass, one side and then the other, and then my hips. Both hands, then, the phone squeezed between his ear and shoulder.

"Can we wrap this up, Craig? I really do have to let you go." A pause, his presence towering behind me, heat billowing against me, his scent wrapping around me, expensive cologne and something more indefinable but distinctly masculine. "Okay, cool. So,

I've let my assistant and secretary know, but I'm shutting my phone off and I'm going to be incommunicado for the rest of the day. And I do mean that, literally—I will not be able to be reached until at least tomorrow morning, so try to not have any emergencies. Okay, cool. Bye."

A silence as he ended the call—another moment or two of silence, one of his hands resting on my hip, the other likely doing something with his phone. Then, he strode away from me, turned to face me with his back to the island in the kitchen, making a show of shutting his phone down.

"Your turn," he said. "Can you do that? Shut your phone down and cancel all appointments until tomorrow?"

I didn't answer him, instead went to my purse and withdrew my phone. Called Teddy, who, as the most junior and most recently hired agent at the brokerage, often acted as my assistant when such was needed.

"Teddy, hi. So, um. Can you access my schedule please? Okay, so I know I have Jeremy Lennon wanting to see the Markus hacienda at two, what else?"

A pause, and then Teddy answered: "Linda Carls at four for a discussion of lowering the list price, and then Amy and Brendan Yates at five thirty for a second showing at the Kaplinsky place."

"Okay, can you reschedule both? The Yates is

priority—Jeremy is a friend and I'm only showing him the Markus place because he's looking for remodel ideas."

She knew something was up. "Yeah, got it. Did something come up?"

"Yes, you could say that." I smirked at Braun, who was eyeing me hungrily, impatiently.

"Is it Braun?"

"All you and the others need to know is that I'm shutting my phone off until tomorrow morning."

"*Off* off? Like *actually* off?"

I laughed. "Yes, Teddy, as in actually *off*."

"Has your phone ever been actually powered down before?"

I sighed. "Not that I know of, but there's a first time for everything."

Apparently, he was out of patience, because Braun paced over to me, his bare feet silent on the thick carpet underfoot. I smiled up at him, pinched my phone between my ear and shoulder—reached up and brushed his jacket off his shoulders, caught it as it slid down his arms. I took it, folded it neatly, and set it across the back of a chair at the nearby desk. He reached for me, standing facing me, and his fingers ran around the circumference of my waist until they came to the zipper of my skirt at the small of my back. He lowered the zipper slowly, millimeter by agonizing millimeter.

"What if there's an emergency?" Teddy asked.

"It's real estate, Ted, what kind of emergency could there possibly be that can't wait till morning?"

She sniffed a laugh. "True. Should I at least know where you are, you know, just in case?"

"In case he turns out to be, like, a serial killer?" I asked.

"Exactly."

I kept my gaze on Braun as he brought the zipper of my skirt down to snug into the base of the opening. The skirt was now looser, but the swell of my hips and the tightness of the garment kept it from simply dropping to the floor. It would need help—I'd had to dance and jump and wiggle to get it on, and it usually required a similar series of maneuvers to get it off.

Braun pinched the fabric of the skirt at each hip between thumb and forefinger of each hand, tugged down; it didn't budge an inch.

I muted the call for a moment. "Gonna have to work harder than that to get this bad boy off," I said, to him, and then unmuted the call again. "I'm at the Viceroy L'Ermitage in Beverly Hills. But unless you don't hear from me for at least forty-eight hours, assume I'm fine. And unless it's a literal life or death, flood, fire, or earthquake emergency, don't even think about trying to get ahold of me."

"Yes, ma'am," Teddy said, and I could hear the grin in her voice. "Get it, girl."

"Oh, I plan to get it. A lot of it." I bit my lip

over a grin as Braun tugged more firmly on the skirt, which moved it downward a teensy bit. "On that note, Teddy, I'm hanging up. Talk to you...probably tomorrow. Maybe. Depends on how this goes."

"We've got you covered."

"I know you do."

"And Lizzy?" She paused a beat. "Leave room in your heart for what-if. Okay? Just humor me on this."

"Bye, Teddy." I hung up and showed Braun the act of powering the device off and tossing it into my purse.

"How the hell did you even get into this skirt, woman?" Braun asked.

"You ever try to stuff too big of a pillow into too small of a pillowcase?" I asked. "It's like that. It requires a careful balance of force and finesse to wedge all *this*…" I smoothed my palms over my hips, "into a skirt this tight."

"Worth the effort," Braun muttered. "But now how the hell do I get it off you?"

I shrugged, a coy grin on my face. "I dunno. You're a smart guy—I'm sure you can figure something out."

He stared down at me, and then a smirk crossed his lips. Before I knew what was happening, I was airborne—he had his arms under my knees and around my shoulders and was carrying me into the bedroom, each step resolute.

"Rather forward of you, Mr. Bennet," I remarked, grinning up at him.

He didn't answer, just tossed me to bounce onto the bed. His hands cradled my calves, slid up to caress behind my knees, and then he gripped the hem of my skirt in both hands and jerked roughly. I yelped at the suddenness of the move, and then the skirt was off and I was lying half off the bed, legs bare. His palms skated up my thighs. I bit down on my lip, watching his hands scrape and slide slowly up my legs to my hips, over the deep purple lace of my thong.

"The question is," Braun murmured, "do I want *this* off first?" He tugged at the waist of my thong, then ran his palms up my belly to cup my breasts over my shirt and bra. "Or this?"

"We should..." I gasped, trying to remember the one important thing left before the fun could start. "Agreement. Sign...sign the agreement."

The sudden discombobulation was because he'd abruptly made a decision, of sorts. That being neither—he pressed kiss after kiss to my thighs, from my quad around to the upper, inner silk, going from one thigh to the other, back and forth, slowly angling my legs open until I was only sort of covered by the tiny triangle of lace over my sex.

"Screw the agreement," he muttered. "I don't give a shit at the moment. Right now, all I care about is getting my mouth on this sweet little pussy of yours."

He suited action to words, tugging the thong aside with one finger, baring my wet core. His tongue lapped at me, flicking upward slowly from opening to clit. I cried out, and then the cry morphed into a groan as he drilled a finger inside me, and then another, and then a third, so I went from empty to spread open in an instant.

"Oh fuck, Braun."

He did not relent. This was not a slow tease, this was a sudden and wild assault with a singular purpose: to bring me to climax as swiftly as possible.

And god, did he succeed. His tongue flicked me, his fingers squelched in and out, and I could only whimper and flex my hips in time with him. Then his tongue went flat and broad, lapping at me, swiping up and up and up, licking me faster and faster. His other hand slid under me, lifted my ass up. I wrapped my legs around his neck and gave in utterly, totally, flexing against him, grinding on his mouth and accepting all the ecstasy he was offering.

"Ohh fuck, oh fuck, oh god, Braun, yes, god, just like that, don't stop, just like that, right there*ohSHIT!*" I locked my legs around him and squeezed, and I worried I'd pop his head like a grape between my thighs, but he didn't protest, instead doing exactly what I'd said, which most guys get wrong: when I say oh yes, right there, just like that, usually they do whatever they were doing harder and faster, when what I actually mean is…right there, just like that.

Weird how I mean what I say.

Braun, however, kept licking and sliding his fingers in and out at exactly the same tempo, with the same force. And I came so hard stars burst behind my eyes, and my whimpers and cursing detonated into a hip-thrusting, body-thrashing paroxysm of clenched-teeth screams.

He kept me there for a time I couldn't measure, pushing me over the edge of orgasm and into something else, tongue still wild and fingers steadily grinding inside me, until the wrenching bliss was too much, until it felt so good it hurt.

I grabbed at his face, pulled him away. "Okay, okay, stop—stop, please, stop for a second."

He sat up and away, gently setting my legs onto the bed, feet on the floor. He stood up, still fully dressed but for his suit coat. His black stubble was dotted with my essence, and he swept a palm over his mouth to wipe it away.

I gasped for breath. "Jesus, Braun."

He shot his cuffs. "Been wanting to do that since I had you up against the wall in that alley."

"Was it everything you imagined?" I asked, flippant.

"It was everything I've fantasized and more." He wasn't flippant—he was dead serious.

I sat up, pressed my thighs together and braced my palms on the mattress. Smiled up at him. "I've been fantasizing about a few things myself, come to think of it."

"That right?"

"Weird question, maybe, but…do you have your glasses with you?"

He grinned. "Yeah, why?"

"Could you put them on for me?"

He shrugged. "Sure. They're in my jacket—be right back." He left and returned immediately, now wearing a pair of round, black-framed glasses.

I bit my lip, grinning. "There we go. Sexy nerd."

He pushed them up higher with his index finger, wrinkled his nose and snorted, spoke in a nasal voice. "I could talk about Star Trek, if that will aid you in your fantasy. Or perhaps I could quote *Lord of the Rings* in the original Elvish."

I paused with my hand on the topmost button of his shirt. "You can speak Tolkien Elvish?"

He bit his lower lip and curled his upper lip, snorting again in a parody of an archetypal über-nerd. "Why certainly I can. I can read and write fluently in Elvish and Dwarven."

"That is surprisingly arousing, actually." I unbuttoned a button, baring more of his chest. "Let's hear something in Elvish."

He adjusted his glasses, unironically this time, using thumb and forefinger around the frame. "Let's see…" and then cleared his throat and began speaking in what I figured was Tolkien's Elvish, although not being fluent in anything but English, he could be speaking Italian for all I knew.

I listened, and then undid another button.

"What did you say?" I asked, when he finished speaking.

"I said, 'My lady, your beauty is as breathtaking as the splendor of dawn breaking in the east. Your skin is like porcelain, your eyes like stars. Though I live for an age, I shall never see the equal of your beauty in this world, nor any other. I worship at the altar of your skin, lady. I bathe in the shine of your eyes, I glory in the blinding vision of your body.'"

I had the last button undone as he finished the translation, and felt my belly clench, my mind twist, wobble, and topple. I blinked up at him. "You said all that? About me? In Elvish?"

"I said all that about you in Quenya, specifically—High Elven."

"Was it a quote from the book or something?"

He chuckled. "No, I just made it up."

"On the spot? Just like that?"

He smirked, shrugged. "Languages are kind of a pastime for me. When I'm burnt out on coding, I take a break and read something in another language."

"How many do you know?"

He glanced up and to the left. "Um? I'm fluent in Quenya, Sindarin, and Khuzdul, which is the language of the Dwarves. As for real languages? Spanish and Portuguese fluently, Italian and German passably, and I'm in the process of teaching myself Russian."

I stared up at him, blinking. "Seven languages, and you're learning an eighth?"

A shrug. "Like I said, it's a hobby."

"Most people, like, learn guitar or play tennis as a hobby."

"I'm not most people."

I slid my hands up his bare torso, feeling the ridges of muscle; I liked the smattering of dark chest hair covering his pecs and belly. I slid my hands under the shirt at his shoulders, reaching way up to do so without standing. The shirt billowed off of him and floated to the floor like a wisp of flyaway silk—the sun chose that moment to peek out from behind a cloud and stream in through the wall of floor-to-ceiling windows to limn Braun Bennet in a cloak of brilliant noon light. My breath caught, staring up at him—his skin was perfectly sun-kissed golden, his physique toned but not hyper-shredded, muscular without being bulky. The chest hair caught the light, and suddenly I was a believer in the masculine beauty of it, when I'd been on the fence before. Or maybe it was just him. His hair was gloriously messy, rumpled into sexiness by his hands passing through it, jet black and wild, errant locks sweeping across his forehead in artful curves. His eyes were the exact shade of burnt caramel, intense and heated.

"No," I whispered, after a moment. "You certainly are not."

"So...was this your fantasy, then?" he asked, his eyes teasing. "Get me shirtless in my glasses?"

I shook my head, hands scraping circles over his chest, down to his stomach. "No, not exactly." I slid the end of his light brown, thin leather belt out from the buckle. "My fantasy did not stop at you being shirtless."

"No?"

I slowly drew the belt out of the loops, coiled it neatly, and set it aside. Reached down, plucked his shirt off the floor and folded it, lay it over the belt. "Wouldn't want it to wrinkle."

"Indeed not," he muttered. "What did it concern, then, if it wasn't merely me shirtless, wearing my spectacles?"

I laughed. "Spectacles—such a funny word to me, for some reason." I palmed the hard wedge of his waist, and then let my fingers trip around to the front, grasping the clasp of his trousers. "Well...in order for me to show you the fantasy I've indulged in, regarding you, we'd have to help you out of these silly pants."

"Silly?" He faked an offended tone. "These are custom-made, I'll have you know. Imported from Italy at great expense. It's my 'impress the investors' suit."

I tugged the zipper down. "It's a beautiful suit. You look positively scrumptious in it, as a matter of

fact. But the pants are silly to me at this particular moment because they're still *on* you. And I want them *off*,
for what I have in mind."

He nodded, making an "a-ha" face. "I see, I see.
You want me in just my underwear and *spectacles*." He
stepped out of the slacks, and I folded them and set
them with the growing pile of clothing.

I rubbed his chest again, because it was a very
beautiful chest, and I enjoyed touching it. "Well, I do
like the sight of you in your underwear and glasses.
Very sexy, I must admit." I leaned back and admired.
"You really are a beautiful man, Braun."

He batted a hand and gave a cutesy shrug. "Awww
shucks. You're makin' me blush."

"But no, this is still not exactly my fantasy." I
hooked my index fingers into the elastic of his underwear at his hipbones—this time he was wearing
tight gray Calvin Klein boxer-briefs. "Still wearing too
much."

"Ohhhhh," he said, nodding. "I see. So these have
to come off too?" He popped the waistband with a
thumb.

"Indeed they do." I tugged them down.

He popped free, unfurling to bob and weave in
front of my face, pointing horizontally away from his
torso, only partially erect at the moment, but still im-
pressive. Actually, much, much larger than the video
had even revealed, and he was only semihard. I folded

the underwear as well. "And now, finally, we can start talking about my fantasy."

"Me naked but for my glasses is not the fantasy?" Once again, he adjusted the glasses with one hand.

"Nope." I held on to his hips, and then ran my hands up his belly to his chest, down to his hipbones, down his thighs, and then back up, running my palms up the hard angles of hips just to either side of his hardening arousal. "You see, my fantasy isn't so much how you're dressed, or as the case may be, *not* dressed, as it is what I'm doing to you in that state—which being you naked but for your spectacles."

"I see, I see." He feathered a finger over my temple, through an intentional flyaway tendril of hair draped down my cheek. "And what are you doing to me, in this fantasy of yours, Miss Stephenson?"

I clutched him and felt him harden in my fist; one hand around his arousal, I cupped his sac with the other. "Why don't I just show you?"

He groaned. "I...yeah. I—I think maybe that would be most effective."

"Show rather than tell, you know." I stroked him, root to tip, slowly, admiring him as he reached full erection—his fully aroused size was mind-boggling, shocking, incredible.

"Indeed." He ran a finger over my ear. "May I take your hair down, Lizzy?"

I had it in an updo, a neat chignon. "You may."

He gently worked the hairband free of my long, thick blond locks, taking exaggerated care, holding the mass of it until the elastic band was free, and then he let it drop free, ran his hands through it to loosen the tangles.

"Good and holy goddamn," he whispered, "you are so fucking incredible."

I felt my chest squeeze at that; Teddy's final words to leave room in my heart for what-ifs racketed around my skull. I ignored it.

Caressed him again, twisting my fist around the plump pink round head. "Thank you, Braun."

He buried his hands in my hair, letting it filter through his fingers. "I mean it."

"I know, I can tell." I cupped his sac again, this time with both hands. "You're pretty incredible yourself."

He snorted. "What, that old thing? Had it for ages. Barely use it."

I cackled. "Yeah, I bet."

"For real. I'm no monk, but I'm not a player, either." He sucked in a deep breath. "I need your shirt off."

I smirked up at him. "My shirt, huh?" I let go of him, grasped the hem of my shirt and peeled it up and off. "There you go."

Now in just my plum-colored bra, which did a frankly miraculous job of lifting and separating the girls, showing them off to pretty fantastic effect. Case in point, the member in my hands twitched, jerked.

"Jesus fuck, Lizzy," he breathed.

I stroked downward, twisted at the root. "You like?"

He nodded, eyes locked onto my tits. "Like? More like love. Want. *Need.*" He reached down, cupped me with both hands, thumbs brushing over my nipples through the lace. "Now that I think of it, there was another fantasy I had."

"What's that?" I asked. "Because right now, we're still on mine. It's not just this, getting my hands on your cock while you're naked but for glasses."

He tilted his head backward, gasped a groan. "God, the way you're touching me is fucking magic." He straightened his head to look at me. "Well, the thing is, I think perhaps this other fantasy of mine just might intersect with yours. Why don't you show me the rest of your fantasy, and we'll see if it matches mine."

I used both hands on him, twisting at the root and plunging my fist up and down in short strokes around the head. "All right." I reached around to clutch at his butt, pulling him closer. "You ready?"

He held up a finger. "No, wait. Not yet. Just…one more thing."

He reached around to my back and unclasped my bra, fumbling a bit before managing to release the hooks from the eyelets; when he'd gotten it undone, he pulled it away, and I withdrew my arms from the straps. He tossed the bra onto the pile of his clothes, and now we were both naked. My breasts hung heavy, swaying. My nipples were peaked, aroused, and he reached down to cup a breast in each hand.

"You may continue, Miss Stephenson." He sounded shaky, breathless. "What was the rest of your fantasy?"

I pulled his cock away from his body, whispered one word, the sound hissing against the precum-leaking tip. "This."

And lowered my mouth onto him.

CHAPTER NINE

"Fuck, ohh…fuck." He growled, groaned. "Lizzy, holy shit, Lizzy. Your mouth—it's…god, feels so good. Too good. So hot, so wet, so tight."

I pushed down, taking him and taking him until I couldn't take any more, and he held my head, hands in my hair, keeping it pulled back away from my mouth, and his eyes were hot and wild on me, watching me take him into my mouth.

He lifted up on his toes as I slid my lips lower and lower until I was at the edge of my ability to breathe and swallow around him; I flicked my tongue against him as I pulled back, gripping his base with both hands, and then tucking one hand under to cup his sac, squeezing and kneading, twisting my fist around him. When only the tip of him was left in my mouth, I bobbed, sucking hard, tongue swirling.

"Jesus Jesus Jesus…" He squeezed his eyes shut. "Lizzy, you should stop. I can't—fuck, fuck. I can't hold out. You're too good, Lizzy, it feels too good, so fuck-ing good."

I kept going with that, pumping at his shaft and massaging his sac, bobbing and suckling at his broad plump tip.

He tried to pull away, but I didn't allow it. I wanted this, liked the helplessness in his eyes, in his voice. The desperation, the confusion. He wanted me, wanted to fuck me, wanted to come inside me, wanted to ex-ert control over himself and this situation, to prove he could hold out at will—he wanted more, he didn't want this to end already. But he also just wanted to come, to let me do this to him as long as I was willing, until he exploded.

His hips were flexing gently, slowly, as if he was holding back his need to thrust only with great effort.

"Lizzy, god...oh god." His eyes opened momen-tarily; he was shaking all over, gasping with the effort of holding back; he raked his hands through his hair, let them fall to his sides, leaning back and burying his hands in his hair again, gripping it hard, pulling at it with desperate ferocity. "You—have to...you have to stop. I'm gonna...god, I—can't—I can't..."

I grabbed at his arms, pulled them down, grabbed his hands, guided them into my hair. Let him pop out of my mouth, smiled up at him as I caught my breath. "Can't what, Braun?"

And then I caught at his butt, cupping a cheek in

each hand and guiding him to me, taking him into my mouth again, and he groaned as he filled my mouth. No hands, now, all mouth, just bobbing on him, tongue swirling, sucking, pulling back to lick up the side and then roll over top to take him deep.

"Lizzy, Lizzy, ohhh my god ohmygod oh god, Liz, I can't stop it—please...please, don't—don't, oh god, don't...please don't stop."

He called me Liz. I'm Elizabeth or Lizzy to everyone, exclusively. From him, and only him, for the first time, I liked Liz.

I felt him tense, pulled at his ass, encouraging him to let go, to thrust. He did, but carefully at first, gently, small shallow thrusts. I took them, and he growled, and I knew the moment had come.

He groaned, a long wild snarl and whimper as he lost the battle to stop from coming. "Lizzy, Liz—I have to—I'm, oh god I'm...*fuck*..."

I tasted it on my tongue, thick and wet and hot and salty, and brought my lips to suction around his head and sucked it out of him, one spurt, and then two, a third, and then I slid my mouth down his shaft and swallowed around him as a fourth stream gushed against the back of my throat, and I swallowed that too, and shit, he was still coming, and I had to breathe, and I let him fall out of my mouth and used my fists around his shaft to pump the last of his cum out of him, and it dribbled over his tip and down his erection and over my fingers. He shuddered, pulsed in my fists, thrust again, and I stroked more, and more, until his knees wobbled, gave out.

He staggered to one side, and sat heavily on the bed beside me. Sat swaying, and fell backward. "Holy hell, Lizzy," he gasped.

I leaned on an elbow beside him, grinning. "*That* was my fantasy, Mr. Bennet."

"Mine…" a breathy gasp as he caught his breath. "Mine too."

I touched his chest, one finger tracing the lines of his muscles. "Just one brief word of business."

He reached across his body to capture my nipple with his fingers, tweaked it until it stood up. "And that is?"

"This whole thing…me sucking you off. It's all outside the parameters of our agreement, which we haven't signed yet."

He eyed me steadily, expression giving nothing away. "Does this mean once we officially, formally enter the agreement by signing the contract, this…" he pointed from his now-flaccid member to me, "won't happen again? Because the goal is to get you pregnant?"

I nodded, shrugged. "Essentially. I'm not saying it won't happen ever again, but since the goal of this is to get me pregnant, wasting it like that seems…inefficient." I wiped my lips with one finger, popped the finger into my mouth. "As much as I enjoyed doing it."

He nodded. "Understood. And I should say, I wasn't expecting that. Blew my mind, is what you did."

I smirked, flipped at his slack member. "No, Braun, I blew your cock." I tapped his forehead. "Your mind is in here."

He snorted. "Smart-ass." He closed his eyes, sighing deeply. "For real. That was...beyond incredible. Most amazing thing I've ever felt. I still can't totally feel my toes."

I grinned, shrugged—his eyes followed the movement of my tits as I shrugged. "Glad you enjoyed it."

I was, for my part, enjoying the ministrations of his fingers, the way they toyed with my nipple, keeping it erect, twisting it, tweaking it, flicking, rubbing it with his thumb, and then caressing and cupping the whole pendulous globe.

"Enjoyed it?" He shook his head. "*Enjoyed* is not even close to the right word. I don't know a word in any language strong enough."

I snorted. "You must not have gotten many blow-jobs in your life, then."

He rolled a shoulder. "I mean, honestly, no. I'm usually more focused on giving my partner pleasure than letting her give it to me like that. But, of the few I have gotten, yours is, by an order of several magnitudes, the best."

"Interesting, because I honestly don't give very many of them."

He turned his head to look at me. "Have I told you yet that you're fucking gorgeous?"

"You maybe did mention something like that at least once."

"Well, you are. Breathtaking. I literally can't breathe, looking at you. It feels like the most amazing privilege of my life getting to see a woman as stunning as you, like this. Naked, so sexy, doing this stuff to me. Like, is this my life? It doesn't seem real. You're…you're like a goddess."

I shook my head, momentarily wordless. "Braun…" I shook my head again. "You're gorgeous, you're rich, you're smart…surely you have the pick of any woman you want."

He shrugged. "I dunno, I don't really think about things like that. In my head, most of the time, I'm still the awkward, pimply, gangly nerd with braces I was in middle school, reading Tolkien alone at a lunch table."

I reached out, brushed his hair away from his temple. "You're not that anymore, Braun. Not at all. Not even close."

"Being here with you, you doing what you just did…I feel as disbelieving and lucky as I would have felt then, had the hottest, most popular girl in the school done that to me."

We lay just looking at each other for a while, Braun toying with my breasts.

"You have a contract with you?" he asked, eventually.

"I do."

"I don't need one, you know." He held my gaze. "It can just be…an understanding, between us. If you want. It doesn't have to be so…transactional."

My heart was doing weird things, and I stood up. "It's protection for us both. So we have what this is in writing."

I went to my purse, withdrew the folder with the two copies, and grabbed a pen from the desk. Braun was sitting up, hair wild, watching me as I reentered the bedroom. I sat on the edge of the bed, handed him the folder, one copy on top of the folder for him to read and sign.

He read it swiftly, took the pen from me, and read it through again. "This is very nicely worded," he said.

"It was Kat. She was prelaw before I convinced her to go into real estate with me."

He nodded, read it again. "I have no exceptions to this." He scrawled his name, and then I scrawled mine. I switched it for the unsigned one, and we both signed it again.

I set the folder with both copies aside.

It was suddenly, tense, awkward.

Usually, after sex or in between rounds, the guy and I would drink to keep the awkwardness at bay. I remember him handing me a glass of wine when I entered, but I had no memory of where it went, or if I finished it.

The bottle was on the little bistro table in the corner of the room, another glass beside it. Braun followed my gaze.

"Want a glass?"

I shrugged. "Sure, if you do. I honestly don't remember what happened to the first one, actually. If I finished it or where it is or what."

He went and poured a glass. "We can share it, if you want."

"Sounds good."

"You drank it—the first glass I mean. While talking to your assistant or secretary or whoever that was, Teddy."

"She's actually an agent at my firm, and one of my best friends, but she's the newest and has the fewest listings, so she sometimes handles my schedule when I'm on the run."

Braun took a sip, and then handed it to me. I drank, and then he took it back. Pressed against my breastbone, indicating that I should lie down. I did so, wary, unsure what he had in mind. He held the glass of wine in one hand, dipped a finger into it. Traced it over my breast, leaving a reddish smear on my skin; dipped again and ran his finger in circles around my nipple, down the valley between them.

He bent, resting the glass on my belly, and licked

the wine off my flesh. Glanced at me, his eyes hot, hungry, eager. Dipped his finger in the wine again, traced patterns on my breasts, one and then the other, and licked that away too.

Then he tipped the glass over, spilling a puddle on my skin between my breasts. I gasped—it was cold and messy. I laughed, giggling breathily as he guided the glass into my hand, slurping and licking red wine off my skin. Then his tongue circled my nipple, and I stopped laughing, cupped the back of his head as he latched on, suckling, drawing my nipple out and making it strain, twinge, ache. He covered my other breast with his palm, squeezing, kneading. He left the glass in my hand, kissed one breast, the other, his hand always cupping the breast he wasn't kissing, that thumb brushing and rubbing and flicking over the nipple, keeping it erect. And then he kissed lower, across my diaphragm, then my ribs, dotting kisses and tongue touches here and there, haphazardly. He did all this leaning on one elbow, beside me. Kissed my side, then the other. My hipbone, the other. My thigh. The other. Then the apex of the upside-down V where my thighs met my sex. I gasped, reached to touch his head, caress his hair—I felt a thought flitter through my head that even my nonsexual touches of him were unlike me, out of my norm. I didn't touch hair, didn't caress foreheads.

A Klaxon sounded somewhere inside, but Braun's

tongue and lips silenced it. He was kissing my navel, now, his hands skating up my thighs. I lifted up, doing a crunch to awkwardly take a fortifying sip of wine. Which I nearly choked on as he flicked a teasing tongue against my sex, suddenly, unexpectedly.

He nudged my thighs apart, kissed the tender inner, upper part of my thigh, so close to my sex that his stubble brushed it. Did the same opposite.

Reached up, dipped a finger into the wine—no, he's not. Yes, he is. His wine-wet finger ran down my seam, smearing wine on the outer edges of my nether lips and he immediately licked them clean—kissed, licked, kissed, licked, tongue probing into me further with each swipe of his nimble, eager tongue.

I managed to take another drink, because god, I'd need it for how hard he seemed to be able to make me come.

This time, he drew it out. Slow, tender. Teasing. A tongue flicking up, over my seam, but stopping shy of the nexus of nerves that would make my pleasure sing. Then a finger diving in, but right out again immediately. Then two fingers in as that tongue sought me, found me, teased me.

Occasionally, he'd provide just enough to make me flinch, flex, gasp.

But not enough. Never enough. Not until I was nearly mad with the need for him to quit fucking around and make me come, but before I could say anything, he gave it to me. As if he just knew, without needing to be told. And then, when he began to devour me in earnest, even that was slow and building, working me to a frenzy, guiding me to a screaming crescendo. I knotted my fingers in his hair and spread my legs as wide as they would go, and he lay between them and gave me an orgasm for the ages—when it finally crashed over me, I was wild and screaming, begging him to let me come, but the screaming and begging were silent, it was in the way my hands caught at his head, the way I guided him where I wanted him, it was in the way I flexed to grind my sex against his hungry mouth; and there was no mistaking the hunger in him, the eagerness for me. He *required* my pleasure, needed my screams. He devoured me like I was his final meal, like he'd never eat again.

And when I did come, wailing, nearly sobbing, he thrashed me through it and refused to quit until I'd given him another, a second and even wilder climax that left me aching and whimpering, unable to even scream.

And when I fell down from the height of climax, he was kneeling between my thighs, upright on his knees, and he was hard for me, cock spearing straight up against his belly, breathing hard, my essence on his cheeks.

Gasping, sweating, shaking, thighs quaking with a fresh orgasm so powerful I'd seen heaven, I grasped him and brought him to me, drew him closer. He bent forward, fell to his hands braced on either side of my face.

This wasn't sex as I knew it—nor for him.

I pushed that away, focused on his lush caramel eyes as they sought the depths of mine. I grasped his hard thick length and guided him to me, lifted my feet to lock my heel over my ankle around the small of his back. I wiped at his face, and he nuzzled my palm with his lips. I dried my juices off of his stubble and he kissed my palm—he wasn't following the script. This was supposed to be fucking, plain and simple.

It wasn't.

I swallowed hard and tried to focus on physical sensation. His heavy weight over me, his heat blasting against my skin, his sweaty flesh tangled up on mine, his cock throbbing in my fist, the broad tip of him pressing, nudging against my seam. Parting me. His hips angular and hard against mine.

But I was losing myself in more than the physical. I was drowning in his eyes as he furrowed his brow, in the gust of his groan when I tilted my hips to take him into me, just an inch.

God, he split me apart, even that little bit of him.

I felt my jaw drop open, wonder at the feel of him in me.

"Lizzy..." he whispered, awed.

I couldn't handle whatever poetic knives he was

about to pierce me with, so I kissed him to shut him up.

Big mistake.

He tasted like me, and like wine.

Pussy and Malbec—what a flavor combo.

He groaned as our lips meshed, as our tongues tangoed. His groan became a growl, and his kiss deepened into something beyond a kiss. And when he did so, he pushed all the way into me, and I whined into his mouth, and he ate that sound and kissed another whimper from me.

A thrust. Slow, deliberate, questing.

I clawed at his shoulders and rocked my sex against him. Felt myself stretch around his impossible thickness, aching to take him, glutting on him.

I couldn't sustain the kiss, the breathing, the anything. I had to fling my head back and scream as he filled me.

He arched his spine and buried his face in my tits, suckled them and nuzzled them and gasped against them as our hips met, and then he withdrew and his mouth was slack open against the inside of my breast and he drove in, and I met him with a scream.

Was I a screamer, he'd wanted to know, in his video.

Yes, I was.

And god, did he make me scream. Like never before.

We found a slow, rocking, rollicking rhythm, flesh meeting with a quiet slap and pulling apart with a wet squelch and meeting again, and it was punctuated by his groans and my whimpering screams.

Then it rose, the intensity of it.

That was my fault: I started to come. It made him wild, the feel of me tightening, squeezing around him, pulsing, clenching, and the sound of my panting screams, and the heave of my breasts and the claw of my fingers against him.

I came, screaming his name, and that made him all animal, all wild primal fury, and he lifted up on his knees, pushing my feet up, draping my knees over his elbows, then pushing my knees forward against my belly to stretch me out, pushing me apart, preparing me for his onslaught.

He slid out, almost all the way, growling the whole wet slick sliding time, paused, hesitating, and I watched him, fraught, between the frame of my thighs. He gripped my hips in his hands and let my thighs drape wide over his arms, and he slammed into me.

Once, hard.

I screamed.

And then he was growling my name—*Lizzy, Lizzy, Lizzy*—and pounding into me, hard and fast and without finesse or subtlety, just fucking me to his release. His thighs slapped against my ass, and his thick sex speared into me and filled me and ripped me apart so beautifully that I quaked and readied to detonate again, another spasm of clenching orgasm from the angle of him inside me, from the way he rubbed me just there, just so, from the primal, dominating, masculine beauty of him taking me, owning me, fucking me with utter abandon.

I came—again or still, I wasn't sure—and then I felt him near his own climax.

Oh god, there has never, ever been anything like that moment. Braun, filling me, ravaging me, pounding hard and fast, and I'd never felt this, never felt a man bare inside me like this, had always been careful, protected. Never felt this, and god, now it was all I could ever feel again.

Him, like this.

Bare.

And when I felt him throb thicker, harder, I knew he was about to come. I wanted to meet his thrusts, wanted to fuck him back, but he had me at his mercy and all I could do was take his thrusts, and come, and come, and come around him still.

He bellowed, a hoarse wild cry, and his thrusting stuttered, pounding deep into me and now pushing deeper, and I felt all of him spasm, felt his sac against me pulse, felt him throb inside me, twitch and jerk, and then I was flooded, and he pulled back and slammed in again, harder, deeper, pushing my thighs farther apart to get deeper yet, spasming inside me again.

Oh fuck, oh god, I was ruined for sex.

After this, fuck me bare, or don't fuck me at all.

And only him, only Braun would do.

But those crazed, desperate, ruined thoughts were burned away by my own climax returning, harder than ever, maybe it was the same one or another I didn't know or care, just that him inside me, so deep he couldn't physically go any deeper, holding me apart and pushing in and coming, coming, groaning as he leaned against the backs of my thighs, sagging heavily.

He released my thighs and I accepted him as he collapsed onto me, his heavy weight pinning me. I was drowning in insanity—that was the only excuse for it.

I cupped the back of his head and snarled my fingers through his hair and scratched his back as he heaved on me, gasping. I had my thighs around him, my heels clinging to his ass. One hand on his back, circling and scratching, one in his hair.

Who is this, with this man?

What am I doing?

It's not me—I don't do this.

But I fucking *loved* this feeling, him, limp and breathless on me, his seed within me, seeping hot and wet and thick through me, leaking already.

Messy.

He pressed a hand to the bed, fought to push

up. Made it to his elbows, weight still entirely on me. Eyes bored into mine, seeking the truth of me, of us, of this.

"Liz."

"Braun."

What to say? Neither of us knew.

He kissed my belly, kissed my breasts. Nuzzled my throat. Took my mouth and kissed me, then, his slack cock still captured inside me, and we kissed and we kissed and I have never kissed a man like that, with my insides scooped out and burned away by the raw furious sun-hot intensity of our sex.

I clutched at his hair and demanded he kiss me, locked my legs more tightly around him.

When we could not kiss anymore for needing to breathe, we clung to each other and just lay there. Him on me, his weight beautiful and crushing.

The sun shone.

A hawk soared past the window, floating on a hot California updraft, circling on a wingtip.

He rested his cheek on my breasts. "I'm crushing you," he mumbled.

"No," I whispered; he was, but I liked it. "Stay."

I felt his breathing slow, and I watched almost disconnectedly as my fingers danced gently in his hair and over his broad back. Watched the hawk dip and rise and pinwheel on the updraft, soaring, until it drifted out of sight.

I did not recognize myself, with Braun.

Did I like this new, different me? I wasn't sure.

I drifted, mentally. Time slowed. Did I drowse, with Braun on me? Perhaps. I must have, for the sun shifted angles, and then Braun stirred. Rose up on one elbow. Peered at me. What had happened to his glasses?

Oh yes, I remember now: at some point during sex, they'd kept slipping off his nose and I'd reached up, drew them off of him and set them aside on the bed.

He brushed his palm against my cheek, sliding forward so he was above me. Blinked down at me. There was a world of words in his eyes, but he said none of them.

CHAPTER TEN

DROWSING IN THE LATE AFTERNOON SUN, MY HEAD ON Braun's arm, I felt...oddly content. So content I did something I've not done in years...perhaps not since I was a little girl: I dozed off in the middle of the day.

It was a slow, warm, yellow drowse, sunlight on my face, a contented tiredness seeping through me, sucking me under. Consciousness was like a thin, delicate film, a meniscus which I floated just above for I knew not how long, and then slowly slid under.

When I felt myself drifting back upward, it was even more slowly than I'd slid under into sleep. It was just that warmth again, that slow heavy contentedness. But I gradually became aware of more.

Of myself, as a person. Of Braun.

I was on my stomach, head turned to one side, away from the window. Naked.

His hand was on my buttock, resting easily. I

murmured wordlessly in my throat and wiggled and sighed to communicate that I was awake-ish.

"Hi," he mumbled.

"Mmmm."

His hand began rubbing in circles, cupping a cheek, squeezing it, appreciating the soft weight and squish of it in his hand before switching to the other side. I felt a small smile tip the corner of my lips at the way he touched me, as if memorizing the feel of me, as if taking the time to simply appreciate being able to touch my nakedness.

"I really like your ass."

"Mmm-hmmm?"

"Yeah. A lot."

"Mmmm."

I blinked my eyes open, flipped my head the other way, to look at him: he was propped up on one elbow, chin in his hand, naked and gazing at me. My hands were tucked under the pillow. I was so comfy, drowsy. Happy.

I smiled at him.

He just kept petting and patting and playing with my butt.

My eyes drifted to his sex, slack, draped to one side. I tucked one shoulder slightly under me and reached out, letting my hand drift to him. I picked him up and let him topple to the other side; it twitched, rousing. I let a little smile curve my lips. This was something I'd rarely gotten to do: see and touch and play with a man from slack to erect.

I rarely slept with a man more than once in a session, because most men couldn't hold my interest past a single fuck—it wasn't that the sex was necessarily *bad*, just that it was rarely good enough that I wanted a repeat. The one exception to that was Ahmed, and we didn't exactly cuddle between sessions, when we did have sex more than once in a night.

Braun?

I was just getting started enjoying him.

Trouble—this was big, big trouble.

But I ignored that, pushed the whole mess of thoughts and feelings aside. Focused on him. On the now. On his hand caressing my ass, his eyes caressing the rest of me. On his gorgeous body, his manhood, now a little bigger, a little thicker.

I twirled it in circles with a finger, and it grew yet more. How long did we do that, him just enjoying my ass, me slowly nudging him to life. Then, at some point, he was roused to full erection, and I let my fist circle him, slip and slide up his length and down again.

He rolled over me without warning, pulling out of my grip. Threw a leg over me, lying on top of me, his front to my back. His fingers delved between my thighs, to my sex, and found my opening, and he fed himself into me. I groaned at the feel of him sliding into my tight sex, still messy from our last round, and then he was over me, lying against me and grinding into me, and he filled me differently like this, at this angle, and I arched to meet him, lifting up to take more of him. He moved slowly, unhurriedly, and I groaned through his slow, leisurely thrusts, and he sighed and panted, growled and murmured.

But I needed more.

I wedged a hand under my body, found my sex. Swirled a finger against myself, and felt a whimper escape me as I began to soar.

"Yeah, that's right, dirty girl," he whispered, "touch yourself. Make yourself come for me."

Ohh god, he was a dirty talker. And a good one.

"Yeah?" I asked. "You like it when I touch myself while you fuck me?"

"Yeah, I do. I like it a lot."

I clamped down with my nether muscles, squeezing around him. "Feel that?"

"Fuck, so tight when you do that."

I did it again, and he growled. "Gonna make me come faster if you keep that up."

I lifted my hips to press my ass against him, to make room for my quick-circling fingers, and then I felt him shift to his knees. He grabbed my hips and pulled me upward and backward, ass in the air, face and shoulders and breasts against the mattress.

I squeezed around him again, and then it started to become involuntary as the quaking of my sex quickened, as the lightning rapture of orgasm began to rip through me. He groaned as I came around him, as I began to clench wildly against his thickness within me.

"Shit, Liz, god, you feel so good."

"Give it to me, Braun," I whispered. "I liked it when you got rough."

He gripped my hipbones hard and slammed into me, once, roughly. "Like this?"

I cried out. "Yeah, god yeah, like that."

He pounded into me again. "You like it like this, Lizzy? You like it hard?"

"Fuck yes, Braun. More. Give it to me harder."

He growled and pounded into me harder, and my fingers were still busy against my sex, bringing me to another, higher, harder orgasm and his erection inside me was throbbing and so thick, filling me and driving into my wet hot slickness.

"Let me feel you come again, Lizzy," he growled.

"You first," I panted.

He groaned, and his thrusts became staccato, wild, hard, rough, frantic. "Shit, I can't help it…" he murmured, "I can't help it. You feel so fucking good like this, from behind like this. So fucking good."

"Let me have it, Braun," I whimpered. "I want it, I want it. Give it to me."

And then he gave it to me. I felt my body shake from the clenching lightning heat of my orgasm, felt my body quake with his wild rough thrusts as he slapped into me, our bodies meeting with loud wet claps as he drove into me harder and faster and harder and faster, growling with each thrust now, cursing endlessly as he chased his climax.

"Liz, oh fuck Liz, Lizzy, god, god, oh god Lizzy—"

I wanted to say his name but I was still tangled up in the long, drawn-out shudders of my own orgasm and I couldn't, could only shove back against him to meet his last frantic ragged thrusts, one, two, three, and then he shouted, a wordless roar as he released into me in a hot wet flood.

I felt it, and oh god, it was so much. So thick and hot and filling me to the brim and he kept coming until I overflowed around him, making a sticky mess of us.

He thrust once more, and then collapsed onto me, kissing between my shoulder blades. "God, you're incredible."

"Me?" I laughed. "You're the one who just made me come three times."

He rolled off me, and I rolled with him—somehow, I ended up on my belly, my chin on his chest.

"You make me come harder than I've ever come in my life. For real."

"Same."

He brushed at the now-crazed mass of my hair. "Thank you for this, Lizzy."

I gave him a half frown, half smile of confusion. "Why the hell are you *thanking* me?"

A shrug. "It just…seems like such a huge privilege to be with you. Just feels right to say thank you. I don't know."

"I'm the one who should be thanking *you*, Braun." I let my hand do what it wanted, which was to slide over his chest, his shoulder.

My stomach growled, then, and he grinned. "Hungry, huh?"

I nodded. "Haven't had much time to eat today. I grabbed a quick salad and ate it on the go earlier this afternoon, but that's it."

"So the question then becomes whether you want room service, for me to go get us something, or to get dressed and go out to eat."

"In the interest of full transparency," I said, "normally this is where I'd tell you to go get carryout and I'd be gone when you get back."

"But this isn't a normal situation for either of us."

"No, it's not," I agreed. "What do you feel like doing?"

"I think you should go take a shower while I order room service."

I smiled. "Sounds good to me."

"Any special requests?"

"Real food. Something moderately unhealthy and delicious. No mushrooms. Beyond that, it's up to you."

"All right, then." He tucked a lock of hair behind my ear.

"Do you want to rinse off first? I may take a while."

"Yeah, that may not be a bad idea."

He showered in what seemed to me record time and emerged wearing the hotel-provided robe. "Okay, your turn."

I sniffed his throat. "Mmm. You smell good." I kissed his jaw. "Shower time. I'll be out in…well, it could be a good forty-five minutes, honestly."

"No hurries, take your time." He took the cordless hotel phone and dialed room service, heading out onto the balcony to place the call.

Once the door closed behind him, I promptly freaked the fuck out.

I grabbed my phone from my purse, turned it on with shaking hands, and shut myself into the bathroom, calling Kat.

"Hey, I thought you were incommunicado until tomorrow?" she asked, by way of hello.

"I was," I hissed, keeping my voice low. "But he's ordering us room service. I'm supposed to be taking a shower but I'm having a freak-out instead."

"Why?" I heard the volume of her voice change, from speakerphone to either the handset against her ear or earbuds connecting. "It was bad?"

"Worse than bad," I whispered. "It was *magical*."

"Oh." A pause. "Oh shit."

"Yeah."

"Magical?"

"He speaks seven languages, half of those fictional languages from *Lord of the Rings*. He's sweet and nerdy and hot as fucking sin. He *thanked* me when he was done giving me three orgasms in a row. Which, by the way, was round two." I heard my voice going shrill. "I sucked him off...and *liked* it. He's confident, and sexy as hell. His body is incredible. He talks dirty."

"Oh Lordy," Kat breathed. "This is bad."

"I took a fucking *nap* between rounds, Kat. It was that good, I needed to sleep afterward." I swallowed hard. "We...*snuggled*," I hissed the last word.

"No." She said it with a laugh. "No, you did not."

"We did."

"And he's gone, now?"

"To get us carryout."

"You're...*staying*?"

"I told you it was bad."

"You *like* him," she murmured.

"I like him. As a person, he's just easy to talk to. We joked. We flirted. There was witty banter, goddammit."

"You're a sucker for witty banter."

"I'm a sucker for being fucked so hard I forget my own name, is what I'm a sucker for."

"That's always a good time."

"Like, involuntarily limp, helpless, and trying to remember who you are, where you are, shit...*when* you are."

"That good?"

"That good."

"Well shit, girl. Stay your ass there, eat some food, and get yourself more of that good dick."

"What if..." I couldn't finish. Couldn't get the rest out.

"Nope. Limited time offer, Lizzy. That's the deal. Enjoy the good dick until you're pregnant, and then it's over. That's what you want, right?"

"Right." I sounded convincing even to myself.

"You'll have more hot sex with Mr. Dirty Talking Nerd with the Wonder Dick, and the magic will wear off."

"The magic will wear off," I repeated. "It always does, doesn't it?"

"Sure does."

"By the way, in case you were curious, I do *not* recommend bare sex."

"No?" she asked, laughing.

"No. It's wet and sticky and messy."

"Sounds horrible."

"It is. It's no good. You'd hate it."

Another laugh. "You're lying."

"Through my teeth," I said, with false bright cheerfulness.

"You're dripping cum right now, aren't you?"

"Buckets of it."

"Gross."

"Yup."

She sighed. "I have to go. I'm sitting in my car and my clients are waiting for me to start the showing."

"Okay. Thanks for talking me off the edge."

"Is that what this was?" She laughed again. "Okay, well, you're welcome. And remember, the magic *will* wear off."

"Promise?"

"Nope. But I'm relatively certain it will, just based on history and personal experience. At least eighty percent sure."

"Go show the house, Kat. I'll call you later."

"You better. I want updates on the magic dick."

"Bye, Kat."

"Bye."

I took a long hot shower, and when I got out, Braun had a room service cart, and was pulling silver dome lids off of plates and cracking open two bottles of San Pellegrino.

"Oooh, I smell burgers," I said, coming out with my hair still damp, wrapping a hotel robe around myself.

"Yep." He gestured at the plates. "Burgers with cheddar and bacon, the fixings, and fries." There were two smaller plates. "And for dessert, flourless dark chocolate cake."

I groaned. "You're the best."

I sat at the table and took one of the plates. "Both the same?"

He nodded, taking the other and digging in with huge, ravenous bites.

"Thank you," I said.

"No problem," he answered, around a big bite. "God, these are good."

"So." I grabbed a napkin and handed one to him, took another for myself. "Now what?"

"Well, I've been thinking about that, actually." A pause to bite, chew, swallow, wash it down. "Do you have any business coming up the next couple days that you can't reschedule? Because I had an idea."

I went over my schedule in my head. "Um, yeah. I have a closing coming up, and a showing for a VIP client. I can get those both done this week, and then I could rearrange things to have the week after that mostly clear, depending on what you had in mind." I eyed him, waiting, but he was lost in thought. "And? What did you have in mind?"

He sipped from his sweating bottle. "Oh, um. How about we leave it a surprise?"

I had to think about that; I'm not much for surprises, generally. "Umm...I don't know. I kinda like to know—"

"Everything, all the time," he interrupted. He leaned toward me, elbows resting on the edge of the table. "We don't know a whole lot about each other just yet, but I'm going to venture a guess that you're used to being the boss. Being in charge. Having all the information at your fingertips, making the decisions and being responsible for everyone around you and everything that happens."

I dipped a fry into ketchup. "Um. Well…yeah, I guess you'd be right."

He reached out and covered my wrist with his hand. "Take a risk, Liz. Just…trust me."

"Just…blindly trust you."

He nodded. "Yes." A shrug, a grin. "Just blindly trust me."

I set down the fry I was dragging through ketchup. "That's kind of a big ask, Braun. You know?"

He laughed. "Lizzy, we're having unprotected sex and we're essentially strangers. How is trusting me to take you somewhere more of an ask than this whole thing is? For both of us, I might add."

I sniffed a laugh. "I guess you're right. But…" I sighed. "Yeah, no—you're right, full stop."

"So, you're in?"

I nodded, grinning. "Yeah, I'm in. Just tell me when and what to pack."

He finished his beer with a swishing swallow. "Monday. That'll give us both time to wrap things up and shuffle our schedules around." He tipped his head side to side. "As for packing? Just be ready for anything. Casual stuff, fancy stuff, swim stuff, sexy stuff. I said I have an idea, not a fully realized plan."

"So my whole wardrobe, then," I said with a laugh. "Any hints?"

"Nah. More fun if you're clueless."

"More fun for whom, precisely?" I asked, one eyebrow lifting.

"Well, me for sure, but you too, if you give into the spirit of things."

I sighed. "Okay, okay." Finishing the last of my food, I leaned back. "But when I said 'now what' I actually meant, like, right now. Today."

He barked a laugh. "Oh, right." A shrug, eyes on mine. "I have no idea. Watch TV? Each of us go home? I don't know. What are you thinking?"

I shook my head, lifting one hand palm up. "I have no idea either. This is way outside anything like normal for me, so I don't know."

"Sick of me yet? I mean, do you want to just call it an evening? Or keep hanging out? I have the suite till tomorrow afternoon."

"Honestly…I'm mixed up. This thing is weird, and intense, and I'm still sort of figuring out how I feel."

He picked at the label of his bottle. "Same. If knowing where I stand is any help, I'm having a lot of fun hanging out with you. So, we can hang out and talk, watch TV, we could go somewhere. Whatever. It doesn't have to be all sex all the time. We can be friends when we're not...you know...screwing."

I laughed. "That sounds complicated. But honestly, I haven't had any real time off in a long, long time. I'm kind of a workaholic, honestly. So...let's just chill."

"Workaholic is an understatement where I'm concerned, so I get it." He toed his shoes off and extended his hand to me; I took it, and he helped me to my feet. "To the couch, then."

And so, we hung out.

Both of us in hotel robes and not a stitch else, we watched National Geographic, and just...hung out.

There was surprisingly little talking, and it was surprisingly nice.

My feet ended up across his legs, and his fingers found my arches and began kneading.

There was a movie, at some point. Something with guns and car chases and explosions, which I only partially paid attention to. Most of my thoughts were focused on not thinking about what we were doing... or not doing.

This was relationship activity, this not-sex hanging out.

It was scary, mainly because of how not scary it was.

If I had to put it into words, I'd say it felt like being alone, except with someone. No pressure, no expectations, just...hanging out.

I fell asleep at some point.

Woke up in bed, with a large male body behind me.

I lay with my eyes closed, half asleep, panicking because I liked the feel of it.

The knowledge of his presence.

I liked that we could have the most intense and incredible and mind-altering sex of my life, and then just not worry about it the rest of the evening. There was this underlying, unspoken understanding between us that it was okay, the desire was there, the need was there, and it was okay to just...let it simmer until it boiled over again. I knew it would, and not knowing when was a delicious anticipation.

I fell back asleep wondering what the hell was happening to me, and why I liked it so much.

CHAPTER ELEVEN

I WOKE UP ALONE WELL AFTER NINE THE NEXT MORNING, later than I've woken up since high school. There was a note on the pillow next to my bed:

Lizzy,

I'm so sorry that you're waking up alone, but I got a text early this morning that there was an emergency issue with work. I won't bore you with the details. Suffice it to say, my plans for you this morning have been sadly derailed. And what lovely, debauched plans they were, too.

The suite is yours until 2, so take your time. Order breakfast.

I'll be in touch later, but if you're still up for my little adventure, tidy up your to-do list and arrange to have time off from Monday of next week through Friday. That will give us plenty of time for what I'm planning, and then you'll have the weekend to get yourself back into work mode for the following Monday.

I know, I know: 5 days alone with me? It'll be fun. We won't spend the WHOLE time in bed, I promise. Just most of it.

No hints. Pack light, but for a variety of things, because the itinerary is going to be...loose.

I had the most amazing time with you yesterday, and if I never saw you again—perish the thought—it would stand forevermore as the single best day of my life.

I suppose I could have texted you, but I didn't want to wake you up.

Til Monday,
—B

Yikes.

A whole business week alone with Braun... somewhere.

I searched myself, and discovered I was excited.

And horny.

And hungry.

I ordered room service, ate, got dressed, and didn't check my phone once. I only turned it back on while I was checking out—he'd taken care of the bill.

I had several messages from all the girls demanding updates, an email from clients regarding closing questions, a query for representation of a property in Orange County...the usual, and more of it than usual since I'd been out of communication for almost half a day.

I sent a reply to the group thread: *on the way to the office. Anyone who wants updates can meet me there.*

Kat replied within seconds: *We're all here already, so hurry the fuck up! We need details!*

Once at the office, I walked into a barrage of overlapping questions. I held up my hand and yelled over the din: "I have to change, first, so just hold on and give me a damn second." Under my breath, I muttered, "Bunch of damn piranhas."

I took my garment bag into the bathroom and changed, dragged a brush through my hair and tied it up, brushed my teeth, and did a quick but passable application of minimal makeup.

Emerging feeling more put together, I sat primly at my desk and pivoted to face the room. "So." I smiled at the girls, drawing out the moment until it looked like Laurel was about to launch herself at me. "Did Kat tell you guys anything?"

"She mentioned something about a magical dick," Laurel said. "But then clammed up and wouldn't say anything else, because you'd want to give us the details yourself."

I didn't blush, but close. "It was the hottest sex I've ever had, and I'm pretty sure I'm never going to be the same," I said, holding up my hand to forestall more questions. "I'm not going to give you a play by play, so don't ask. Yes, he's hung like a fucking horse.

He's also sweet and one of the smartest human beings I've ever met in my life."

I reached into my purse and withdrew the note, which of course I'd saved.

"There's also…this." I extended it toward the middle of the room, and Laurel was out of her seat as if she had a rocket-powered ejector seat.

She snatched it out of my hand and was immediately surrounded by the others, and there was a brief combat to get it from her.

"I'll read it out loud!" she shrieked. "Back off! Jesus."

She cleared her throat dramatically, and then read it out loud. When she was done, there was a moment of silence, and then another overlapping barrage of questions.

Like a cranky substitute teacher in front of an unruly class, I waited silently until they quieted. "That is literally everything I know. Where, what, why, how, I don't know."

"And you're *going*?" Teddy asked. "Alone with him, for five days, to an unknown location."

"Yes." I laughed. "As he pointed out when he first mentioned the idea, he was inside me without a condom, twice. At this point, what else do I have to be afraid of? I've got plenty of my own money and a passport, so if things go sideways I can always hop the next flight home. What do I have to lose?"

"It's just not like you to..." Teddy shrugged, searching for the right words. "Go into anything blind. To take time off at all, for that matter. You work seven days a week all year except major holidays. The most amount of time other than going home at night I've ever seen you take off is to get a manicure and blowout for viewing parties."

"This whole thing is unlike me," I said. "I'm having unprotected sex with a complete stranger. On purpose. Taking time off and trusting someone is...I don't know. It just seems..." I trailed off. Started again. "It's weird how not weird it is. And that applies to the whole thing with Braun."

Teddy's eyes were shining, and she was clenching her hands together under her jaw. "I *knew* it!"

I pointed a finger at her. "Teddy—*don't*. Do *not*. It's *not* that."

She held both hands up, palms out. "Fine, fine. Just...you're *sure* you want to do this with this guy?"

"You remember when Ahmed invited you to spend a weekend with him at his penthouse in Dubai?" Autumn pointed out. "That was a weekend, Friday through Sunday, and you didn't go. And you'd been seeing Ahmed on and off whenever he was in town for months by that point. You just met this Braun dude literally a week ago and you've met with him in person exactly twice. I've never understood why you didn't go with Ahmed, honestly, because hello, Dubai!"

I shrugged. "I know. It doesn't make any sense on the face of it, I totally see that. I guess I'm just throwing caution to the wind. Why not? What do I have to lose? I've got a contract with him pinpointing an exact cutoff date for things between us. I may as well enjoy the shit out the time I do have with him."

Zoe and Teddy exchanged significant glances.

"Just for the record, Lizzy," Zoe said, "I think you're playing with fire. You want to keep this purely sexual, going on trips with him is not the way to do it."

"What, like I'm going to develop *feelings* for him?" I asked, my voice sarcastic and snarky.

"Uh, yeah," Teddy said. "Exactly that. And then you're going to freak out and run away and get hurt...*and* you'll be pregnant."

"Thank you for your concern, but I'll be fine. I'm a professional when it comes to keeping feelings out of sex. I'll be fine."

"I'll be fine," Autumn echoed, making a droll, sarcastic face at me. "Famous last words."

I eyed the group. "Okay, let's take a poll. Who here thinks I'm going to, like, fall for this guy if I go on this trip?" All hands except Kat's raised. "Thank you for being on my side, Kat."

She raspberries. "I'm *not* on your side, dummy. Based on our conversation yesterday, I think you're already halfway falling for him."

I let out a sound that was part howl and part groan. "Gah, you're all so annoying."

"We love you," Autumn said. "You're our boss, our coworker, and our best friend. I just know personally how…against relationships you are, and I'm worried that you're painting yourself into a corner with this guy. I don't want to see you upset."

"I'm not against relationships," I said, knowing it was bullshit even as I said it.

"Yes, you are," Zoe said.

"Sorry honey, but yeah, you kind of are," Kat said.

Laurel finally chimed in. "I don't know if it's that you're against relationships, exactly, just more that you're…happy being alone. You like sex, you like men, but you don't want one involved in your life, cramping your style."

"That I would agree to," I said. "I don't know. This guy is different. This whole thing is different."

"Famous last words of a single woman," Autumn said, repeating her sentiment from a moment ago.

I sighed. "Look. I hear what you're saying, I'm grateful for all of you, but I'm going. So what I need is for my schedule next week to be cleared. I'll reschedule as much for this week as I can, and hopefully the rest of it I can either push out to the week after I get back, or you guys can take it for me. So I'll be spending most of the rest of today working on my schedule."

And so it was—by the time five o'clock rolled around, I had packed my days the rest of the week full from dawn to dusk, pushed other appointments out, or handed them off to one of the other girls.

I barely had time to sleep or shower the rest of the week, spending it either in the car, showing houses, or meeting with prospective new clients; when I wasn't doing one of those things, I was on the phone or whipping off an email. I didn't have time to even think about Braun, much less engage in any digital hanky-panky.

I got one text from him, late Thursday night: *working just about around the clock, the issue that came up turned out to be a pretty major thing, so my team and I have had to rewrite half the code from scratch. I'm assuming you're as busy as I am. Looking forward to next week. Call or text if you want, but don't feel pressure to do so.*

It was honestly a relief to know I could just focus on work and not feel pressure to stay in constant contact with him. That was one of the most frequent issues I had with any man I'd ever tried to see more than once: they always demanded too much of my time and didn't seem to understand that I couldn't always just stop in the middle of a showing to answer his call or text, and that when I finally was off of work, I was dead beat and just wanted to go home and relax, not have to entertain him and deal with his needs. Braun was just as busy, and being a creative sort of guy, probably absentminded. I could see him forgetting to answer a text or missing a call because he was so focused on his own work.

I was on the run all of Friday and Saturday, and had a closing Sunday, which required a lot of coordination with the title company—with whom I had to beg and plead to do it on the weekend—the bankers, the sellers, and the buyers. By the time we got everyone in place at the same time, it was midafternoon; by the time all the paperwork was signed and copied and sent and received and the whole crazy outside-business-hours deal was done, it was late evening, and I was dragging ass back home, as exhausted as I've ever been.

I drew myself a hot bath, plunked in a bath bomb, poured a whole bottle of wine into my extra-large goblet, set my custom-made wood tray across the middle of the tub with my iPad on it, and climbed in. Piping-hot lavender water swirling around my chin, a nice dry Cabernet Sauvignon to sip on, and some Real Housewives to take my mind off of things…doesn't get much better, if you ask me.

Then my iPad burbled with an incoming FaceTime call.

Braun.

I accepted the call. "Hi."

He had his glasses on, and his hair was wild, sticking straight up—he looked like he hadn't slept more than a handful of hours all week, and judging by the rumpled state of his dress button-down, he probably hadn't changed or showered recently either.

"Hey," he said, smiling at me briefly before his eyes flicked to a different screen; they immediately drifted back to me, and a smile graced his lips as he realized I was in the bathtub. "Tough week, huh?"

I took a mouthful of wine, swallowed before answering. "Hell yeah, it was. I crammed a good eighty percent of next week's appointments into this week. I don't think I've had a crazier week since…shit, ever. You?"

He tugged his glasses off, let them dangle from his crooked finger as he pinched and rubbed the bridge of his nose. "It was a week of damage control, is what it was."

"What happened?"

"Eh, you don't want to hear that boring-ass shit."

"Sure I do. Try me."

"I sold an app I wrote, I think I told you this…which is how I came to be eligible for your ad requirements in the first place—I sold it for a shitload of money, because what it does is something businesses across the globe need and are willing to pay a mint for. And I'm the only one with a working model. Catch is, the corporation I sold it to wanted to make some tweaks. They ran them by me, okay cool, whatever. But they hired junior programmers who were just not in any way, shape, or form cut out for the work required. It's technical, complicated, lots of tricky behind-the-scenes code that has to be absolutely just right for the whole damn thing to work. And whaddya know? They fucked it up. Days, literally *days* before the app was supposed to roll out and go live to all the people and companies slated to buy the suite of programs…and it doesn't fucking work. Like, they made a godawful fucking mess of it, and I had to come in and personally rewrite and patch and fix all the code they messed up, which means totally redesigning it from scratch in some places because of the idiotic, unnecessary so-called 'tweaks' they insisted on." He leaned back in his chair and groaned. "God, sorry, I'm unloading on you."

"No, it's fine. Makes my week seem like a piece of cake. I just ran around like a crazy person, showing houses and meeting clients and signing paperwork— the usual stuff, just a lot more of it than I'm used to. And it's fine if you unload on me. I don't mind."

He glanced around, as if checking to see if he was alone, then leaned toward the screen. "Wish I was there with you, I'd really unload on you."

I bit my lip, eyes going hooded, dirty ideas flitting through my brain. "You would, huh?" I sat forward, letting the water sluice down my chest, leaving me bare and exposed from the waist up, a thin scrim of bath bomb froth coating my tits. I cupped myself, rubbing soap all over my slippery skin. "You'd unload all over me? All over these?"

"Fuck." He gritted his teeth. "Lizzy, you're a bad influence on me, you know that? I'm in a public office building, my associates are just in the other room getting coffee, and I'm sitting here with a fucking woody the size of Ohio, this damn close to jerking off like a pervert."

"Well…" I quirked an eyebrow. "When are you done? Are we still on for tomorrow?"

He seemed to be adjusting himself with a wince. "Yeah, we're still on. I just have to check over this last batch of code once more, run some tests, and then I can get the fuck out of here."

"You're very sweary right now, Braun."

"Sorry. Frustrated, tired, irritated, and stressed."

"It's cool. A few curse words don't bother me any." I remained sitting upright, the layer of bubbles slowly popping and sliding off me, leaving me more and more bare. "How about I text you my address and you just come over here when you're done?"

"Will you still be in the bath?"

"Ha, um…maybe? Depends on how long you are. I've been known to stay in the tub for an hour or more."

"Shit. I'll be a couple hours at least."

"No rush. If I'm not still in the tub, I'm sure I can think of a few ways to help you decompress."

"Are you packed?"

"I have a few things in a bag, yeah."

"So am I. My bag's in my car."

"The Shelby?"

"Well, that's not really my daily driver. I drive it as much as I can because it's sexy as hell and fun, but it's so valuable I don't dare put too many miles on it."

"So what's your daily driver? You mentioned a GT3 for tracking."

"It's not what you'd expect."

"So far, your taste in cars is exquisite."

"It's an '86 Mercedes 560 ragtop, and it's far, far from mint, with almost a hundred thousand miles on it. It was my grandfather's, bought new. He gave it to me in his will when he passed."

"That's really cool. The car, I mean. Not the fact that your granddad passed."

"I knew what you meant. Some people think it's dumb. Like dude, can't you afford a better car? But here's the thing: yeah, obviously I could, and I have some sweet rides that I've paid a ton of money for, but despite my net worth, I'm still the dorky, frugal nerd I was in college. I'm not gonna spend half a mil on a car that'll only lose value every mile I put on it, and I need a car I can just…drive, and not worry about it. The 560 is that car for me. Plus it was Grampy's, and it reminds me of him."

"No, those eighties Mercedes are cool as hell."

"There's a song about eighties Mercedes, I think." He sang a few bars of the selfsame song.

"You have a nice singing voice, Braun," I said. "Anyway. You finish your work. I'll text you my address and you just come over here whenever." I heard a door open and voices erupt in overlapping chatter; I slid back down under the water. "So, I'll see you soon?"

"Sure will." He put his glasses back on. "Soon as possible."

"No rush. Don't introduce any new errors. I'll be here."

He smiled at me. "You're the best. Okay, gotta go. Bye."

"See ya."

OMG. I just invited Braun over to my house, and implicitly promised him sexy fun time.

He just looked so stressed, so tired, and I'm horny as hell after a long week of running my ass ragged.

I sent him my address, and he thumbs-upped the message. I lingered in the bath until I was pruney and wrinkled, showered off, braided my wet hair back, and considered what I should wear or not wear when Braun showed up.

Lingerie?

Nothing?

Robe?

I settled on a short silk kimono, the hem of which only just covered my ass, and which even when tied closed couldn't entirely contain my boobage, which I figured he'd enjoy seeing. Something for him to take off, sexy, and comfy.

Without any clue whether he was on the way or when he'd be here, I decided to pass the time cooking. I had some chicken breasts I'd thawed a couple days ago that I had to use before they went bad, so I seasoned them, sliced them open, and wedged a chunk of cream cheese inside them, set them to bake with some broccoli. While that was going, I put some frozen, pre-shaped cookie dough on another baking sheet and set those to baking in the other oven.

I was pulling the dinner out of the oven when my phone dinged. *I'm here, down in the lobby.*

I sent the elevator down for him—my penthouse wasn't set up to have the elevator open directly into my living room, instead, there was a foyer with the elevator and a set of French doors. More private, which I liked, even though you couldn't access the penthouse with my code. I left the doors to my condo open for him and went back to plating our dinner. The cookies finished right then as well, and I pulled those out to cool.

I heard the elevator slide open. "Come on in!" I called.

He entered, and my heart skipped a beat: he was wearing faded blue jeans, a white button-down, and battered sneakers. His hair was still wild, and he had a well-worn leather messenger bag on his shoulder.

"Smells amazing in here," he said.

"I hadn't eaten dinner yet." I plopped the plates down on my table, arranged forks and knives to either side, poured us each a glass of white.

"Me either." He rubbed the back of his neck, chuckling. "Or breakfast, or lunch. I think I had a bagel yesterday?"

I frowned at him. "You're serious?"

He shrugged. "I'm a programmer." As if that explained everything.

"Well." I slid a spatula under a still-steaming cookie, juggled it to cool, and brought it to him. "A bagel in twenty-fours is ridiculous. Eat this, to start. Wash your hands, take off your socks and shoes, and take a breath. Vacation starts now."

He held the cookie, standing just inside my condo, bag hanging from his shoulders, staring as if he'd entered an alternate dimension. "I, um."

I threw away the tinfoil I'd lined the baking sheets with, washed my hands. "You, um, what?"

He laughed, a soft huff, and shook his head. "Nothing. I've just never…"

"Don't read too much into it, Braun. I was hungry. I always make extra because what I don't eat I save so I don't have to cook every night." I smiled at him. "Plus, it was a little effort on my part to do something nice for you. So, don't overthink it. Okay? It's just dinner."

He seemed relieved, tension flooding out of his shoulders and face. "Well, thank you."

He set his bag on the floor by the door, toed his sneakers off without untying them—by the looks of them, they'd not been untied in years. Hesitated, and then with a self-conscious grin, pulled his socks off.

"Taking your socks off at someone's house is kind of weird." He curled his toes against the hardwood floors. "Super personal. You know? Like someone says, make yourself at home, but they don't actually mean, literally, make yourself at home. When I'm home alone, I do things that if I did them at someone's home in which I'm a guest, they'd never invite me over again."

I laughed. "You have a point, now that you mention it." I gestured at the cookie still in his hands. "You gonna eat it, or hold it?"

He blinked at it, then snorted. "Oh, right." He took a bite. "Sorry, when I've been crunching code that intensively for that long, I kind of have trouble transitioning back to the real world. Plus, I'm exhausted. So...I'm a little out of it, and not great company, I'm afraid."

I patted the chair. "Sit, eat with me. And don't worry about it. The nice thing about this arrangement between us is that there's no reason to put on airs. It's limited engagement, you know? You don't have to impress me or try to keep the honeymoon phase going as long as possible."

"So just be, like, unapologetically myself, warts and farts and all?"

I cackled. "Maybe not the farts. But otherwise, yeah. I mean, why not? What do you have to lose?"

He finished the cookie, brushed crumbs off his hands into the sink, and then washed his hands. "Because this is LA. Pretending we're perfect and that our lives are Instagrammable from wakeup to pass out is *de rigueur*."

"This is Malibu, as a matter of fact, not LA. But I take your meaning." I gestured at the condo with a sweep of my hand. "Consider this a fake-free bubble, in that case. Or, at least, wherever we are. Not just here."

He sat down, smiled at me as I took my seat kitty-corner to him. "This looks amazing."

I shrugged. "It's just chicken and broccoli."

"Well, seeing as I haven't eaten in I'm not really sure how long, it looks like the best of my life." He let his eyes scan me, slowly. "I take that back. I see something else that looks like the best meal of my life."

I shifted, did a shoulder wriggle and deep breath calculated to loosen the constraint of my robe, so my cleavage spilled out a bit more. "See something you like, do you?"

He narrowed his eyes, his jaw flexing, clenching. "It has been a hell of a long, hard week, and the only thing that I had space in my brain for other than code was you. Specifically you naked, and underneath me."

I pressed my thighs together under the table, heat gathering in my sex as desire flooded through me—the hunger in his eyes was not for food...it was for *me*. "Funny. The only thing I had space in my brain for this whole week other than houses and clients and closing paperwork was you, naked, underneath *me*."

He growled. "Fuck. If I don't eat food, I won't have the energy to do any of the things I'm planning."

I tugged the edges of my robe closed. "So I shouldn't distract you, is what you're saying?"

He sliced a bite of chicken, shoved it into his mouth, chewed slowly. "Fucking incredible." His eyes closed briefly. "No, that's not what I'm saying. I don't think there's anything that could distract me from eating this truly delicious chicken right now, but I welcome you to try."

I let the edges fall open again, and now I was all but bare, the robe draped just over the peaks of my breasts, only just hiding my nipples, leaving the whole inner swell of my breasts bare.

He paused in his chewing, shook his head, sighing noisily. "How are you real?"

I started eating, took a couple bites before answering. "What does that mean?"

He speared a few pieces of broccoli and ate them, then set his fork down. "I mean, it doesn't seem possible to me that anyone could look the way you look and be as funny and smart as you are. Not to mention as good in bed. You made me food when I needed it most, just because. You're successful. You're not high-maintenance." He bit the inside of his cheek, as if contemplating whether he should say what he was thinking. "On top of all that, you gave me a blowjob that I've literally woken up in the middle of the night thinking about." A laugh. "You just don't seem like you could or should be a real person. All that, and you're *looking for* no-strings-attached, unprotected sex, and a lot of it. So I repeat—how the hell are you even real?"

I felt funny inside. Mushy. Like a wet sponge being wrung out. "Braun…" I sighed. "You're just not seeing my flaws."

"Which are what?"

I cackled. "I'm not telling you! You seem to think I'm perfect—why would I want to ruin that?"

"Nobody's perfect, Liz."

I set my fork down. "You know, no one ever calls me Liz. Professionally, socially, and to my best friends, I'm Lizzy, and my parents call me Elizabeth, because they're *fancy* and like the trappings of formality."

"I know someone like that. The guy who's the CEO and founder of the company that bought my app is like that. Calls me Mr. Bennet." He sipped wine, a small careful mouthful. "So, should I not call you Liz? I won't if it bothers you."

I shook my head with a little smile. "No, it's fine. From you, I like it."

He went back to eating. "You want to know some of my flaws?"

I laughed. "Well, you already said you have warts and you fart."

"You've had a chance to examine me pretty... um...thoroughly. I do not have warts, that was a joke. I'm a human, and a guy, so yeah, I have been known to let one rip every now and then, but my mama raised me well enough to never do so in any kind of a social setting." He grinned at me. "I'm the quintessential distracted artist computer nerd. When I'm lost in my world of coding and programming, I'm not even on this planet. People have had to literally shake me and shout my name to get my attention."

I laughed. "I'm a workaholic, I've never been in a serious, monogamous, long-term relationship, I don't trust easily, I have a nearly debilitating penchant for very expensive things, and I drink more than I should."

"What's your notion of very expensive things?" he asked.

I shrugged. "I have an issue with purses and shoes. I've got nearly as much invested in my purse and shoe collection as I do this condo. I've put off buying a new car for years because I'd rather keep driving my little old Miata and be able to afford the newest Chanel or Louis Vuitton, and the occasional Birkin."

"The occasional Birkin?"

"Well, yeah. You have to be accepted onto a wait-ing list to get one, and it's not easy. For a new one, I mean. And even the pre-owned ones cost as much as a car."

"And you have one of these?"

I shrugged. "I might." I let a smirk roll across my face. "One which I bought new, after my first really big, lucrative commission, and another I bought used from a client."

He shook his head. "I understand cars being worth a lot of money, but even those depreciate. And require maintenance to upkeep, and the really valuable classics are just a shitload of time and money and resources to just own, much less operate. But a purse, a bag for holding things in, being worth as much as a car? I'm sorry, I just don't get it."

I grinned. "I'm not sure I could explain the eco-nomics of it, but I can tell you that the most expen-sive designer purses are actually a better investment than stocks, and certainly than classic cars. As long as they're stored indoors, in a reasonably temperate room and away from direct sunlight, they'll last just about forever...and they'll actually *appreciate* in value. If something were to happen to my career, some sort of freak thing where I was facing sudden poverty, I could sell off my bags and have enough cash to buy a reasonably priced condo. And I'm not exaggerating."

I knocked on the table. "Heaven forfend such a thing ever happen, because my purses are third on my list of most important things. My Miata and my condo are the other two."

"The Miata. What's the story there?"

"It's almost a classic, at this point. It was the first car I ever bought, and I bought it new. It was the first thing I ever bought when I first started selling houses with my uncle. He owned a brokerage, and hired me as his PA the day I was old enough to legally work. I started working on my realtor license as soon as I was of age, and was selling under my uncle's tutelage before I was twenty. I became his top seller, and then when he was ready to retire, he sold me the brokerage, building and all. The office where I work was his office, where I started." I smiled at the memories of my uncle. "He passed a few years ago, unfortunately, but it wasn't unexpected—he'd been sick for years. Anyway, I saved my money earned PA-ing for him and bought that Miata. So, it's kind of a mixture of reasons that I've refused to sell it or buy a new car. I have it gone over with a fine-tooth comb twice a year by my mechanic, so it runs as well as it did the day I got it. It reminds me of my uncle, reminds me where I came from, and also, I just love it. It's cool, it's fun, it's retro at this point, and I guess it's also a point of pride that I've owned the same car for almost twenty-five years."

"That is something to be proud of," Braun said.

"Very similar to the reason I still drive Grampy's Mercedes as my daily driver when I obviously could go buy anything I wanted."

"I've been telling myself for years that I'm going to buy myself a 911 Cabriolet, but I've never actually been able to convince myself to pull the trigger." I went and got the plate of cookies, brought them to the table, munched on one.

He took one, bit into it thoughtfully. "Same. It's weird, though. For me, I feel like buying a brand-new car is stupid. Like, yeah, the money is no object, so the fact that a car depreciates the moment you drive it off the lot isn't really a financial issue for me, but mentally, it is. My mindset hasn't changed all that much. I'd still prefer a vintage car, or something a few years old, that someone else has taken the deprecation hit on. I've been thinking about a new or newer car as my daily driver for years. Something faster, something sleeker, something cooler. But I never do. I'm just...content driving that old 560. I just like it. It's comfortable and familiar."

"You're very down-to-earth and practical, for a billionaire."

He laughed. "Well, in the interest of full transparency, I'm not actually a real, true billionaire. Just a multimillionaire. My net worth is somewhere around six hundred million, something like that? Close enough, for all intents and purposes, I just don't make the list of actual billionaires. Which doesn't really mean jack shit to me." He eyed me. "Does that change your perception of me?"

I kept my face blank. "Yes. You should leave. I only fuck with actual billionaires."

His brows lowered. "I can't tell if you're kidding or not."

I couldn't hold it any longer, and started cackling. "Yes, I'm kidding," I said between laughs. "Totally joking. The whole thing started as a joke, and I just went with it, because I…" I sighed, started over. "I guess it was one of those situations where you're drunk and joking around, and you say you're just kidding, but really what you're saying is the unvarnished truth you'd never otherwise be able to admit even to yourself, much less out loud, but you're fucking hammered and it comes out, and you have to cover it up to yourself by saying you're just joking."

Braun yawned, a jaw-cracking, back-arching, full-body stretch kind of yawn. "God, I'm beat."

"Why don't you take a long hot shower?" I suggested. "And then we can crash."

"Our flight is at ten tomorrow." He rubbed his eyes. "Lizzy, when you invited me over, I know you were kind of hinting at us doing stuff. I don't want you to think that just because I'm tired—"

"Braun." I cut in over him. "It's fine. If anyone can understand being too tired to even feel like having sex, it's me. And I *always* feel like having sex…except when I'm too tired."

"Still. This whole thing was supposed to be about you, and—"

"I'd like to think that we're friends, right?"

"For sure."

"So as your friend, I'm saying go take a shower. And then we can crash." I smirked, wiggled my eyebrows in a silly and suggestive way. "Maybe in the morning we can make up for what we're too tired for tonight."

"As long as you're sure."

"I'm sure." I pushed aside the rumblings of concern in my belly at the decidedly nonsexual turn things were taking. "It's fine. More than fine."

"A shower *would* be amazing."

"All I have is girly shampoo and stuff. So you might come out smelling like a fruit salad."

"That's fine," he said, laughing. "My natural male musk will dominate your girly shampoo." He said the last part in a falsely deep, gruff, macho voice.

"Yeah, I bet it will," I said, not at all joking. "You do have a pretty awesome masculine musk going on."

"Are you saying I stink?"

"No. I'm saying you smell like a man. It's a good thing."

"I mean, I *am* a man."

"Well, yeah. But not all men smell good. It's more

than hygiene. It's…I don't know. A combination of natural smell, being clean, and what kind of scents you use. Deodorant and cologne and aftershave or beard oils or whatever. You just have this natural smell that's…" I shrugged. "You just smell good."

He shied away from me. "Well, I don't smell good right now, I guarantee. I wouldn't recommend sniffing me just now."

I was in the middle of clearing our plates and putting them in the dishwasher. Before he could stop me, I leaned close and sniffed him, right at center mass, over his chest.

I ruffled his hair playfully. "You do need a shower, but considering the week you've had, I'd say you smell remarkably normal."

He stood up, intercepted me and grabbed me by the shoulders. "Thank you, Lizzy." His eyes were deep and earnest, and made the pit of my stomach drop away, made the middle of my chest, where my metaphorical heart was, expand in a disconcerting way. "For real. Thank you. I really, really appreciate you making dinner for me."

I pushed at his chest. "It's fine, no worries." I moved past him, abruptly, heading for my room. "This way."

I felt him trailing behind me as I led him into my bedroom, which was embarrassingly untidy—I was normally pretty fastidious about making my bed and keeping things neat, but the week had been absolutely bonkers, so my bed was unmade, there were dirty clothes spilling out of my hamper, bras I intended to wear a few more times before washing hanging from both the inside of my bedroom doorknob and the bed-room facing side of my bathroom door's knob. My underwear drawer was half open, a bright pink thong hanging out.

I stopped before he could enter. "Wait, hold on. Don't come in." I pushed him backward. "There's no way in hell I'm letting you see my bedroom like this."

He laughed. "Lizzy, it's fine. The last person to judge a messy bedroom is me."

I closed the door between us. "Just—just hold on."

Why did I care? He'd probably never be here again, in my room. We weren't dating and never would, so again...why did I care?

I just did.

So. Tornado Lizzy—ENGAGE.

I went into whirlwind cleaning mode, cramming the dirty-but-not-ready-to-wash bras into a cubby with my cardigans and stacks of folded leggings, shoving clothes down into the hamper and hiding the hamper in my closet, hastily making my bed, or at least neat-ening it to a minimal degree, closing drawers, making sure nothing else embarrassing was out.

I opened the door. "Okay. You can come in, now."

He snickered. "You're funny. What do you think

I'd do or say, if I'd seen it? Which, by the way, I sort of did. Unmade bed, some bras, some dirty clothes. It's just life, Lizzy. No one's perfect."

I peeked into the bathroom, and tossed my various hair appliances into drawers, shoved my makeup into a corner, yanked my wet towel off the rack and set out a new clean one for him. "It's the principle of the thing."

He shook his head, laughing. "Next time, just leave it messy."

Next time?

I waved at the shower. "It's a shower. You're an adult, you can figure it out from here. Take as long as you want."

He was already unbuttoning his shirt. "Thanks." He grinned at me. "And just as an F-Y-I, you don't have to go out of your way to give me privacy. I don't see much point in us being modest around each other, you know?"

It was too familiar. There were too many feelings happening.

"Have a good shower," I said.

He hesitated, and then flicked open his jeans. "You're welcome to watch." He arched an eyebrow. "Or join me."

I bit my lip. I wanted to say something snarky, or witty, or sarcastic, or…something. But I couldn't think of anything. So I just pivoted on my heel and walked out without a word. Soon after, I heard the shower turn on, the glass door thump as it sealed closed.

I found myself in my kitchen, almost frantically cleaning, wiping down counters and straightening already straight things.

What was wrong with me?

I'd invited him here for sex. Under the idea that it would relax him, but instead I'd made him dinner and sent him into my shower and all but taken sex off the table, because he looked so tired and worn out and stressed that I just wanted to…

Take care of him.

Dammit.

I was being *nurturing*. I was acting like a wifey.

I'm not that girl.

It's totally normal to want to be nice to a friend, right? That didn't mean I was catching feelings. I was just being a good friend. We could be friends and still have totally meaningless, casual sex, and I'd get pregnant and we'd never see each other again and that would be *fine*.

A weird, perverse part of me wanted to rip off my robe and go in and fuck him just to prove a point to myself.

But…what would that point be?

Argh.

Now I just plain *wanted* him. He was all wet and naked, in my shower, in my bathroom. Did he jerk off in the shower? God, how hot would it be to watch him jerk off? So hot. Like, live and in person, not just via video.

But if he was live and in person and jerking off, there was literally no chance I'd be able to keep my hands off him.

I braced my hands on the island and fought my libido. Because if I went in there and did anything right then, I couldn't be sure what my real motives would be. Sex, meaningless and fun, with my fuck-buddy-with-a-purpose? Proving to myself that it was just the afore-mentioned sex? Or would it become something else?

Safest thing would be to just stay my horny ass out here, and get some sleep and figure it all out tomorrow.

Except I'd invited him to crash at my place. And the obvious was that he'd crash in my bed. With me.

Clean, freshly showered. With no clean clothes to change into, as he'd left his bag in the car, I assumed.

So he'd have to sleep naked.

And I was naked, basically. The robe only just barely counted as a covering, and I'd only put it on to drive him crazy, to make him want me.

Despite all these thoughts banging around in my brain like a bird trapped in a house, there was one thought, one question, one burning crazy need to know:

Was he jerking off?

I had to know.

I mean, he'd said he didn't need privacy.

I had to know.

I forced myself not to tiptoe.

I wasn't sneaking or spying.

Who was I kidding? I hesitated in my room, just outside the bathroom; the door was partially open, but from my current angle I couldn't see anything. What was I doing?

I exhaled slowly.

You know what I was doing? I was about to peek. He'd said he didn't need privacy, so why not just go in, bold as brass balls?

Why stop there?

I lifted my chin, set my jaw, and let the needy flood of hormones wash over me. Why fight it? That's what this whole stupid thing was about: sex. Just sex. I wasn't proving anything, because I didn't feel anything for him except lust.

Pure, unadulterated, simple sexual desire and physical attraction. Nothing else.

My thoughts thus sorted out, I entered the bathroom, already tugging at the knot of my robe's belt.

The glass of the shower was fogged, but not to opacity. I could still see him clearly, and god, I was struck again by how sexy the man was. Flat stomach, hard, with a hint of abs, a V angling over his hipbones, hard thighs, strong arms. He was in profile to me, and his manhood was at rest. Funny things, limp like that: thick, dangly, jiggly, swaying flesh tubes.

I watched him for a second. He was rinsing his hair, head tipped back, eyes closed, water sluicing down his back and chest, streaming off the tip of his dick making it look like he was peeing. I wondered if he peed in the shower. Hair rinsed, he wiped his face with one hand, blinked his eyes open. Caught glimpse of me out of the corner of his eye.

My robe was untied but still on, hanging open, a two-inch gap between the edges down my center. His chest rose as he sucked in a deep breath, jaw setting.

I had no idea what to say.

He didn't either, it seemed—he nudged the shower door open in invitation.

I rolled my shoulders, and the slippery silk whispered off me, floated to pool around my feet, leaving me naked. My nipples hardened, and my sex dampened.

I stepped into the shower, closed it behind me, kept Braun between me and the water. Gazed up at him, let my hands reach for him. Palmed his chest, his waist. Cupped his manhood, and felt it twitch, begin to unfurl. Reached behind his shoulder for the bottle of body wash. Squirted some into my palms and rubbed, smeared it onto his belly. Scoured his chest and shoulders, a thick lather smearing onto his skin where my hands had been. Down to his waist, his hips. Around to his buttocks, down his thighs. Saved the best for last:

lathering his erection, smearing soap over the burgeoning length of him.

He let me soap him up, then turned to face the spray, rinsing it off; pivoted back to me. His eyes spoke volumes—he wasn't about to let me get him off before he'd gotten me there first. His body blocked the spray of water, but a fine mist had still coated my skin, my loose hair. His hands captured me, pulled me closer, until the tips of my breasts brushed his chest. He bent, and his mouth covered my nipple, and his fingers sought my sex, found me wet and waiting, scissored inside me. I felt him gather my essence and smear it over my clit, and then my knees dipped and he was working me to a quick and rising climax, gasping, my back against the wall.

I grabbed his erection and pulled him to me. "Inside," I gasped. "Want you—inside me. Now."

He ignored me, fingers circling and rubbing back and forth, up and down, and then pausing to slide inside, curl, rub, and then smear over me, and my knees gave out briefly as my climax stole through me, subtly and slow at first—I'd gotten close quickly, but the actual slide over the edge to coming was slow, and his fingers never hurried.

I was just clutching him, squeezing his thickness in one fist as I came, head tipping back and a cry leaking out of my clenched jaws.

He kept me shaking through it, bent to nibble at my nipples, licking and flicking, tonguing and suckling.

And then, as I began to subside from the quaking peak of orgasm, he turned me to face the wall. Instinctively, I pressed my hands against the cold wet marble and arched my back, extending my ass toward him. Braun felt for my opening, gripped himself in one hand and fed himself into me.

He didn't just shove in, though. Oh, no. He notched himself into me, just the very tip. Then his hands rose to cup my breasts, which hung pendulous and heavy, and he pinched my nipple, the other. Kept one hand at my breasts, playing with one and then the other, while his free hand descended my front and found my still-throbbing and sensitive clit.

He pulsed against me, sliding in another inch, and began working me toward climax yet again. Slowly, un-hurried. Water sluiced against his back, spraying a mist that moistened my back.

Slowly, deliberately, he gathered my orgasm to him-self, bringing me higher and higher, skillfully working me to groaning, gasping rapture.

"One more, Liz," he breathed into my ear. "Give me one more."

I flexed against him, seeking more of him inside me. "You first."

He growled, renewed his circling assault on me. "Unh-uh. You first. Once more, Lizzy, let me feel you come. I want you to come around me. I want to feel you squeeze me while you scream."

"Then I need you to...to fuck me," I gasped. "I need it."

He plunged in, sudden, filling me to whimpering fullness. "Shit, shit, shit," he moaned, a low, lost sound. "You feel too good. You're gonna make me come so hard...I want to wait, but I...oh god, Liz. You feel too good."

I felt him throbbing, felt him at the edge. I'd already come once, and I wanted his pleasure. His release. "Give it to me."

"It's too soon," he gasped.

I pushed back against him, ass cheeks meeting his thighs, hips. "Braun, I want it."

"Come first."

He fumbled for me, one hand gripping the crease of my hip where I was bent forward, the other reaching for the nexus of pleasure. I whimpered at his touch, but he had a bad angle, had to reach around my bent body. I nudged his hand away and took over, because no matter how good someone else's touch is, they'll never know your body like you.

I had myself there in seconds, ridging the edge, and somehow me touching myself seemed to give him permission to let go.

He gripped my other hip and began to slide against me, a slow, gentle thrust at first. Then another, harder. "Oh fuck, Liz," he groaned.

"With me," I gasped, and then whimpered, knees

shaking. "With me. Right now, Braun. You feel it? You feel me? I'm coming, Braun. Come with me."

He bellowed, a wordless roar as he felt me, and let go of his restraint. Pounded into me, hips meeting my ass with loud wet claps, and then he was coming and I felt the hot rush of it, a flood through me. I clenched around him and cried out, screaming through my second climax, this one wild and intense, leaving me thrashing backward raggedly against his plunging erection as it speared deep into me.

"Liz..." he whispered, a hoarse, broken sound. "God, Lizzy."

Finished, I straightened, pressed my flushed body flat against the cold marble. He moved with me, stayed inside me, pressed his hot wet body against my back. Gasped with me.

Kissed me on the temple. The back of my neck. My nape. My shoulder. His hands rested on my hips, and then circled around me, an embrace from behind, one arm under my breasts angling up to cup one, the other low around my belly to clutch my opposite hip. Still inside me, thick but softening.

"What the hell do you to me, Lizzy?" he murmured.

I felt him let go of me with one hand, twist away, and the water turned off. He cupped my breasts again, and his lips touched my nape in a soft warm damp kiss. Between my shoulder blades. The left shoulder blade itself. My hands were still pressed against the marble to brace myself, and he kissed the round of my shoulder. That part just beneath my underarm, the piece of skin that would hang out over the edge of a dress. That was too much, that kiss, to that tender, intimate place. I shivered, shuddered, but he wasn't done. He kissed my rib, a hand's breadth down from my underarm. His palms rested on my waist, then the bell of my hips and his kisses trailed over my spine, across my lower back. The upper swell of my buttock.

"Braun..." I whispered.

This was too much.

But god, it felt so...nice. So gentle. So tender. Like he hadn't just been chasing his own pleasure. He cared about *mine*.

About *me*.

He boldly, unabashedly kissed more of me. Kissed me in places nobody had ever kissed, not even in the wildest, most unhinged moments of intimacy; he kissed my buttock. Here, there, everywhere. The plump roundness of it, just inside, where the cheeks met. The outsides, then down where the underside curved in to meet my thigh. Across to repeat the kissing exploration.

"Braun..." I whispered again, pleading.

Pleading what, I wasn't sure. Keep going? Stop?

He twisted me, pressed my back to the wall. His kiss slid over my quad, then my belly. Just above my sex. My other thigh. He was on his knees, his palms now holding my waist. He kissed my navel. My diaphragm. Between my breasts.

"Braun...what are you doing?"

He didn't answer. Just gently lifted my breast and kissed underneath it, then did the same to the other side. My hands naturally, instinctively rested on his head, and he kissed my breastbone. Lifted to his feet, and now he was crowding me against the marble, and his hands cupped my cheeks and I had no time to think, to turn away to demur to beg him not to—he kissed me.

He kissed me breathless.

Kissed me stupid.

I gasped into his mouth at the volatile tenderness of his lips against mine, his tongue seeking mine.

I felt things crumbling inside me, and I broke away from the kiss.

Left him standing in the shower, naked and dripping and beautiful and confused.

CHAPTER TWELVE

I SNAGGED MY ACTUAL ROBE ON THE WAY, THE ONE I'D bought from a spa, enormous and thick, enveloping me like a quilted comforter, draping to brush the tops of my feet and the sleeves rolled twice to even leave my fingertips exposed.

I went straight to the cabinet over my fridge, where I kept the in-case-of-emergency hard stuff. This was an emergency. Top-shelf whiskey, which I reserved for the most epic of freak-outs.

I snatched a juice glass from another cabinet and clumsily splashed some whiskey into it, tossed it back.

Poured more, but a big hand intercepted it. Took the glass from me, and I turned to see Braun with a towel around his waist, still dripping.

"Why are we shooting whiskey?" he asked.

I took the glass after he was done and poured myself a second measure, hesitated, searching Braun. Tossed it back. Swallowed with a hiss.

I shook my head. What to say? How did I put into words what I couldn't even quantify to myself?

"Did I do something wrong?" he asked.

"No," I murmured. "Maybe too right, if anything."

"I'm lost."

"The way you were kissing me." I set the glass down, feeling my heart thump too hard, my hands shaking. "It was…" I sighed. "I don't know."

"Don't know, or don't want to say?" He screwed the top back on the whiskey and put it away.

He took my hand. Drew me toward the bedroom.

I followed, feeling dazed. "I…this is just sex, Braun."

A beat of silence, just a touch too long. "I know."

Did he?

"The way you were kissing me…" I felt a lump in my throat.

"You didn't like it."

I swallowed hard, because I couldn't say that. I had. "It's just sex."

He sat me on the bed, toweled off his hair, scraped it to one side, and then tossed the towel over the tub and returned to sit beside me on the bed, naked and comfortable. "Do you want me to leave? Do you want to cancel our thing next week?"

Did I?

I shrugged. Sighed. Had to shake my head. "I… no, I don't."

"But you're freaking out a little."

Or a lot. "Braun, I just…" I looked at him, a bead of nervous sweat sliding down my spine. "It's more intense than I was anticipating."

"For me too," he said. "I guess I'm just…going with it."

I had to drop my gaze. Pick at a cuticle. "Stay. Sleep here. With me."

He hesitated. "If you're freaking out, wouldn't that just…um…confuse things worse?"

I already was confused. I wanted him. I wanted him near me. I wanted more time with him. But…I was scared it was becoming something I didn't know how to…do. I didn't do *more*. And the way he'd kissed me had been *more*, had hinted at *feelings*.

I couldn't bring myself to make him leave, though. I just couldn't.

I shook my head, then laughed. "I don't know. Maybe. But it's silly for you to leave." I sighed. "I'm sorry I freaked out."

"Don't worry about it." He glanced behind us at the bed. "Which side are you?"

"Bathroom side," I answered.

"Good, I like to be by the door."

I met his eyes. "This is a really, really weird thing we've got, you know?"

He nodded, not quite smiling. "Yeah, it is. But hey, I'm okay with that."

He slid under the covers, tucked a hand behind his head. "You gonna sleep in that giant robe?"

"Don't laugh at me. I get cold as I'm going to sleep, but then I always get hot in the middle of the night."

"Well, I turn into a furnace when I sleep, so you'll probably get hot even faster."

"So I should just take it off now, is what you're saying."

"Probably, yeah."

I smirked, more comfortable in this territory. "You just want me naked again."

He grinned, shrugged. "I mean, yeah. Always."

"Fair enough."

I removed the robe and hung it up again, tried to not feel self-conscious as I got into bed beside him.

This was so, so weird.

This wasn't casual sex behavior. Far, far from it.

"We got the sex out of the way," Braun said, settling lower and turning to his side, facing me, hand tucked under the pillow beneath his cheek. "So now we just...chill."

"I've never just *chilled*, naked, in bed before."

"It could be that." He yawned again, prodigiously.

"Yeah, you're gonna be asleep in a minute." I held the blankets against my chest, lying on my back, head turned to look at him. "I'm just feeling awkward."

"Why?"

I sighed. "I've never actually had anyone here. I

always…it's always been their place or somewhere neutral."

He frowned at me. "You've never had a guy here? Ever?"

"Nope. My condo is *my* space. My private little haven. I have my girls over now and then, but mainly, it's my one place to just be…me."

He blinked. "So why invite me over?"

I shook my head, huffing a laugh. "I don't know, honestly. It was an impulse."

"You regretting it?" He held my gaze, his open and real and earnest. "Don't. Nothing about this whole thing is normal, so I'm just sort of going along with the weirdness."

He reached out and brushed my hair away from my eyes, teased a strand away from my lips. "You're all stiff and uncomfortable, Liz. Just…relax. You don't have to…entertain me. Just be you, how you would be, if you were alone."

"But I'm not, and I don't know how to be like this, with you."

He closed his eyes. "Just breathe. Close your eyes, and just…breathe."

I closed my eyes and let tiredness wash over me.

It was pure instinct to flip over, to my belly, but then I ended up twisting again immediately, to face away from him.

A moment, a pause, a silence.

He shifted toward me.

I shifted backward.

This wasn't normal. Liking it was even less normal.

He was starting to fall asleep, I could tell. I felt his breathing slow, felt him loosen. He scratched his face, and then his hand came to rest over my waist, palm on my belly.

He was behind me, big and hard, strong and kind and…just so *there*. Even just sleeping, he was still enormously present.

It was a long time before I fell asleep, feeling him behind me, breathing.

A man, in *my* bed.

Naked, but sleeping.

Holding me.

Have I ever been just held like this? How often have I ever gotten this kind of nonsexual, comforting touch? I haven't. Not in my entire adult life, not from a man. The only nonsexual touch I get is from my girlfriends. The only form of care or compassion I get is from them.

Is that messed up? Is that why I'm so messed up about relationships and sex?

This was spiraling way out of control, out of bounds of what it's supposed to be.

Why was I not stopping it?

CHAPTER THIRTEEN

T HERE WAS A PRIVATE JET WAITING FOR US ON A PRIVATE section of tarmac at LAX. It was a large jet, meant for international trips.

There was champagne on the flight, and movies, and imported chocolate, and an elegant charcuterie. Conversation between Braun and me flowed easily, as if this was normal.

It wasn't.

I was well off, doing great for myself. But I wasn't at a level of booking private jets and penthouse suites at five-star hotels, not by a long shot.

I'd asked him a dozen times where we were going, and he'd declined to answer. So, I decided to just roll with the surprises.

The flight was long, and with no idea how long it would take, it was hard to fully relax. But eventually, I settled in. We watched a movie together, and I dozed. Woke up, and we started another, and this time he dozed.

More snacks, brought by a quick, quiet, efficient flight attendant, a pretty woman perhaps ten years older than me.

At some point, we both dozed off at the same time, and when I woke up again, I had the ear-popping sensation of descent.

I looked out the window and saw the lights of a city, but it was impossible to know which. We'd been flying most of the day, and without a clock in the cabin it was impossible to know how long I'd slept.

The jet descended, and there was no announcement, perhaps by Braun's request to keep our destination a surprise. We landed, and there was a brief roar as we slowed, and then quiet again as we taxied for a few minutes before coming to a stop. There was another moment or two of quiet and then the flight attendant opened the side door, revealing a staircase. At the base of the staircase waited a car, long and black and sleek, with tinted windows. A uniformed driver stood beside the passenger door. We each only had one small carry-on bag, but the driver took them both from us as we reached the bottom of the stairs and stowed them in a trunk.

"Welcome, *Senhor* Bennet." He had a distinct accent that could have been Spanish, but I wasn't expert enough to be sure. "*Senhora* Stephenson." He said my last name *Steeeff-en-SOHN*.

"Where are we, Braun?"

He grinned. "My favorite place on earth." A brilliant grin, and he inhaled deeply. "Ferragudo, Portugal."

"Portugal?"

"Yup. A cousin had a destination wedding here, and I fell in love. Bought a place." He leaned close enough to whisper into my ear. "I lied—this is now my second favorite place on earth."

"Oh?" I smirked at him, playing along. "And what took the number one spot?"

"Being inside you," he murmured, low enough even with his lips to my ear I barely heard him.

I felt a rush of heat. "Oh," I said, and then felt stupid for the lame response.

He tugged my hand and pressed a palm to my lower back, guiding me into the car. "Home, Emmanuel."

"*Sí.*"

The car was a Rolls Royce. Smooth, powerful, quiet, luxurious. Beyond the windows, the industrial surroundings of the airport gave way to a rural two-lane highway leading up a coastline, and the view took my breath away. Sheer cliffs, sun setting fiery golden into the rippling sea, which threw itself ceaselessly, violently against the cliffs, as if the ocean was resentful of the land and was trying to bash it away, wave by wave.

The ride was only perhaps twenty minutes,

maybe closer to thirty, and then the cliffs slid closer to the sea and the waves settled and there was a small city ahead, white buildings stacked one atop the other, following the curve of the shoreline. Up, into the village, then, into the old-world cluster of close-set buildings, the big Rolls sliding between pedestrians and motorcycles and little cars and delivery trucks and squeezing around seemingly impossible corners, the streets narrower and narrower the higher into the village we went.

I lost track of the turns, switchbacks, ascents and descents, and then we slowed to a stop, and I watched a section of wall slide apart, a cleverly disguised gate opening. Beyond it, a cobblestoned courtyard, at the center of which was a round fountain, a statue of a fish leaping from the water, spitting water to spray high into a glassy umbrella. Two stories of colonnaded porticos ran the perimeter of the courtyard, up to the wall where the gate was. As the driver parked and scurried to let us out, I saw through the glass doors on this ground floor a hint of the view beyond—sea, as far as the eye could see, and the village spread out beneath.

Gaslights flickered on every other column, the light dancing off the stucco. Palms waved in a dull warm breeze, carrying hints of sea spray and brine.

"What an incredible place," I breathed.

Braun chuckled. "Wait till you see inside. Your little realtor's mind is going to explode."

I held up a hand. "Just...let me soak this in for a moment."

I pivoted in a slow circle, taking in the courtyard one more time, breathing the peaceful sunset air, absorbing little details. The home was *old*. The cobblestones told the story, as did the columns, the barrel-tiled roof, the elegant, wrought iron railings around the balconies, the stucco walls.

"When was it built?" I asked.

He smiled. "It's got a complicated history. The original structure, this area around the courtyard in particular, goes back to the seventeenth century, some sort of local governor's palace. It was updated and added onto around the turn of the nineteenth century, and then again turn of the twentieth century, and then it was blown back to the exterior walls and completely modernized and expanded again a little less than ten years ago, and I bought it last year, as is." He smiled at me. "Ready to see the inside?"

I nodded. "Lead the way, Mr. Bennet."

The main entrance was enormous, arched French doors twice the height of a person, crafted from aged, weathered, dark wood with black wrought iron straps, heavy matching knockers in the shape of fish tails. More flickering gas lamps on either side of the door. Despite the enormity of the doors, when Braun pushed it open, it did so easily and silently, on exquisitely balanced hinges.

"These doors are from the fort down by the water's edge, salvaged after a renovation a couple hundred years ago. They'd been just sitting in a storeroom in a basement collecting dust, and the guy who renovated this place took them for a song and had them refinished," Braun explained. "He had the entrance redone to accommodate them. They're one of my favorite things about the house."

"They're amazing," I said. "A real selling point."

"They were for me." He led the way in, and I was dumbstruck.

I'd sold houses going for nearly a hundred million dollars, from coastal mansions to sprawling celebrity palaces. But never, ever had I seen anything like this. Barrel-vaulted ceilings some twenty feet overhead, with heavy black exposed beams. Mediterranean-style terra cotta floors, a mosaic of colors and patterns. White walls, huge windows open to the sea air. A wrought-iron spiral staircase leading upstairs; to one side of the foyer was a glassed-in office near the foyer with floor-to-ceiling built-in bookcases running three walls, and on the other side was a library, a true library: two stories, with a sitting area underneath the arched, stainless windows, rolling ladders, a second level of shelves accessible through a pair of staircases—it was truly a library worthy of The Beast's in Disney's *Beauty and the Beast*. Through the foyer and past the spiral stair and office was a short hallway featuring a powder room, and then it opened into a sprawling, open-concept main living area, a chef's kitchen with acres of marble and stainless appliances, a living room open to the air. Outside was an extension of the kitchen and living room, with further seating and an outdoor cooking area. An infinity pool, built-in hot tub. The landscaping was pure Mediterranean garden wonder, towering trees, flowering shrubs, a profusion of shade and sun and color, a fountain tucked in here, a little lily pad-dotted pond there. A concrete bench under a rose-wreathed arch, a wooden swing with thick ropes hanging from a thick branch. All of it overlooking the sea.

"Wow," I breathed, standing just outside the house, looking at it all.

"Yeah." He stood next to me. "I can't take credit for a single thing, other than having the good sense to buy it the moment I laid eyes on it. It's magical."

"How do you ever leave?" I asked, looking up at him.

He laughed, shook his head. "Only with great difficulty. I'm planning to live here full time, eventually. I have some things back in California I can't abandon, or I'd already be here. My app still needs me to be there in person till it rolls out and the bugs are worked out, and my other project needs me in person for a while yet as well." He sighed deeply. "But trust me, every time I leave, it's harder than the last." He laid a hand on the small of my back. "Come on. Come see the master suite."

It was definitely worth seeing. Sprawling, taking up a good half of the upper story footprint, it featured a bed in a nook that could be opened on three sides to let in the breeze, so you were almost sleeping outside. A sitting area, huge his-and-hers walk-in closets, and a bathroom so luxurious it defied description. The soaking tub was also in another little nook with three walls which opened entirely, a shower big enough for six people, with a baffling profusion of spray nozzles on the walls, and a rainfall showerhead directly above that occupied most of the ceiling space. A built-in heated towel rack, double vanity, a makeup station… everything you could want in a luxury home, just done to a level of mind-boggling perfection that was several steps beyond anything I'd ever seen.

"This is beyond incredible, Braun." I shook my head, marveling. "Just…incredible. And I sell some of the most expensive luxury homes in the world."

"It's only four bedrooms, and it's not actually all that large—only, like, seven thousand square feet. Which, I recognize, is a big house, but not, like, palatial."

"I sold a place two years ago that was over twenty thousand. Just between you and me, it was awful. You needed a damn Segway to get from the kitchen to the stairs up to the bedroom. You want a midnight snack?

Better pack a bag, you'll be gone all night." I laughed. "It was a custom build, and the sellers were like, yeah, we went overboard. It's too big, we want something smaller."

He laughed with me, and then his gaze went serious. "It's just you and me—and the staff, which consists of a chef, a groundskeeper, and a housekeeper, and none of them are live-in, all locals who show up when I need them. So most of the time, we're totally alone here."

I smirked. "And I'm guessing you have plans for all this alone time."

He arched an eyebrow. "I mean, other than my immediate family, you're the only person who's ever been here. So yeah, I've got some ideas."

"Such as?"

He sighed, tucked a lock of my hair behind my ear. "How about dinner first?"

"I'm famished, so that sounds good."

"I've given the chef standing order to just wow me with whatever magic he feels like working, so I have no idea what we're having. I just told him when we'd arrive, approximately, and that we'd be hungry when we got here." There was a rattle of pots and pans from the kitchen, audible due to the open-air nature of the house. "There he is, now."

"And what shall we do until dinner is ready?" I asked, my grin giving away what I was thinking.

Braun rubbed his thumb over my lip. "I can think of a few things…"

A few things to Braun meant peeling my clothes off item by item, kissing my skin as he bared it, until he had me naked and panting and begging for his mouth. Which he gave me, slowly.

He had to press a hand over my mouth to suppress my screams—at least until I found another, tastier way to make use of my mouth. That kept me quiet for a while…until he pulled away and slid into me, kissing me as he came, hard and fast, within seconds.

The whole thing had been less than ten minutes, and yet I was as sated and glutted on him as if we'd been at it for hours.

He traced his finger over my nipple, as I lay beside him, catching my breath. "I meant that to take longer," he said. "You just do something to me. You make me crazy. You make me come so hard, so fast, and I just…I can't seem to hold out when I'm with you."

I just smiled. "You're not gonna hear me complain, Braun. No matter how fast you come, you always make sure I'm there first, and at least twice."

A silence, then.

"Lizzy…" he trailed off. "I'm glad you're here." Something in his eyes told me he'd been about to say something else, and had changed his mind. "Let me clean you up. Be right back."

I wanted to know what he'd been about to say. But

also, I didn't. I was scared it would be too much, too personal.

He was so gentle as he cleaned me—so tender and delicate that I took the washcloth from him and did it myself. Why, I wasn't sure. He was thorough enough. Just...too gentle.

"I'm gonna rinse off before dinner," I said. "You made me all messy."

"Should I apologize for that?" he asked.

"Nope." I stood up, headed for the bathroom. "That's what this is all about, after all."

He watched me fiddle with the shower controls, getting the water going and adjusting it. "You know, I watched a movie a while ago where the couple was trying to get pregnant, and the woman did all sort of weird stuff to make sure she stood the best chance of getting pregnant. Like, she'd lay on her back with her feet up for fifteen minutes, afterward, to make sure the...the stuff...got where it was supposed to go."

I laughed. "Yeah, I've heard about things like that. But I guess it seems silly. I figure people have been doing it the old-fashioned way with none of that nonsense for thousands of years, and women get pregnant just fine. I'm as fertile as can be, according to my doctor, so I don't see any reason for that." I smirked at him, winking lasciviously. "If I'm gonna be on my back with my feet in the air, it's gonna be for a much different reason."

He just grinned at me, laughing as I got into the shower.

He went about cleaning himself up, then, and got dressed in different, clean clothes from the closet—a pair of khaki shorts and a short-sleeve white button-down. I got clean quickly and dried off, and discovered that while we'd been touring the property, someone had unpacked all my things. Next to his.

It was all so...intimate. Familiar.

Leave room in your heart for what-if. I heard Teddy's voice in my head, as I unbraided my hair and brushed it out so the kinks became waves and curls.

This was starting to feel like what-if.

CHAPTER FOURTEEN

B RAUN HAD A SAILBOAT, WITH A CAPTAIN AND A CREW. THE next day, our first full day in Ferragudo, we spent it on the deck, sipping wine and watching the Portuguese coast slide slowly past. We put in for a late lunch in another port, with a name I forgot as soon as the captain told us. It was another adorable, pastoral little fishing village. We ate at a little place on a wharf, barely big enough for three or four tables, where the server, chef, hostess, and bartender were all the same two people, the husband and wife owners. The food was mind-blowing. The wine was even better.

Conversation flowed as easily as the wine, changing directions as swiftly and effortlessly as the sea breeze. Childhood stories, school embarrassments, first crushes, the trouble we'd gotten into, first professional accomplishments.

Talking to Braun wasn't a conversation…it was an on-going, living thing. An extension of just being together.

We sailed back, arriving well past dark, and after the boat was tied up, the captain and crew left us, and we christened Braun's sailboat—the bedroom, and the saloon, and the deck…and the galley.

The next morning, we had a late breakfast at a little cafe. We walked there, hand in hand, like a couple. Which freaked me out, but holding hands seemed harmless enough, right? It didn't have to mean anything. It just felt as natural as breathing to walk with him, holding hands. The café was small and quaint, with a little outdoor seating area that overlooked the ocean, small wrought-iron tables with marble tops. It was almost unbearable romantic. We had delicious frittatas and magical espresso and some kind of sweet, flaky pastry, and we barely spoke, just enjoyed the shimmer of the sun on the water, the warm air, the chatter of people in the café and the occasional passersby.

Walking back, we ended up behind a couple a few years younger than us, the man pushing a stroller, his wife holding his arm with both hands and gazing down into the stroller. I couldn't understand what they were saying to each other, but I didn't need to in order to understand the gist.

The woman paused, leaned over the stroller, reaching in to tickle the baby within, and there was a giggle, and the man said something. She stood up, and she gazed up at her husband and palmed his cheek, and said something soft and sweet, and the adoration in her eyes was so palpable I could feel it from here. Braun and I passed around them, but I only got a couple steps before I stopped, and looked back at them. The woman had removed the baby from the stroller and was holding her, a little girl a few months old, and she was cooing at the baby—baby talk sounds the same in any language, I think. Her husband then watched, his smile as adoring as her gaze had been.

Braun was looking at me.

"What?" I asked.

He shook his head, shrugged. "Nothing."

"What?" I started walking again. "You were looking at me like you were thinking something."

He sighed. "You'll be an amazing mother."

I swallowed hard. "I don't know. I hope so." I swallowed, felt history I rarely spoke of trying to come out. "I didn't exactly have the greatest example, growing up."

"Of motherhood, or of marriage and relationships?"

I swallowed again, hard, the lump in my throat hard and hot and acidic. "Both."

"What you saw and experienced as a kid doesn't have to be how you are. You want a baby. You want to be a mother. That's good. And you'll be good at it."

"I didn't even know I wanted a baby until recently," I said. "I always figured I was a pretty self-aware sort of person, but I'm discovering there's a lot about myself that I didn't know."

He eyed me. "Is it *just* the baby you want?" He was watching me intently. Too intently.

My stomach flipped, and I kept my eyes anywhere but his. "Yes."

"I see." A hard, tense pause. "Good to know."

I didn't look at him. Couldn't. There was something in his eyes, in the silence, something he wasn't saying, and I felt it. Heard it. Knew it.

I could feel the shape of it, and it was something I didn't dare examine.

We finished the walk home in silence.

Later that day, Braun had his driver get "the car" ready. Which, I discovered, meant not the Rolls Royce Ghost we'd been met at the airport with, but a vintage roadster.

"This," Braun said with obvious pride, running his hand along the elegant, sweeping line from the sloped tail to the boxy front end, "is a 1936 Hispano-Suiza K6. There's only a handful of these in the world, and this one is a survivor. Matching numbers, rebuilt and restored about twenty years ago."

I breathed a soft sigh. "You have incredible taste in cars, I must say."

He grinned. "I like nice things. Selling my app has only enabled my predilection for very expensive, very rare things. This one was owned by the same family from the day it was purchased until I bought it a few years ago." He opened the passenger door. "Shall we explore?"

I didn't need any further encouragement. Apparently driving a car from 1936 was a touch more complicated than I'd ever imagined, and for once I was glad to let him do the driving; normally, I like to be behind the wheel, especially if it's a cool, fun, fast, or otherwise interesting car.

With the top back and the Portuguese sun warming us, we followed the coast north, in no hurry. The noise was too much for talking, but the silence was as easy as the conversation. Apparently, the chef had put together a picnic, and we pulled off the road a ways, hiked a mile or so up a hillside and spread our blanket beneath a gnarled old oak with leaves as big as my head.

With no one for miles, no one to see or hear but the seagulls and the squirrels, when our picnic lunch turned into Braun snacking on me, I was able to scream as loud as I wanted, and scream I did.

And you can bet I made Braun shout and bellow as loudly as I'd screamed.

We stayed there for a long time, underneath the tree with the sea in the distance. We lazed naked in the shade, chatting, dozing—that turned into kissing and touching, and then it was a quiet and intense moment together, no longer screams and yells but something deeper, slower. Not a sudden explosion of heat and wildness but a slow build to mutual gasping kissing climax, sweating together, clinging to each other through manic furious whimpering groaning shuddering quaking ecstasy.

When it was over, I was panting and sweating and still shaking with aftershocks. Braun was gasping as if he'd sprinted a quarter mile.

His eyes slid to me. "I swear, every time we have sex, it's better than the last time." He was serious, his voice low, a rough rumble. "Is that normal?"

I swallowed hard, rolled a shoulder. "I don't know, Braun. I've never had this much sex with the same person before. Not all at once, at least, this close together."

I was thinking of Ahmed, but didn't bring it up. Because somehow, what I'd had with Ahmed wasn't in the same realm as what I had with Braun.

He stared up at the canopy of leaves, through which the sun glowed brilliant green. "Me either."

"You've never had a serious girlfriend?"

He shook his head. "Not really. I had a girlfriend I thought was serious. She had other ideas."

"Oh." I wasn't sure if asking was allowed. If it fit in the parameters of this whole thing. If I wanted to know. "I'm sorry."

He didn't smile, didn't shrug. "We were only together a few months, and she was at UC-Davis while I was at Caltech. We only saw each other on the weekends, usually. Mainly Saturdays. We'd hang out Saturday, but we both had to go back for homework and classes Sunday…I thought it was going somewhere, and she thought it was casual. That was the last time I was with anyone in any kind of sense that could be termed a relationship. I've been too busy, had too much on my plate. And honestly, haven't been all that interested."

Until now—those words hung in the air, palpable but unspoken.

"I've been married to my job since high school," I said. "There's been time, if I had wanted to make room in my life for it. There's been opportunity, too. Decent guys with whom I could probably have had something good. But…" I felt a truth, nascent and soft, rolling around in my head, my heart. "But decent isn't good enough for me. It's like with my car. I *love* my car. It fits me. It's perfect for me. It's comfortable. I understand it. I could buy a new car, but it wouldn't be the same, and I think I've never been quite convinced anything I would buy would feel as comfortable and familiar and perfect as what I have. So I stick with my Miata."

"You've never had a serious relationship?"

"No." I looked away. "There was one guy. Quentin. In college."

"I thought you worked for your uncle since you were fourteen?"

I nodded. "He made me get a four-year degree before I could work for him full-time. He wanted me to have experience outside the real estate world. So I went to college, which is where I met Kat—she was my roommate. So yeah, I have a bachelor's in business, but as soon as I was done with that, I went back to working for my uncle."

"I see." He held my gaze. "Quentin. He broke your heart?"

I shrugged. Looked away, at the sparkling sea in the distance. "I broke his. I was the girl in your story, more or less. The one who assumed things were casual when he assumed they were serious." I hated thinking about Quentin—it made my stomach roil, made shame and guilt burn like boiling acid in my gut. "We didn't even see each other that much. He went to a different college, so we only saw each other on the weekends. I met him at a bar. He was cool. A little geeky, into obscure jazz and record players and art films and one-off whiskies from indie distilleries. He thought we were falling in love, and I thought we were just hooking up on the weekends."

"How'd it come apart?"

"He finished his midterms before I did and came to my dorm to surprise me. He had flowers and chocolates, and I had a different guy over." I rubbed my upper lip, letting out a harsh sigh. "He was so hurt. So angry, but hurt more than anything. Said he was falling in love with me, and how could I do this to him, and…" I shook my head. "The hurt in his eyes, it was…it killed me."

"You were young."

"Yeah, but I think I still knew deep down that he thought we had something different than how I saw it, and I never bothered to make that clear to him."

"And after that, you never wanted to hurt anyone like that again."

"It's easier to keep guys at arm's length." I shrugged. "Quentin was good. He was decent." I sighed yet again. "Since Quentin, decent has stopped meaning what it meant, then. Good, too. Good enough and decent became the norm. Good enough for tonight." I finally looked at him. "This thing with you is...it's different."

Braun looked at me. Steady, serious, with understanding and compassion and acceptance. "New is scary. Different is scary. And when you have a standard of excellence, decent and good enough are akin to bad words."

"Exactly." I sighed, rolled to my back and stared up through the green-lit canopy. "And that's how I'm forty, single, and put out an ad for a random stranger to impregnate me."

"I'm not a random stranger anymore, though," he said.

"No," I agreed. "You're not."

"This—whatever it is, whatever you want to call it—this thing we're doing, this thing we have..." he paused. "Is it decent, or good enough?"

I knew what he was asking. I watched an ant

crawl across the underside of a leaf, a few feet over-head. "No, it's not decent or good enough. It's…" Which word was the right one? Which word was the truth? Which word was one I'd be willing to use? "I've never experienced anything like it, to be perfectly hon-est, and I don't always know what to make of it, what to do with it."

He let out a breath, and his voice sounded tight. "Especially considering the essential nature of what we have, defined and inherently limited as it is."

"Exactly."

Something in me shied away from exploring that line of thinking any further. I dressed, and we col-lected our things and headed back to the car. The drive back home was different than the drive out—the si-lence was less easy, more thoughtful, his thoughts and mine coruscating in palpable waves, each of us on the verge more than once of saying something, but then not saying it.

We just slept, that night. In the same bed, close.

Dawn found us both awake, by habit.

I wrapped up in a button-down of his, stood at the railing of the balcony overlooking the courtyard, watching the sun rise over the wall, watching the pink-orange light play on the splashing fountain. Braun floated up behind me, set a mug of thick dark black coffee on the wrought iron bistro table near at hand.

His palms floated over my shoulders. Toyed with

my hair. Tugged the edges of the shirt apart, baring my breasts to the warm dawn air. I leaned my head back, rested it on his shoulder. His lips touched my temple, my forehead; his fingers tweaked my nipples erect, and then danced down my bare front. Lower, and lower. Stirred my sex to heated, throbbing, dripping life.

He tugged the shirt off my shoulders and it fluttered to the floor at our feet; I reached behind me and tugged his underwear down. He kicked them off and nestled himself against my backside, and he kissed my shoulder and my neck, bringing me to gasping, knee-dipping climax, and his lips found mine as I came and he swallowed my cries and he kissed me and kissed me until I sagged against him, and then he bent at the knees and I guided him to me, gasped with my lip caught in chattering teeth, and sank down on him. His arms encircled me, held me up, and his mouth was at my ear as he powered up into me, and I rose up on my toes as he filled me, sank down as he seated deep. Cried out and reached up to clasp at his head, the messy locks of hair.

"Liz," he breathed.

"God...Braun!"

It was moments. That's all it took. A few touches of his finger, and I came apart. A few thrusts of him inside me and I was coming again, and he was there with me, and he filled me and filled me to overflowing, and I was crying out—I was crying, plain and simple. I hid it, swallowed it, shoved it down. Ignored it, denied it to myself.

Replete with him, still anchored on his fading but still firm manhood, I lay back against him and breathed. Held on to the railing and caught my breath. He held me, breathed against me. He reached over, brought the coffee in front of me, and I took it, and sipped. Coffee while still impaled on Braun was…a new kind of amazing, honestly.

Everything with Braun was just…better. Coffee, sex, food, cars, houses, conversation, silence…it was all just *better*.

But there was unease in my gut, a rippling, constant flutter of something deep within.

I was scared.

What-if had come to pass, and I wasn't sure if I had room in my heart, if I knew how to make room in my life.

I didn't know what I wanted, and I knew I was too scared to even examine it.

"Liz?" His voice was a whisper; he took the coffee and sipped.

"Yeah?"

"What are you thinking, right now?"

"I don't…I don't know."

"Yeah you do."

"Braun…"

"Fine. What are you *feeling*, right now?"

"A lot."

"Like?"

I felt suffocated, suddenly. By him. By his questions. By the intimacy. By the glut of him within me, the perfectness of him inside me, even stilled and softening. By my own desire for him.

I wiggled, made it clear I needed to get away, and he let me. I paced to the other side of the balcony, held the railing in white-knuckled fists.

I dripped with him.

Ached for him.

Ached *because* of him, and I didn't mean physically, though that was true.

"Liz?" he repeated. "Tell me what you're thinking—or feeling. Please."

"A lot, Braun. A fucking lot."

"Well, can you *elucidate*, at all?"

Oh, the inside joke. It made my heart squeeze.

I felt him beside me, but I shrank away and held up my hands, palms out, facing him. "Please, Braun. I need—I need a second. I need space."

"Okay." He sounded hurt, and that made my gut twist and my heart ache even more.

I went inside, away from the bright beautiful sun. My emotions didn't deserve the beauty of the morning. I felt him. I felt every move he made, smelled him, heard him.

"Braun, I…"

"You can't, can you?"

"Dammit, Braun."

"Getting you to tell me what you're feeling is like pulling teeth." A bitter bark of a laugh. "And that's coming from a dude."

"I'm sorry." I couldn't face him, look at him. "I think I need to get back home."

"We still have one more day here."

"I'm sorry. I just…"

"Can you tell me why?"

"Braun…"

"You can't, can you?" He sighed, bitterly. "You're just…*done*, and you won't even tell me why."

"I'm sorry."

"We were going to go into Lisbon. I was going to take you shopping."

"I like shopping, but…" I sighed, frowning. "You don't need to take me shopping. That's not what this is."

He tensed, his face hardening. "I know. I know what the contract says. I guess I thought…" he trailed off, backing away. "It doesn't matter."

"Braun?" I whispered.

He was still a moment. Then he shook his head. "No. It's fine."

"It's fine?" Fine, in this context, was a bad word, like *good enough* or *decent*.

"Yeah. It's fine. I'll make the arrangements."

"Thank you, Braun. For the trip, for sharing your amazing home with me. And…for understanding."

"I get it. It's fine, Lizzy." He dressed quickly, and I watched as he slipped his Patek Philippe over his wrist, facing away from me, clicking the clasp in place.

"Braun." I hated the distance in his eyes, the slight coldness in his bearing. "I just…it's…"

"Contractual. It's okay." He came back to face me, towering over me, gazing down at me. "That's what this always was." He brushed my hair away from my mouth. "I understand."

He backed away; I could see clearly that he was carefully hiding his emotions.

So was I, for that matter. From him—and from myself.

The flight home was long, bitterly tense, and icily silent.

CHAPTER FIFTEEN

I HID FROM EVERYONE UNTIL MONDAY. I DIDN'T CALL ANY of the girls and tell them I was home early, or that I was home at all.

I didn't call Braun.

When Monday came, I was in a terrible mood. The girls sensed it, and left me alone.

Braun didn't call or text, and I found myself scrolling on my phone, hoping he would.

I had appointments and showings all week, to make up for the days I'd taken off, which now felt like a dream.

Sailing the Mediterranean, making love under a tree on a blanket, waking up with him the bed next to me.

Him behind me on that balcony. God, that had been...*so* much more than just sex. I could admit that, now, alone at home.

Had it *always* been more than just sex, with Braun?

It seemed like it had. From the get-go, I'd done things with him that I'd never allowed in any of my other…dealings…with men. I kept sex in its own little bubble. I messaged on Tinder enough to find a local hookup, and we met, had drinks, went somewhere to screw, got it on, and I went home. I didn't stay. I didn't cuddle naked in bed with him after we were done. If round one was good, we'd put on some kind of clothing, if just underwear for him and a robe for me, and drink more and watch TV until he was ready to go again. But that was rare—I had high standards. And, if I was being honest with myself, I didn't like letting anyone that close for that long. It smacked of…risk. And the rewards just weren't worth it—I'd seen that live and in person. You let someone close, they fucked you over. Broke your heart and ruined your life. Why would I *ever* let anyone that close?

A week of appointments turned into closing on a property, lining up another new client, several parties in the LA area to angle for new listings.

Two weeks.

He never called, or texted.

Neither did I.

But it *had* been more than sex, had become more than sex early on. I'd come to grips with that much, at least.

Late at night, alone in my apartment, I thought about him.

About how that picnic under the tree in Portugal hadn't been sex. It hadn't been fucking. It had been *making love*, and that scared the unholy hell out of me.

And I was SO MESSED UP.

I wanted Braun. I wanted his smell, I wanted his voice in my ear. I wanted his hands—I needed him to touch me. His touch made me feel…beautiful. Wanted. Treasured. Like it would be okay. I forgot to be scared when I was with Braun. I forgot about the difference between just sex and fucking and making love. It was all just…him and me. And I wanted it. It wanted what he had. I wanted his jokes, his secret self-consciousness, his wry confidence, his mouth and the dirty things he said and the dirtier things he did with it.

But now that I wasn't with him, I was fucking terrified.

I wasn't allowed to feel that way. I'd never allowed it. I'd made a vow as a kid, not even a teenager, that I would never ever fall in love. I'd seen what love did— I'd watched Mom love Dad, watched him shit all over that love, and I'd seen what that did to Mom. And I'd promised myself I'd never love a man, never let a man love me. It wasn't worth it. It would never be worth it. And I'd never found a man capable of changing my mind.

Until Braun.

But…what if. What if.

What if I let him in, what if I let him love me, let it become something? He'd hurt me.

He'd leave. He'd run.

I'd sold so, so many houses because of that—man and woman get married, man gets bored, man cheats, there's a divorce, they sell the house. He buys a new house with his new wife. The former wife buys her own house. I've made a ton of money off the whole cycle. I've stood in dozens and dozens of houses as the woman fights tears because she's selling the house she thought she'd raise her family in, but her shitbag husband found someone younger and prettier and tighter and picked the new shiny thing and left his wife broken. I've seen it, and I refuse to be that woman.

Sure, Braun and I had good sex. Great sex...who am I kidding? Epic, fantastic, incredible, life-changing sex.

But it was still just sex.

It doesn't mean he can love me.

It doesn't mean he *wants* to.

It doesn't mean he wants...*me*. The real me. The deep-down me that I've kept hidden from *everyone* in my life, my girlfriends included. The me that craves... *more*.

That scared little girl listening to her parents fight, watching Mom sign tear-stained divorce papers, watching Dad move his stuff out and wondering what I'd done, what Mom had done to make him leave.

That little girl was in there, wanting desperately to believe in…something else. That something could matter, could last.

But the fear was stronger.

Two and a half weeks after returning from Portugal, I was in my office sorting through paperwork and answering emails. Teddy was the only other one in the office, busily doing her own work. The bell over the front door dinged, and I looked up.

"Delivery for…Lizzy?" The voice was hidden behind an explosion of flowers, the biggest bouquet I'd ever seen in my life. He could barely get his arms around the vase.

"Uh yeah, that's me." I stood up and cleared a space on my desk. "Just…set them down."

He set the bouquet down and shook out his arms—he was young, Hispanic, handsome, with a friendly smile. "Someone really likes you. Or he *really* fu…um, messed up."

"Ha, yeah," I said, my voice faint. "Do I need to sign anything?"

"Nope." He handed me an envelope. "This is from the sender." He smiled at me. "Have a nice day, ma'am."

"You too, thanks."

Teddy was at my side, eyes wide. "Ohmy*god*. I didn't know they made arrangements this big. That's intense." She wandered to the front door, watching the delivery guy climb into the van "He's hot."

I laughed at Teddy. "He's too young for you."

"He's legal." She snorted. "I'm kidding. He's way too young." She returned to the flowers. "Seriously, though. These are from Braun?"

"I'm assuming." I was holding the card, reticent to open it.

She stared at me. "Well?"

"Well, what?"

"What does the card say?"

I was afraid to look. The flowers said it all.

Slowly, I slid my finger under the flap and pulled the card out. It was expensive linen cardstock, with a watercolor painting of a courtyard which strongly resembled the one in Braun's Portugal home. I swallowed hard, hesitated, and then opened it. Inside, a handful of lines in neat, slanted, all-caps handwriting.

Liz,
I miss you. I miss Portugal. I miss us.
Braun.

"He calls you...Liz?" Teddy's voice in my ear.

"Yeah."

"No one calls you that."

"I know. He does."

"And you let him?"

"Yeah." I closed the card.

Set it on my desk. Stared at the flowers. It was... everything. Red roses, yellow, orange, pink, lavender, white. Gerber daisies. Irises. Tulips in every hue. Sprays of baby's breath. More flowers than I knew the names of, in so many colors it took my breath away.

"He's thinking of you, Lizzy." She took my arms, spun me to face her. "He wants more of you. He wants *you*."

"I know," I whispered.

"So…?"

"I can't, Teddy."

"Why not?"

"It's complicated."

"In my experience, that's just an excuse for 'I don't want to explain.'"

"Teddy…"

"Why can't you just be with him?"

"It's not what I want."

"Then why'd you go to Portugal with him? You've let him closer than anyone I've ever seen you with. You've done things with him you normally never do. I think you *do* want that with him. You're just scared of it."

"I'm not scared."

She snorted. "That's some bullshit and you know it."

I picked up the flowers, but it was too heavy to lift. "Help me."

"Help you what?"

"Throw these away."

"Why?" She grabbed my hands to stop me. "Lizzy, no. This is, like, hundreds and hundreds of dollars worth of flowers and they're *gorgeous*. It's a meaningful, heartfelt gesture. You can't just...chuck it, just to prove a point. And prove a point to whom? Yourself?"

"I don't know!" I snapped, then sagged, wilting. "I don't know," I said again, more quietly.

"Yeah, you do."

"He *wants* you, Lizzy." She took my hands and held them. "He wants *you*."

"He just thinks he does."

"And he still would, if you let him in."

"I don't know how. I don't want to. I can't." I shook her hands off. "And you don't know that. You can't know that. He'll want someone else, eventually. That's just how it goes."

"Not necessarily." She paced away. "Why can't you just...try?"

"Because it won't work. It'll...it'll come apart. It'll fail."

Teddy faced me, several steps away. She was wearing a sundress that flattered her curvy figure, and the sundress had pockets at the hips, which she shoved her hands into. "And that's it, isn't it?"

"What do you mean?" I asked. "What's it?"

"There is nothing that scares you more than failure." She moved closer to me. "That's why you work the way you do—you refuse to risk failure. It's why you don't date, why you don't let anyone close—a relationship not working out is failure. There's some failure in your past that you won't talk about, not even to us. We've known you for years, Kat since college, and you don't let *any* of us in, don't and won't tell us that deep-down stuff. Because even with us, you're afraid of getting hurt and afraid of failing, even at a friendship. You work with us, you party with us, you're a great boss, a great friend. You're always there for us. You've given us all careers. But you don't talk about *you*. You don't talk about your past. I don't know why you're so afraid of failure, so afraid of relationships...of love. All I know is you've been avoiding it and running from it for as long as I've known you, and now it's here, in your lap—he's *pursuing you*, Lizzy, and you're running from it." She sniffled, turned away. "I'd give *anything* to have someone want me the way Braun clearly wants you."

"Teddy..." I trailed off, because I had no clue what to say.

She was right. I was terrified of failure. I'd watched Dad fail Mom, watched their marriage fail, and it had broken me as a child, left me in shambles the rest of my life, afraid of repeating their mistakes.

"Just *try*, Lizzy." She blinked away tears. "What do you have to lose?"

"Everything," I whispered.

I went next door to the dress boutique and had the hired girl behind the counter help me carry the giant bouquet into their shop. Teddy watched, disapproving.

"You're making a mistake, Lizzy." She shook her head. "Just so I'm on record as calling you out for this. It's a big, huge, epic mistake. He loves you. You could have something amazing with him."

It was all too much. Perhaps part of me wondered, and wanted. Perhaps. But...the walls were too high. They clamped down, fear shuttering the windows into my heart.

What I wanted wasn't strong enough to get past what I was afraid of.

CHAPTER SIXTEEN

THEN, A MONTH AFTER PORTUGAL, I WAS PUTTING ON makeup before work, wearing a skirt and a bra, waiting to put my blouse on till after makeup.

My stomach revolted, and I had to drop to my knees in front of the toilet, felt my stomach empty itself in a hot bitter sour stream.

Coughing, I leaned back to sit on my feet, wiped my lips on my wrist.

Oops, no, not done yet.

Again, I was sick.

Had I eaten something the night before that didn't agree with me? No, just a piece of fresh salmon I'd picked up on the way home, and some air-fried cauliflower. Both had been fresh, and well-cooked.

What else could make me sick?

It seemed like the sickness was fading, so I stood up and glanced at my phone: 7:36 a.m.

A.m., antemeridian. In the morning.

I was sick…in the morning.

I felt faint.

Had I missed my period?

I counted—the last one had been…beginning of last month. I'd missed my period this month.

And now I was having morning sickness.

Come to think of it, my breasts were tender. And swollen.

What now?

I closed my eyeshadow palette, leaned forward against the vanity and struggled to breathe, to keep calm. Rinsed my mouth, brushed my teeth for the second time that morning.

I was pregnant.

I was pregnant?

I called Kat. "Hey, boss," she answered, on the third ring. "What's up?"

"I'm not feeling well."

"Did you eat something bad?"

"Nope."

A pause.

"Did you throw up?"

"Yep."

"Just now, this morning?"

"Yep."

"Girls!" I heard her shout. "Lizzy is pregnant!"

"We don't know that," I snapped. "It could be a bug."

"Oh pee-shaw," she said; that was a thing with Kat, saying *pee-shaw*. Apparently you read "pshaw" in books but never heard it actually said, and she thought—erroneously, it seemed, to me—saying "pee-shaw" was funny. "You're like, freakishly healthy. You've never even had a cold in all the years I've known you. Even hungover, you're not really sick."

"Kat..."

"I'm on the way. Teddy will handle your morning schedule. Just...I don't know. Lay down, maybe?"

"You just said I'm not sick. And I'm not. I'm queasy, but I'm fine. I don't need to lay down."

"You need to take a pee test. I'll be there in fifteen."

"I need to take, like, four."

"I'll bring six."

"Six might be overkill."

"This is you."

"Oh, good point." I groaned. "I'm not ready for this."

She cackled. "Shoulda thought of that before you hired someone to knock you up."

"I didn't *hire* him, you heartless monster. There was no exchange of money."

"There was an exchange of fluids."

"Kat!"

"Yeah, you're right—it's not really an exchange, is it? More of him giving you *his* fluids. Did you like his fluids, Lizzy? You haven't seen him or talked about him since Portugal, which I take to mean something went sideways."

"Kat," I growled. "Stop."

"What? I'm already halfway to the pharmacy. I'm talking you off the ledge, here."

"I'm not on any ledge, woman. I'm just freaking out because now that I'm actually pregnant, or possibly pregnant, I'm sort of realizing maybe this was stupid."

"You *are* pregnant, and it *was* stupid. But you're in it, now, and we're all here for you." A muffled exchange, and then she was back. "And you're gonna be a great mom."

"Me. A mom."

"Weird." She was silent a beat. "You, a mom."

"That's weird?"

"A little."

"Or a lot," I said, laughing. "Just get here, dammit. And tell the girls not to tell anyone."

"Don't have to tell them that. That's, like, an understood thing." I heard a car door close. "I'm walking into your lobby."

We hung up and within a few minutes she was in my bathroom with me, watching as I peed on stick after stick. I capped them, lined them up one by one on the sink, finished up, washed my hands, and waited.

One by one, the indicators came back.

Pregnant.

It was unequivocal. Each one was affirmative.

"You need to tell him."

"I haven't talked to him in a month."

"Why not?"

"Because Portugal was…" I closed my eyes. Hormones, man, they were making me emotional. "It was a lot. It was…beautiful, and magical, and incredible."

"Portugal was, or he is?"

"Kat, dammit. Not helping."

"Well, if it's true…?"

"The last day, that morning. We're both early risers."

"Annoying." Kat was *not* a morning person.

"I had on one of his shirts. His place has this balcony overlooking a walled courtyard, like, one of those old-world places, you know? The front gate opens right onto the street, and that's the front door, the main entrance, that courtyard. And his master suite looks out onto that courtyard from one side, and out onto the ocean on the other side."

"Super jealous of that," she said.

"You have no idea." I sighed. "He came up behind me with coffee. And he was so…sweet. So soft, so gentle. *Loving*. It's the only fucking word for it. The way he touched me, the way he…there was no thought in me, no choice, no desire but to *be with* him. Standing there, him behind me." I choked, and my voice dropped to a whisper. "I've never felt so...*wanted*. Needed. Appreciated. It was like that every time with him. But that moment especially, sleepy still, just after dawn, the way he was with me...it was too much."

"So you freaked out, and bolted."

"Yeah."

"And now you're pregnant with his baby, and the contract is concluded."

"Yeah."

"And you're having second thoughts."

"I don't know. I don't know what I'm having."

"A baby."

"Well no shit, Sherlock. I meant second thoughts. I don't know. I just found out. And now I don't know how to tell him. What it would mean."

"Lizzy..." She sighed. "Coming from me, I know this is weird. But...honey, you need to do some soul searching."

"Yeah."

"Take the day. Think about things. Figure out how to tell him, and what you want."

"I can't take the day. I took four days."

"Lizzy, honey, baby, sweetie."

I rolled my eyes at her. "Kat, darling, pumpkin, snookums."

"Business will continue without you. We can manage. And we're gonna have to get used to it anyway, because you're going to be missing days for appointments, and taking extended time off when you give birth."

I rubbed my face with both hands. "I'm not ready to think about any of that yet, Kat." I stared at the line of pregnancy tests. "What the *hell* was I thinking? Why did I think I could do this?"

"Because you can."

"I'm not so sure, at the moment. I don't even know how to tell Braun."

"Why? It's contractually over. That's what you wanted. You tell him you're pregnant, thanks for your service, buh-bye. Simple." She held my gaze for a long beat. "Unless it's not that simple."

I had no answer for her on that score. Was it that simple? Or was it more complicated than that? The answer to that lay on the other side of the aforementioned soul searching. Which I was loath to do, because I wasn't entirely certain I wanted to know the answer.

Kat side-hugged me. "You've *got* this, Elizabeth Stephenson. And you have *us*. You're okay."

"Thank you, Kat."

"No problem, boss. Now, I have an appointment, so I gotta hustle. You need anything, you let one of us know. We're here for you. We'll cover your schedule for today."

"You're the best."

"I know."

"That was a you-plural, by the way."

She snorted. "Sure it was. Have some tea. Take a bath. Make some soup. Think. Call Braun."

"I'm pregnant, not sick with the flu. And I have to think about what to say to him before I call him."

"Yeah, yeah. I know you. You're just trying to figure out an excuse to not tell him. That would be marvelously shitty of you, Lizzy, and you're better than that. Woman up and call his ass."

I couldn't help a snicker. "It's not his ass I want to talk to."

"No, it's his magical dick." She smirked at me. "I think you might be…a-*dick*-ted."

I picked up a pillow off my couch and hurled it at her—she closed the door just in time, and the pillow smacked against the door. "I hate you for that joke!"

I did make some tea and a can of chicken noodle soup, because I was still feeling nauseous, but I knew I needed to eat. Especially after having barfed up everything in my stomach.

Ugh.

I had to tell Braun. I should have called him weeks ago, but I was chicken. I was still chicken. I needed outside verification of pregnancy first, though. I mean, every conversation you ever see where a woman is telling a man she's pregnant, he asks two questions, in a specific order: *are you sure?* and *is it mine?*

I called my doctor and scheduled a blood test for later that afternoon—which was lucky, because there'd been a last-minute cancellation; normally, you were lucky to get a slot within two weeks.

I did end up running a bath and was happy to be able to keep the soup down. I took a long lazy bath, watched mindless TV, and avoided thinking about all the things I needed to be thinking about.

Like being pregnant.

Like Braun.

Eventually, though, I had to face the music.

I knew the blood test would only verify what I already was certain of—I was pregnant. In nine months, I was going to produce a whole human. It—he or she—was going to grow in my belly and come out of my vagina. Hopefully. Unless I had a C-section. Regardless, I was going to then be responsible for keeping that human alive. Giving him or her a name. Teaching the child to eat, to walk, to talk, to read and write and be a good human—the child would have his or her own personality, passions, foibles.

I knew nothing about raising a human.

I barely knew what to do with a baby beyond holding it. Diapers, breastfeeding.

Oh god, breastfeeding.

I was in so far over my head.

Before I knew it, my appointment had arrived and I was sitting in a sterile room, having not a blood test, which apparently was unnecessary, but something called an hCG test, which measured some kind of hormones. I received the expected result: pregnant. Around six weeks, my doctor said. Which would mean, if that timing is correct, I was already pregnant in Portugal. Like, one of the first times we had sex, if not *the* first.

I drove home in a daze, but didn't get out of my car—I sat in my parking lot and cried.

Why, I wasn't sure.

Hopefully this wasn't my new normal for the next year, randomly crying in parking lots for no reason.

I had to tell Braun. And for some reason, I couldn't bear the thought of telling over the phone.

I texted him: *Where are you, right now? We need to talk.*

He answered almost immediately: *We do? I figured we were done.*

Me: *I'm sorry, Braun. I really can't excuse it. But we do need to talk.*

Braun: *In person, I assume you mean.*

Me: *Yes. Soon.*

Braun: *I'm in a meeting in LA, and I'm not sure when I can get away to come up to Malibu.*

Me: *I can come down to LA.*

Braun: *It's serious, then.*

Me: *Yeah, it is.*

Braun: *I'm guessing I know what it's about, and I have a feeling it's something I would prefer to hear in person. So, if you're okay to come down to LA, then I could slip away for a while.*

Me: *I'll text you when I'm in LA. Where exactly are you?*

Braun: *I'll send a car and driver for you. They'll be outside your building in a few minutes, and will bring you to where I am. Text me when you're here.*

The car turned out to be a Mercedes S-class, with a silent driver. We arrived a little less than an hour later at a nondescript high-rise in downtown LA. I took the elevator up to the lobby of the building and texted him that I'd arrived.

I didn't receive a reply—instead, I got the man himself, dressed in a beautiful, bespoke, navy blue houndstooth suit, no tie. I spied a Patek Philippe peeking out from under his cuff. For once, his hair was combed back and to one side, making him look every inch the billionaire tech inventor he was.

I think I preferred him in jeans, bare chested and barefoot, but I really, really liked this version of him, as well.

He stood a foot away from me, one hand tucked into his pocket, the other dangling at his side. "Hey." His eyes scanned me head to toe. "You look well."

"Appearances can be deceiving," I said. "Your suit is amazing."

"Thanks." He flicked his wrist to expose his watch. "I have a couple hours. Want to grab an early dinner?"

"Please. Somewhere quiet, and...private."

He nodded, unsmiling. "I have somewhere in mind."

"Lead the way."

There was a private section of the underground garage, accessible only via a special elevator and a unique six-digit code; the private garage was occupied by precisely four vehicles, which totaled together were worth a couple million dollars—I saw a Bugatti, a McLaren, a new Ford GT, and a vintage Rolls Royce drophead coupe.

I smirked at Braun. "Let me guess—the Rolls is yours."

He winked. "You got it. It's like you know me."

"I have to say, as lux as the one in Portugal was, I like this one better."

"I'm a sucker for old cars. My dad was a gearhead, and was always working on something, and I got the bug. Of course, I don't work on them—no time. I just collect them."

"How many do you have?" I asked, unable to contain my car-nut curiosity.

He frowned, hand on the roof of his car. "Um. The two in Portugal, the Shelby, the Mercedes, this, the GT3, an '89 Defender 90, umm...oh, and a '78 Jaguar E-type Roadster."

"I may be jealous of all of them."

Braun opened my door for me, waiting until I was

seated and settled before closing it. The engine rumbled to life, and in another moment, we were outside in the brilliant, blinding, hot LA sunshine. I didn't ask where we were going, because I knew Braun well enough by now to know that I could trust his judgment.

We didn't go far, only fifteen minutes or so across town. Our destination seemed to be a hotel restaurant, which wasn't open yet.

I eyed Braun curiously. "So…a closed restaurant?"

He grinned. "I'm friends with the head chef. I texted him when you said you were coming down here, and he's got something whipped up for us. Being closed for another couple hours, you can't get more private than a totally empty restaurant."

"You know some cool people."

"I've been friends with him since high school. He's one of the few friends I have that doesn't give a shit how much I'm worth."

I nodded. "The best kind of friend, I'm guessing."

"You have no idea. It's so hard to know who to trust, sometimes. Or all the time." He glanced down at me as he held the restaurant door open for me. "Which is part of why I was curious about your ad—it specifically ruled out you being after me for my money."

I wasn't sure how to respond to that, so I didn't. The interior of the restaurant was that of a swanky, dinner-only, reservations-several-months-ahead, suit-jackets-required sort of steakhouse. Most of the tables still had the chairs flipped upside down on them, except one near the entrance to the kitchen. A tall, heavy-set black man bustled out of the kitchen, dressed in the black-and-white checked pants and white shirt of a chef, complete with the fancy hat.

"Hey, B, my man, good to see you!" He clapped Braun on the back, and then turned to me. "He said he was bringing a friend, but he neglected to mention that his friend was as gorgeous as you are."

"Thank you," I said, shaking his hand. "I'm Lizzy."

"Mackenzie. Mack, to my friends. You guys sit, have some bread. I'll have your meals out in a minute, they're just finishing off. B—you know where the wine is. Help yourself to a bottle."

"Thanks, Mack." Braun showed me to my seat, held the chair for me. "So, a bottle of red?"

Moment of truth.

I dearly wanted a glass, or a bottle, but I had to start acting like what I was. "I, um—I'm good with sparkling water."

Braun's eyes narrowed. "Fine by me. I've got to be on my A-game, so skipping the wine is probably a good idea for me too."

"What's your meeting about?"

"Well, it's more of a series of meetings. We're working out the kinks of the rollout of my app, now that I've reworked the code their hacks fucked up." He sighed. "Sorry, it just still chaps my ass."

"You worked hard on that and having someone else mess it up has to be galling, at best."

He went behind the bar and produced a pair of bottles of Perrier from a cooler, two glasses, and a few slices of lime, brought it all back to the table. "Mack started here as a dishwasher when he was a kid, worked his way up and to line cook, went to culinary school, and eventually got made head chef. I used to come here between classes while he was prepping and work on my app." He twisted the tops off, poured, added lime wedges, and slid one to me. "So. You needed to talk to me in person, and aren't having wine. I can put two and two together."

I sipped, but nerves prevented me from breathing, much less anything else. "Yeah. I, um. I'm pregnant. There's no question—I took six pee tests and got an hCG test at the doctor's. Six weeks, she said."

He nodded. Didn't look at me. "Congratulations."

"Braun..."

"How long have you known?"

"Since this morning. I got sick, and I never get sick. The moment I got the results from my doctor, I messaged you."

"So then, you ghosting me after Portugal..."

"Braun, I..."

"Even now, you can't be truthful. You can't even lie."

"I'm a lot of things, but one thing I'm not is a liar."

"So why did you ghost me?"

"I didn't ghost you, Braun."

He sat back, eyes narrowing, a rare display of actual anger on his face. "You ended the trip early, didn't say a word the whole flight back, and I haven't heard a peep since." He stabbed the table with his finger. "That's ghosting, in my book."

I swallowed hard, opened my mouth to speak, but Mack came out then with a plate in each hand. Filet Mignon, roasted asparagus, twice-baked potatoes, some kind of fancy sauce. Mack seemed to sense the tension between us, because he dropped off the plates, gave a little half bow of his upper torso, and backed away to leave us alone.

I was suddenly famished, and started eating, if only to buy time for my answer. Braun wasn't eating, however.

I set my fork down. "Portugal was intense."

"Yes."

"Especially that last morning."

His eyes heated. "Yes."

"It was just…more than I was…more than I—"

"You really did expect to keep the whole thing casual and entanglement free."

"Well, yes." I frowned at him. "Thus the contract."

"I guess part of me wondered if that was a protection proviso, in case things went sideways." He finally took a bite. "I guess I had it backward."

"You thought I was looking for...what? A relationship?"

"I don't know. I took you at your word, I really did. I just wondered if maybe, in the back of your mind, you were thinking something...more...might come from it." He speared asparagus, bit the tip off, chewed thoughtfully, his eyes on mine. "After that last morning in Ferragudo, I guess I thought, maybe..." he trailed off, shaking his head.

"What, Braun?"

"Maybe there was something there, between us. More than just screwing."

I studied my plate—I was almost finished already, but barely remembered eating. "The contract. It states that as soon as I'm pregnant, our contact is at an end. Whatever that last morning may have been, I was already pregnant by then. I didn't know it, but I was. I had to tell you in person. But..."

"It's just contractual." He nodded. Went to eating with business-like efficiency. "I understand."

"Braun, I don't mean that I didn't enjoy and appreciate the time we spent together. It was so much better than anything I'd anticipated." I set my utensils down. Blinked hard. "I'm *pregnant*. My life is about to change. You may have been right, that first time we met in person—I don't know that I knew what I was getting myself into, doing this. You have your app, your other project, your amazing house in Portugal, your whole life. Mine is…" I let out a slow, shaky breath. "It's going to change, in ways I don't think I have any capacity to understand."

"Lizzy," he murmured. "Shit, this is tricky."

"What?"

"I can tell you're getting ready to cut me out again, and I understand. I appreciate you telling me in person." He finished his food, washed it down. "There's a lot I could say, but I'm not going to. Portugal was special to me. This whole thing was. But I have to protect myself, at this point, since it doesn't seem like you're willing to…look at me, or this thing we had, as anything other than a contract fulfilled."

"Braun…"

"Am I wrong?" He leaned forward, dark gaze intense, cautious. "If you can see a way past this moment that doesn't involve me going back to my meeting, and you to doctor appointments alone, then say so. But otherwise, for the sake of my mental and emotional clarity and stability, I think it's best we make a clean break of it."

My chest ached. "I don't know what to say."

I knew exactly what to say, but I couldn't. I couldn't tell him about Dad cheating on Mom—visibly, publicly. I couldn't tell him about how humiliated Mom had been, that the whole town had talked about it. I couldn't bring myself to talk about how Dad had tried to bring his new girlfriend into my life, after the divorce. Shit, the divorce—I *really* couldn't talk about that. It had been long, protracted, ugly, vicious, and brutal. Mom had been angry by that point, past the shock and hurt and humiliation, and had moved into blind rage and hate. It had swept me up with it, made me hate him, robbed me of my father. And Mom, too. She'd drowned in her hatred of Dad, and had gotten back at him by bringing a parade of men into her life, into my life, into her bedroom. And Dad had done the same, after his pretty young secretary had dumped him—dated girl after girl, each younger than the last. I think his current girlfriend was younger than me. And Mom's boyfriends had been...uniformly horrible.

But I couldn't say any of that. It was stuck in my chest, under a hard, calcified layer of pain and child-hood confusion and resentment, under a lifetime of acting out in order to get attention, to get either of them to see *me* instead of their hatred of each other. It was all a big spiky knot of awfulness and I'd spent so long avoiding it, refusing to deal with it, refusing to think about it that I couldn't even begin to broach it with myself, much less Braun.

"I don't know what to say." It's all I could manage, and I felt my eyes stinging, my throat closing. But I couldn't take it back. Couldn't get anything else out.

"And that says it all." He dug a thin wallet out of his suit coat's inside pocket, withdrew a stack of bills—which looked to be all hundreds, and set them down beside his plate. He stood. "Take the Rolls. I'll walk, or have someone come get me, or…or something."

"Braun." I swallowed hard, stood up as well.

He was cold, distant. "It's fine." He set a small keyring on the table. "In fact, just keep it."

"It's a half-million-dollar vintage Rolls Royce, Braun. I'm not keeping your car."

"It was a custom order when it was new, so it's a one-off and worth over two million. But in the end, it's just a car—I don't give a shit." He walked away, both hands in his pocket. "Goodbye, Lizzy."

I watched him walk away, wondering if I was making the biggest mistake of my life.

I did something then that I hadn't done since Mom and Dad's divorce was finalized—I cried.

Because I knew I'd done it again—I'd hurt Braun. The reason I'd kept men at arm's length my whole life, especially after Quentin, was because of how much hurt and pain I'd seen both Mom and Dad go through. Relationships clearly weren't worth it.

And this was why.

Confusion. Pain. Anger. Resentment.

I felt some part of me demanding I go after him. Tell him I cared. Tell him I wanted more.

I didn't.

I couldn't.

And I hated myself, for that.

CHAPTER SEVENTEEN

"EVERYTHING LOOKS GREAT SO FAR, LIZZY," THE ultrasound tech said, moving the wand around my belly.

On screen, colors jumped and shifted, and images twisted and morphed.

"The baby is healthy?"

"Oh yeah." She clicked, tapped, rolled the mouse-ball, clicked and tapped. "See? Two arms, two legs, a head." She adjusted the wand, touched a button. "And…a heartbeat."

A rhythmic rustling, whumping, thumping sound filled the small dark room. My eyes started, tears filling my eyes.

"That's the heartbeat." It was real. My belly was growing and I'd felt little faint stirrings of movement now and then, but this was the first time I'd heard the heartbeat. Despite being forty, apparently, I wasn't considered high risk, so this eighteen-week ultrasound was my first. "Can...can you tell the gender?"

A wiggle of the wand, twist, angle this way and that, and then she found something she liked and held it in place. "I sure can. You want to know?"

I blinked, swallowed hard. "Yeah—yes, please."

She smiled at me. "You're having a girl." She pointed at the screen—if I squinted, I could sort of see what she was talking about. "See the three lines, here? That's the lady bits."

"A girl."

"Yes, ma'am. A little baby girl. I just need to take a few measurements, and you're good to go." She smiled at me. "So. Are you doing a gender reveal party or anything?"

"Um, no."

"Ah, okay. A lot of couples are doing that, these days. Requests for the gender to be a surprise are actually higher than ever, lately. Everyone wants to do the balloon or the cake or the piñata."

"Nope. Just gonna go buy some pink onesies and some pink bedding for the crib and call it a day."

"How do you plan on telling Daddy?"

My heart twinged. "I, um. I don't. He's...not in the picture."

She winced. "Oh. Sorry. Sometimes my friendliness runs away from my tact."

"It's okay. It was by design. It's a long, complicated story."

"I see." Clearly, she didn't, not at all.

More wand work and such, and then she wiped the blue goo off my belly, handed me a stack of clean white towels, stuffed the printouts of ultrasound pictures into a folder, and stood up. "I'll leave you to get dressed. You're all set. Congratulations, and good luck!"

"Thanks."

It was still only just noon, and I had a showing in an hour. I stopped by the office to show the ultrasound results to the girls, who made all the appropriate squeals and cooing and plans for girls' nights out with "our daughter," as Kat put it.

I snorted. "Our daughter?"

"Well yeah," she said, rolling her eyes. "It's a group effort." She pointed at me. "First Mommy." At herself. "Second Mommy." Then everyone else in turn. "Third, fourth, fifth, and sixth Mommy."

I laughed. "Kat, you're crazy."

Teddy, as usual, ignored the obvious to point out what everyone else was refusing to talk about. "You seem sad."

"I'm not sad."

"You're sad." She was flipping through the ultrasound photos. "You miss him."

"Teddy," Laurel said, her teeth gritted. "Enough."

"What? It's true. We all know it. You fucked up, Lizzy. But it's not too late. You can still call him."

I stood up, not without difficulty. "And on that note, I'm going to my showing. After that, I'm going home and eating a metric ton of Mexican takeout."

Kat watched me amble slowly to the exit—I wasn't waddling yet, but if I got any bigger, I would be. "Lizzy, you know—"

I held up my hand. "Nope. Not listening to it. Not a word. Thanks for the concern, but I'm fine."

"You're not fine!" Kat yelled after me, following me. "You're moping, goddammit."

"I am not." I was at my car, but stopped to face Kat.

Because I wasn't fine.

I missed the shit out of him.

But I still wasn't ready to admit I'd been wrong. I wasn't ready to admit I wanted him in my life.

That I felt...*things*...for him.

Braun had said he wanted a clean break. I wasn't about to call him, only to have him tell me he's seeing someone new. Or that he finally moved to Portugal.

My clients in the business community had all been talking about a new business solutions app that was rocking the corporate world, making serious waves. Now that it was out, I imagined that Braun would be finishing up his other secret, mysterious project and moving on.

God, who was I kidding? I'd totally fucked up. I'd gotten attached to him, developed feelings for him, and then had been too scared and too deeply entrenched behind my walls to let him in. And now he was gone and I was too scared of being hurt even worse when it turned out he'd moved on—as he absolutely should have, after the way I'd treated him.

I just didn't know what to do. Or, I did, but I was too scared to do it.

"You're miserable," Kat said. "We all know it. And we all know why, except, it seems, for you."

"I'm not miserable, I'm pregnant. I pee every ten minutes. I have heartburn. I crave tacos literally all the time. I can't drink. I dropped my keys the other day and it took nearly a minute to pick them back up."

She sighed. "Lizzy, being pregnant has nothing to do with your shitty attitude. The others may not see it as clearly as I do—except maybe Teddy, but she has, like, a sixth sense about this stuff, I think. She's right—you miss Braun. You fucked up, you know it, and you're too stubborn to call him."

"He's moved on by now."

"You don't know that."

"How could he not have? I gave him nothing to work with." I shrugged, fighting emotions. "Except some superhot sex. But if superhot sex was enough, the divorce rate wouldn't be what it is."

"Teddy told me about the flowers. And the note."

"Or course she did."

"He said he missed you."

"He missed my vagina. And my blowjobs."

"But it's not out of the realm of possibility that he actually just missed *you*."

"You don't know that. More to the point, I don't know that. The contract is over. He did his part. It's done."

"I put in an escape clause. You can still have him."

"I don't know that I *want* him."

"Bullshit. You do."

"Kat, please."

She pinched the bridge of her nose. "You fucked up, Lizzy. You can fix it."

"Correction, Kat—*I'm* fucked up. And it's not something that can be fixed."

She held my gaze for a long moment. "There's no talking to you about this, is there?"

"No."

"You're making a mistake. For the record."

"Noted."

Her eyes bored into me. "Lizzy, why can't you just be honest with yourself, and with me? With all of us? With Braun?"

I got into my car. "I'm going home."

She watched me go, concern in her eyes.

Maybe she was right. Shit, I knew she was. But yet again, fear overruled reason, and killed hope.

CHAPTER EIGHTEEN

"AND ON THE LEFT, A LIBRARY," I SAID, GESTURING with one hand, while the other cupped my prodigious belly. "Lots of lovely nooks, a nearly hidden door leading out to a secret courtyard only accessible from this library."

My clients oohed and ahhhed. I saw the library, and could only think of another library, across the ocean, which dwarfed this one.

"Through here we have a powder room, and the kitchen. Which, of course, is open to the living room. Backstairs to the upper floor, and would you look at that outdoor living space? It's an entertainer's dream."

Something twinged in my belly. Little Sabrina had been kicking a lot today, but this didn't feel like a kick, or a roll, or a punch, or whatever gymnastics the active little thing got up to all day and all night, every day.

I paused, waiting for it to pass.

"Are you okay?" the wife asked. "How far along are you?"

"Due any day now," I answered. "I'm fine. It's nothing." I smiled brightly. "Shall we see the bedrooms?"

But two steps along, and there was another twinge, this one sharper. I'd been having them on and off all day, but over the past couple hours, they'd been sharper, and more regular. Still pretty far apart, until now, so I hadn't bothered my doctor.

I had to stop. "Ooh, this one stings a bit," I gasped, bracing a hand on the wall.

"Michael, call an ambulance." The woman—Sheila? Sarah? Something like that—put a hand to my belly. "I've had four children, dear, and I think you're in labor."

Michael, the husband, was on the phone before I could stop him.

"It'll pass," I insisted, gasping. "We can continue."

"Yeah, it'll pass...until the next one. That's how labor works." She smiled at me. "Why don't you sit down here, okay? You've had several since we've been here, and they're getting closer together."

I grimaced as I slid down into the chair she'd pulled over from the kitchen. "It's not time yet. I'm not due for another few days. I still have showings to do."

"Babies are no respecters of schedules, dear," she said. "Now just breathe. Squeeze my hand if you like."

"It's passed for the moment." I struggled to get

my feet under me. "This is unprofessional of me, and I apologize."

"It's life, dear," she said. "Is there anyone we can call for you?"

I fished my phone out of my clutch, found Teddy's number. "Teddy. She's closest."

A blink. "Of course." She took the phone and sent the call through. "Hi, no, this is Susan Wright, Lizzy's client. She's in labor. We've called an ambulance…yes, she's okay, as well as can be expected. Okay, yes, thank you. No, it's all right. We can do another showing at a different time."

"I've seen enough," Michael said. "I like it. It's the best location and backyard."

Susan patted his hand. "Now's not the time, dear."

I huffed. "It's always the time. If you like it, we can get paperwork going." I winced again. "My associate, Kat, can help you put in an offer, since it seems I'm going to be…out of commission."

Susan gave me a look that was a cross between admiration and exasperation. "We'll see that you get the commission, but we really do like this house, and we would like to move on it."

"I'm not concerned with the commission," I said, and then gasped as another contraction lanced through me. "God, they're coming hard and fast all of a sudden."

"With my first, it was like that," Susan said. "Slow,

dull contractions really far apart all day—for a couple days, as a matter of fact. And then all of a sudden, boom. We barely made it to the hospital, actually."

My eyes widened. "Oh no, no. No way. I am *not* having this baby at a client's house." I tried to get to my feet again, but the contraction was like a vise, and I couldn't breathe, much less move. "We have to go. I have to go. I have to get to the hospital."

"The ambulance should be here soon," Michael said. "You'll be fine. Just breathe."

Fine was a relative term. If by fine, you meant *in unutterable agony*, then yes. If by fine, you meant *my water broke all over the foyer of the house I was supposed to be showing*, then yes.

Fortunately, the ambulance arrived at the moment of my water breaking, and there were medics and the ambulance ride to the hospital. Voices, encouragement, hands in places hands didn't typically go unless I was naked and in bed.

Something about being at eight and almost fully effaced, whatever the fuck that meant. I knew, but in the moment, the meaning eluded me.

I was transferred from the ambulance to a hospital bed, and there was a race through the halls. An elevator being summoned.

"WAIT!" A male voice. Familiar.

Sweating, panting, gasping, in agony, I knew him.

"Braun?" My voice was hoarse, faint. Braun was

here? Was I scared, happy, confused? It hurt too much to figure it all out.

"Sir, sir, family only." A calm male nurse's voice. "Sir, please, you can't go back there. You have to sign and—*sir*—"

"He's the father," I rasped. "Let him—let him come."

Moments later, Braun's face was hovering over mine. He hadn't shaved since I last saw him, and now sported a well-trimmed short beard, and his glasses. "I didn't miss it. Thank God."

He had my hand.

I squeezed, because another contraction was pulsing through me. "Braun...what...how are you here?"

"Teddy called me."

"Teddy. Of course." I had a million things to say to him, but it took everything I had to catch my breath before the next contraction.

We were on the elevator, and then it stopped and the doors opened and more hallways racing past, drop-tile ceilings overhead and fluorescent lights; the sound of doors opening, remote open plates being smacked, a PA announcement, Braun trotting beside me, pain like waves of lightning and hot vice clamps and pressure—another door, a room, curtains, intensely bright lights being turned on and a flurry of activity. I was being helped out of my clothes from the waist down, and a sheet was draped over me, and there was a young Asian male doctor in full scrubs with a face shield between my knees, probing my undercarriage.

"Okay, Miss Stephenson, this is happening now." He smiled, calm and confident and reassuring. "I'm Dr. Chan, and I'm going to take care of you, okay? We're going to have a great birth. I don't want you to push yet, okay? Not until I tell you."

"It hurts," I snarled.

"I know, and I'm sorry, but the baby is going to crown any second now, and it's way, way too late for any medicine. But the good news is, this will be over before you know it and you'll have your new little baby in your arms. Okay? We just need to finish getting set up, here. Dad, can you go by her shoulder, back there? Good, hold her hands, when I tell her to push, you count from one to ten, nice and slow. One...two... three...about that pace, okay?"

I looked up, and saw Braun, dressed in a suit and tie, sweat dotting his forehead, a wild mixture of emotions on his face. "Braun. Why are you here?"

"I told you. Teddy."

"No...I mean *why*?"

He shook his head. Squeezed my hand. "She told me you were in labor, and I just...knew."

"Knew? Knew whatOHSHIT!" Another contraction, this one volcanic and immense, wrung me, wrenched me.

He held my hand and didn't protest when I surely

squeezed his hands so hard they had to be near breaking, and I was screaming, a feral, shrill scream.

After an eternity that passed in the blink of an eye, it let me go, and I sagged back to the bed. Sweat had my hair pasted to my face.

"What did you know, Braun?"

"We can talk later, okay? I'm here, and I'm not going anywhere."

"BRAUN!" I snapped. "Do *not* argue with the woman in labor!"

He huffed in surprise at my outburst. "Okay, okay. I…I'm in love with you, Liz. I knew it that morning in Portugal. I knew sitting across from you at Mack's restaurant. I've known it the last nine months. Shit, I knew it that first day on the beach! I tried to stay away, for you, because that's what you said you wanted, but…I can't. I love you." He swiped at his face, emotions leaking down his cheeks. "I knew from the start that I wanted more with you. I went into it out of curiosity, but then I talked to you, met you, and I knew. I knew I wanted more. I tried to…to pretend like I didn't. Because I knew you didn't. But I did, and I do, and I'm here because I love you and I want to be in your life and this little baby's life." He put his other hand over our joined hands. "I missed you. I missed your smile, the way it lights up your face, and the whole room. I missed the way you make me feel. I missed everything about you."

I leaked tears. "Dammit. DAMMIT!" I looked up at him. "You have to say that *now*, when I'm as emotionally, mentally, and physically vulnerable as a human being can be?"

"Liz, I just—"

Another contraction, and then the doctor was back, checking me. "Okay, Mom, are you ready? Next contraction, I want you to *push*, push with everything you've got, okay?"

Mom. Mama. Mommy. I was about to be a mommy.

Braun loved me?

I was crying, sobbing, ugly crying. "Look at me, Braun Bennet. I'm a sweaty, crying, half-naked mess. I'm in the middle of having a baby. You don't want any part of this. I gave you the out."

Don't take it. Please, Braun—please don't' take it. Please love me. Please stay. Even still, I couldn't say it, couldn't get it past my lips.

"You're beautiful," he said. "And I took the out. I stayed away as long as I could. But I *do* want this. You're not just having a baby—you're having *my* baby. *Our* baby. I *want* this." He gripped my hands, bent and kissed my lips, soft, delicate. "I love you, and I want this."

"Okay, ready? Here it comes." Dr. Chan was watching a monitor, and somehow knew the very moment the contraction hit. "Push, push, push!"

Oh fuck, oh fuck. They tell you it hurts, and TV and movies show women giving birth screaming and all that, but there's just no way to prepare you for what that moment is like.

There just aren't words.

Then, in the middle of pain the size of the universe itself, something…changed.

Dr. Chan was telling me to keep pushing, and it hurt, it hurt, but it was different and then the titanic, crushing pressure just…*popped*, and there was a moment of intense, profound silence.

And then a sound.

A thin, wavering, tiny sound. Angry, confused.

Dr. Chan rose, holding a wet, messy, bloody, squirming bundle of legs and arms and thick dark hair, a reddish-purple cord still trailing from the baby to inside me. "It's a girl, mama. Congratulations! You're a rock star. You did so good. Here, here she is."

I had my daughter in my arms. Her tiny hands were clenched into tiny fists, and she was screaming and screaming.

My heart, outside my body. I felt the truth of that old adage the moment I saw her, felt her in my arms.

Braun.

He was beside me, looking stunned. Tears marked his cheeks, disappeared into his beard. "You did it, Liz." He sounded faint, awed. "You did it. She's so beautiful. I'm so proud of you—so proud of you."

He had her in his arms, then, holding his daughter for the first time—a tiny bundle of squalling, shrieking, messiness, thick mop of dark hair still wet. He blinked, swallowed, gasped a choked sound, and then tears slid down his cheeks and he couldn't seem to say anything, just stared down at her, awe in his eyes.

A nurse took the baby, took Sabrina from Braun and whisked her away.

He looked at me, then. "The nurses are taking her to be cleaned up and measured, okay? She'll be right back, I promise."

He addressed Braun, next. "Dad, you want to cut the cord?" Dr. Chan attached clips to the umbilical cord, handed Braun a pair of medical shears. "Right here, right between the clamps, between my fingers. Yep, perfect, right there...good job."

I was suddenly crushed by another contraction, not as painful as the delivery contractions and without the intense pressure as before, but still far from pleasant.

"Why do I still feel a contraction?" I snapped, demanding. "I thought I was done!"

"You have to deliver the afterbirth," Dr. Chan explained, patient and calm. "Here it comes. Okay, this is the easy part. Ready? One more, and...there we go."

I felt wrung out, utterly drained, and everything hurt. But Braun was there with me, still holding my hand.

"You meant what you said?" I asked, heart pounding for a different reason, now. "You meant it? You weren't just saying it because I was in labor?"

He wiped at his face with a hand. "Yes, Liz, I meant it. I absolutely meant it."

"Why? How?"

He laughed. "Somewhere between the amazing sex and seeing you in my house in Ferragudo, I just...it stopped being just sex." He shook his head. "You know what? The truth is that it was *never* just sex for me. But then when you ghosted me, it was just super obvious. I missed you every single moment of every single day. And then you made it clear you really didn't care for me, at Mack's, it was like, crystal fucking clear. That was the hardest thing I've ever done in my life, walking away that day."

"I—never said I don't care for you," I managed. "I do."

"I want to be in my daughter's life," he said. "If you don't, can't, or won't love me, I'll manage that. I'll be okay. But I'm not going to let my daughter grow up not knowing me. We could work out how—"

"Braun."

"I just...the moment Teddy called and said you were in labor, I knew I had to be here. I couldn't go one more day without telling you how I felt. The last nine months have been miserable. Fucking awful. They should have been amazing, since my app went live and is killing globally, and my other project wrapped up and that's a success, and I've launched my own company and it's already exploding…the whole world is saying I'm poised to be the next big thing, with Zuckerberg and Gates and Bezos. But it doesn't matter. It tastes and feels like shit, because—because I fucking *miss* you, Liz." He swallowed hard. "This whole time, every moment we were together, you played your emotions close to your chest. I never knew how you felt about me. If it was just good sex, if you even liked me. If you felt what I felt that morning in Portugal. I just couldn't let you have this baby without knowing—"

"Would you shut up for a damn second?" I yelled over him. "I *love* you, Braun, you big sexy amazing nerd. I fought it like hell, but…" I swallowed, but it was too late—I was crying worse than ever. "Of *course* I felt it that morning. Why the hell do you think I ran? Why do you think I ghosted you? I'd fallen for you and I was too scared of you, of feeling that, to…to be able to be around you. You sent me those flowers, and it just scared me even more."

"Why are you so scared? If you had someone break your heart, you never told me about it."

"I haven't. Why do you think I'm so scared? I watched my parents divorce, watched my mom get her heart ripped out by Dad cheating, leaving, knocking up his secretary, the whole cliche shtick. It was a mess. It was so vicious, so ugly. And they…they stopped seeing me. They stopped taking care of me." I felt everything well up, a lava flow of things I'd spent a lifetime suppressing. "And I just…I never wanted to feel that. I never wanted to… to let anyone have that power over me, how Dad made Mom feel. I'm so *damaged*, Braun. My parents fucked me up. They divorced, and it was hell. I know divorce happens, like, a lot, but for me, it just…it fucked me up. And I…I grew up never wanting to let anyone, ever, *ever* have that kind of power over me. I never wanted to have that power over anyone else. The power to rip their fucking heart out, the power to just fucking ruin me the way Dad ruined Mom. Over a fucking *secretary*, a no one. A booty call. A quickie over a desk. And I didn't think I could handle bringing a child into this world because…because I'm so damaged. So hurt. So angry. So closed off. I hid behind work, behind success, behind being a career woman, behind chasing sex. I'm scared, Braun. Scared of you. Of your feelings for me. Of my feelings for you. I don't know how to do this." I swallowed hard, and then the tears flowed because I couldn't stop them. "I've never told *anyone* that. Not even Kat."

He held me, an arm around me. "Lizzy, it's okay. It's okay. I'm here."

"But you shouldn't be. I'm such a mess. I hurt you. I don't deserve you. You're, like, perfect, and

I'm such a mess." I blinked through tears, swallowed hard, let out a sigh. "I can't find any flaws in you, Braun, and that just scares the hell out of me."

He barked a laugh. "I'm so far from perfect, Liz. I knew I was falling for you from day one. From the selfie. You sent me that selfie of you with the kumquat and I just...I heard a voice in my head go *she's it. That's her. That's the one.* But I was too scared to tell you. Because I could tell you'd shut it down. You didn't want me, you didn't want my love. So it was...it was easier and safer to just...hold it in and take what I could get from you."

"You deserve more than that, Braun."

"I ghosted you as much as you did me. After Mack's, I could've called. But it was too hard. I was too angry and hurt. I let you...I let you do the last nine months alone. So...I'm not...I'm not perfect. I'm far from perfect."

"From the first selfie?"

"The moment I heard your voice."

"How did you know?"

"Every moment, I knew. But I wasn't brave enough to admit my feelings. To tell you I wanted your heart, not just your body. I almost did, so many times. But I knew, more and more every moment I spent with you, that I wanted more. More from you. More with you. More of *you*."

I couldn't look away from him. "I didn't want to

love you. I fought it so hard, Braun. So fucking hard. After I let you walk away, I realized I'd messed up. But…I…I was too scared that you wouldn't want me anymore. That you'd moved on."

"Never."

"My dad moved on, and Mom never even did anything to hurt him. He just wanted…something else, I guess."

"I'm not your dad. I'll never be your dad. I never moved on. I just…I was running from my feelings. Trying to pretend I wasn't head over heels in love with you. But then Teddy called and I *knew*."

"Braun." I grabbed his hand. "I'm so afraid. I don't know how to do this, but…I want to. I do. I want to be with you. I want to have more." I cried yet again. "I want to be like that couple in Portugal. I want that."

"Me too," he whispered. "Just be honest with me from here on out, and we can figure it out. We can do it. You and me. We can…we can be together."

I squeezed his hand and blinked tears away. "We can be a family?"

"You and me and our daughter. We can be a family."

That was like a spear of light to all the darkest places inside me. A family. The thing I'd lost in my parents' divorce, the thing I wanted more than anything in the whole world. I'd made a family with my five girlfriends, but we all knew we wanted something more.

I knew I did. I always had, I'd just been in denial for thirty years.

I watched a nurse wheel a little clear cart in, with a tiny bundle wrapped in a white blanket with purple and green stripes.

"Here she is," the nurse said, cooing quietly in a high-pitched singsong. "Six pounds, nine ounces, and twenty-one inches long. She's got all her beautiful, perfect little fingers and toes, yes she does, and she passed all her tests with flying colors." She helped me sit up, arranged a pillow behind me as if she knew exactly where to put it for maximum comfort, and then gingerly settled Sabrina into my arms. "You, my dear, are the proud mommy of an absolutely perfect little angel."

Sabrina squawked.

"She's a hungry little angel, though," the nurse said. "Why don't I help you see about getting her to latch?" She glanced at Braun. "Can Daddy stay, or would you like some privacy?"

"He can stay," I said, feeling suddenly, oddly shy. "I'm still in the shirt I was wearing, so I might need some help getting it off. And my bra." I looked at Braun. "The girls! Where are the girls?"

"You have a waiting room full of very...aggressively...supportive ladies," the nurse said, not quite suppressing a terrified shudder. "Quite a group of friends you have."

"Send them back!"

"*All* of them?" The nurse seemed a bit incredulous.

I thought of all five of my girls in the room with me at the same time, and shuddered. "Good point. Maybe just...Laurel and Kat first, and then Zoe, Autumn, and Teddy."

"I think that's smart." She smiled down at me. "First, though, we need to get your little one nursing. Sometimes it can take a bit to get them to latch on at first."

She helped me out of my top and bra and into a hospital gown, and then she settled Sabrina in my arms and showed me how to tease her little mouth with my nipple. She got confused at first, but after a few tries, she got latched on, and there was a sharp tug. She spat it out, and we tried again, and then the next time, she latched on and started sucking, and suddenly, having boobs made sense in a whole new way.

Braun was watching the whole thing, rapt, fascinated. "That's so cool. She just...knows what to do."

"So does my body," I said. "It's really amazing, actually."

Braun knelt beside the bed, stroked her hair as she suckled at me. "Have you named her?"

I smiled at him, her, them, at life. "Yeah. Her name is Sabrina." I met his eyes. "After my grandmother."

"Sabrina. It's beautiful."

"I haven't picked a middle name, yet, though." I

gazed at him intently, meaningfully. "You have one in mind?"

He swallowed, let out a soft, emotional sigh. "Noelle. After my grandmother. She half raised me, when my parents were busy, which was all the time."

"Sabrina Noelle." I smiled at him, tears of over-whelmed, jubilant, frightened, fragile, bursting emotion hazing my sight. "It's perfect."

He was about to say something, but the door to my L&D room opened, and Kat and Laurel swooped in, chattering over each other excitedly. They both paused on the way in to sanitize their hands.

They both halted abruptly when they saw Braun beside me, a hand resting affectionately, possessively, on my shoulder.

"Um." Kat blinked at him. "Did...did we miss something? What's he doing here?"

I looked up at Braun, still not quite fully com-prehending the reality that he was here, that he loved me...that I'd told him I loved him.

Then at Kat. "Yes, you did miss something. Teddy called him and told him I was in labor, and he showed up as I was being brought in." I sighed. "He's here because he loves me."

Laurel went very, very still. "He loves you."

"I do. I have, for a long time." He straightened, gave each of them in turn a long, level look. "I only stayed away to try to and respect her wishes. But when Teddy called me, I knew I couldn't pretend I don't feel how I feel."

Kat stared at me, keeping her emotions in check. "And you, Lizzy—how do you feel about this?"

"I've had a change of heart," I said, turning my gaze to my daughter, who was still hungrily sucking at me. "I do love him. I think I have for quite a while, I just...I was scared and in denial." I looked at each of them in turn. "You guys were right."

"I don't want to be a buzzkill, here, but...could this just be intensity and hormones and such from having just given birth?" Laurel moved to stand on the other side of me as Braun.

"No." I felt Sabrina let go, and gingerly moved her to rest on my chest, facedown, patting her back gently. "It was there before. It's why I came back early from Portugal, it's why I ghosted him when we came back, it's why..." I swallowed hard, blinked. "It's why I was so miserable the whole pregnancy."

"You were miserable?" Laurel asked.

"I mean, a lot of the time, yeah. Physically, it was..." I shrugged. "Hard, of course. Anyone who tries to tell you being pregnant is easy is a damn fool and a liar, because it's hard as fuck." I glanced down at my daughter, who had let out a tiny little burp and was now sleeping. "But that was just...it was made harder by the fact that I...I missed him. I tried pretending I didn't, but I did. Every moment of every day, I missed him."

"Him, the man—who he is?" Kat asked, now standing next to Laurel. "Not just his, you know... magical peen?"

Braun choked on a laugh. "My *what*?"

Kat glared at him. "This doesn't concern you, *Braun*."

I snorted. "Stop being nasty, Katja Spears. I still love you. You're still my first-among-equals best friend. But it *does* concern him, number one, since it's *his* magical peen you're talking about, and number two, he's right here in the room." I reached out and took her hand. "Of *course* I missed his magical peen, Kat. I was literally unbearably horny for so much of the pregnancy and no way to take care of it properly. I daydreamed of his magical peen so much it was ridiculous, and there were any number of moments I nearly called him just as a booty call to take care of my needs."

Braun groaned, pacing away with his hands in his hair. "I don't need to hear this. You have any fucking clue how bad I've missed you? How many times I nearly called you, nearly showed up begging you to let me just...taste you?"

"*La-la-la-la-la!*" Kat chanted, fingers in her ears. "NOT LISTENING TO THIS!"

"Oh stop," Laurel said, smacking Kat's arm. "Quit pretending you're a prude when you're as much of an incorrigible horndog as I am."

Kat glared at Laurel. "I am a *woman*, not a horndog."

"You're a horndog who would perpetrate dastardly deeds all day long for a man like Braun, who dreams of merely *tasting* the woman he's in love with."

Kat ignored this. Knelt beside the bed. "Can we focus on the baby, please?"

I squirmed further upright, transferred Sabrina in the crook of my arm, and extended her to Kat. "Say hello to Sabrina Noelle."

Kat was almost comically ginger and awkward as she took the baby from me. But then, once she had Sabrina in her arms, she visibly melted. "Hi, little one. I'm your second mommy. We're going to best friends, okay? I'm going to spoil you absolutely rotten. When your mean ol' mommy won't buy you ponies or give you sweets, I'll be there to absolutely ruin you." She blinked hard. "She's so beautiful."

"Sabrina Noelle, huh?" Laurel said, leaning in against Kat to gaze down at the baby. "Sabrina Noelle Stephenson, or Bennet?"

I felt all the air rush out of me at once. "I...I don't know. We haven't gotten there yet. She's not even an hour old yet."

Laurel eyed me. "I mean, if he's on the birth certificate, generally she would take his name, unless you don't want her to."

JASINDA WILDER

Braun grabbed my hand. "We don't have to decide it right now. We can talk about it, think about it."

Kat transferred Sabrina to Laurel, who took her with a confidence and familiarity that made me wonder where she'd had the practice.

"You know," Kat said, eyeing me with a not quite hidden smirk of amusement, "If you were to marry Braun and take his name, you'd be...Elizabeth Bennet."

Laurel frowned at Kat. "Okay...so?"

I giggled. "I hadn't thought of that."

Braun laughed outright. "'It is a truth universally acknowledged, that a single man in possession of a good fortune, must be in want of a wife.'" He grinned at me. "You could call me Mr. Darcy. Could be some fun role-playing in there."

Laurel looked at each of us. "What am I missing?"

"*Pride and Prejudice*," Kat said. "Did you not take English Lit in high school or college?"

"No, actually. I went to a European boarding school and then university in Switzerland before transferring to Stanford." She huffed. "Literature class was a much different thing there than it is here."

"No wonder you're so stuck-up," Kat said, cackling.

"Oh shut up. You guys knew I went to boarding school."

"I didn't know boarding school was still a real thing," Braun said.

"Oh, it very much is. Ultra-rich parents who don't want to bother raising their own kids will always need somewhere to stash their oh-so-inconvenient spawn."

"So…your parents are European?" Braun asked.

"Don't even try," I answered. "Laurel is an excessively complicated person with a bafflingly complex history."

"Oh shut up," she sighed. "It's not that complicated. I'm a hundred percent American. I just…my parents have pretensions of grandeur, is all. Dad is from solidly Midwestern stock, who just happened to strike it rich in oil back in the twenties. Mom is from Old Hollywood royalty, and don't you forget it. She's never done anything like work a single day in her life. The woman can barely dress herself. I wouldn't put it past her to hire someone to wipe her ass for her."

I glanced at Braun. "I've met her. Laurel is in no way exaggerating."

Braun just blinked. "I see."

"No, you don't." Laurel was bouncing gently while rocking back and forth. "But that's okay. Understanding me is a full-time job even for me. No mere mortal male stands a snowball's chance in hell."

I was watching Laurel. "You've done that before."

Laurel froze. "No-I-haven't." It came out in a jumbled rush.

"Yes, you have." Kat pointed. "The bounce-and-rock is a pro-level move."

Laurel resumed the bounce-and-rock. "There's a single mother next door to me. She's super over-worked and underpaid, can't afford a full-time nanny, and takes night classes. Her son is a year, now, and I've been taking care of him at night for free so she can go to class. I had no freaking clue what I was doing at first, but the thing is, babies are actually very forgiving. Their needs are very simple, and as long as those needs are met, it's fairly easy."

Kat and I were staring at Laurel as if she'd grown a second head and was speaking ancient Egyptian.

"Who the hell are *you*," Kat asked, "and what have you done with the real Laurel McGillis?"

Laurel rolled her eyes. "Why do you think I never told you? And honestly, I don't do much. I watch TV, catch up on work, sometimes I tidy up a bit. If Roland wakes up, I change his nappy, feed him a bottle, rock him back to sleep."

"Nappy?"

"Elsa is a Swede who was raised in Britain, so she calls his diapers nappies. So, I do too." She smiled gently down at Sabrina. "I can't believe you had a baby, Lizzy."

"Me either." I sighed, suddenly exhausted beyond description. "Can you guys switch with the other girls? I'm suddenly really tired."

"I mean, you *did* just poop out a human," Kat said, leaning over to kiss me on the forehead—a rare gesture of affection from Kat, who typically showed her affection through insults.

"It doesn't come out of your butt, you idiot," I said. "It comes out your vagina."

Kat rolled her eyes. "I *know*, Elizabeth. Duh. I'm a grown-ass woman." She shook her head, sighing a long-suffering sigh, as if dealing with me was exhausting. "It was a *joke*."

Laurel settled Sabrina back into my arms. "Congratulations, Lizzy," she murmured, side-hugging me. "I'm proud of you." She glanced at Braun. "And happy for you."

"Thanks."

"For real," Kat said. "I'm proud of you and happy for you. You made a people, Lizzy!"

I nudged her arm with my head. "I made a whole person." I glanced at Braun, smiling. "*We*…made a person."

Kat moved around the bed to stand nose-to-nose with a wary Braun. "You take care of her. I slept with a hitman, once. I still have his number." A stony glare. "I can make you disappear."

Braun just laughed. "I believe you, which is a little scary. But…you don't have to worry. I'll do more than just take care of her."

"You'd better." She pointed at me. "Get some rest."

"I plan on it." I blew her a kiss. "Love you."

When they were gone, Braun let out a harsh breath. "So…Kat is a little intense."

I cackled—a little too loudly, because Sabrina stirred, mewled. "Yeah, she's a lot intense."

"Did she really sleep with a hitman?"

"Who the hell knows? Probably? I wouldn't put it past her. But then, if you're a hitman, do you go around advertising that to chicks you bang? Like, 'hey, I'm a mafia hitman, wanna fuck?'" I cackled again. "But it *is* Kat, so nothing would surprise me."

He perched on the edge of my bed. "Can I hold her?"

"Of course." I leaned into him, snugging her into the crook of his arm.

"Hi there, beautiful," he murmured, his voice soft and tender. "I can't believe this is real. You're real. I'm a daddy."

I choked, eyes burning. "You really, truly, absolutely without question want to be with me? Baby and all?"

He stilled. His eyes lifted to mine—his dark, deep eyes swam with emotion. "Liz…yes. I wish I knew how to put it more emphatically, but I don't. Yes."

"Why? What is it about me? What do you love?"

He gazed at me. "Everything. You're smart. You're driven, and successful. You understand me being a workaholic. You're funny. You're loyal to your friends, and a great boss. You like nice things, but you're not, like…a gold digger, or…or shallow." He took a deep breath, held it, let it out slowly. "You're so sexy, so beautiful. You're naughty, and you talk dirty and you're bold about what you want, what you like. But you're sweet, too. Caring, thoughtful."

"Emotionally unavailable, scared of commitment, terrified of vulnerability," I added, "addicted to stupid expensive purses and shoes…"

"Not unavailable, just wary. Scared of commitment and vulnerability with good reason, and if I never worked another day in my life, I have enough money to buy you all the purses and shoes you want and never even think about it."

I sighed. "You have an answer for everything, huh?"

He smirked. "I mean, I'm trying. I wasn't sure you'd want me, when I showed up, so I spent the helicopter ride here coming up with reasons why you should give me a chance."

"Helicopter ride?"

He grinned. "You're here, I'm in LA, so I figured a helicopter would be a good way to make the commute shorter." The grin faded. "You have your life and career and friends here, and mine, for now, is in LA, and I know it's only forty minutes each way, but yeah, I bought a helicopter and installed a landing pad on the roof of my building."

"You have a building?"

He smirked. "It was my first major investment. I lease a good ninety percent of the building to other businesses, which more than pays for the cash I put into it, and I own the top three floors—two for my growing businesses and the top floor is where I live."

"I'd like to see it," I said.

"I would love that." He glanced at Sabrina, then back at me. "We don't have to jump into this, Liz. We can take it slow."

I laughed. "Braun, we fucked bare and had a baby together. I've slept with you—just sleep. That's huge for me, you know. So, I don't know that taking it slow makes much sense. I mean, like, how much is there left for us to take slowly?"

"Getting married and moving in together," he said.

I swallowed hard. "Oh. Right."

He arched an eyebrow. "See? You're panicking."

"It's a lot." I let out the breath I realized I was holding. "I...I don't know. I love my condo. I have her nursery all set up, already. It's close to work. And getting married? I...god. I don't know."

"That's what I'm saying. We don't have to even go there, yet. Not right away. We had a physical relationship first, so now we can work on the emotional one. Combine our lives little by little." He hesitated. "I'm only currently living in five thousand square feet... there's, like, fifteen thousand more that's pretty much blank, unused. So, when and if you're ever ready to live with me, or to have your own space there, we can make it whatever you want."

"For real?"

"Blank check, honey. We can make it part of what I've already built, we can make it a whole separate condo, whatever. It's not bare metal rafters and empty space, but it's raw enough we can move walls and re-route electrical, plumbing, all that, without it being major reconstruction."

"That's...that would be millions of dollars, Braun."

He shrugged. "Whatever. What's the point of having more money than Midas if you don't use it for what matters? What am I going to do with it all by myself? I can only drive one car at a time. I can only live in one house at a time. I'm investing left and right to diversify my income streams, and my app is selling like mad and part of my deal was royalties. I actually took less up front so I'd get those royalties into perpetuity. I had billions in investors lined up when I sold it. My next project isn't as big, but it's still lucrative. And I have pages and pages of notes for ideas for future projects. So, you want to spend a few million designing your dream house with me? Cool. I'll help, if you want, or be hands-off if you prefer. As long as you're with me."

"Are you real?" I asked, laughing.

"That's what I keep asking myself about you." He looked away, blinking. "The last few months, I sometimes wondered if those weeks we spent together were real. If I'd dreamed them—" he paused. "I dreamed for so long of…not of you specifically, obviously, but of…someone. To share life with. Someone who got me. Who wanted me, and me for *me*. I dreamed of that for years. I'd all but given up on it. And then I answered your ad out of…curiosity, interest, whatever, and then I saw you—in that coffee shop, and it was like…there she is." He shook his head. "Just…*there she is—she's* what I've been dreaming of. And every moment I spent with you reinforced that. I saw *you* and I know you saw me. I could be myself with you. I wasn't worried about money, about your motives. I could just be totally and unapologetically myself. And every little hint of *you* that I got showed me more and more that I want *who you are*. Warts and all."

"God, Braun—"

Teddy, Zoe, and Autumn burst in, then; they sanitized their hands on the way in, and Teddy was the first at Braun's side, peering over his arm at Sabrina.

"God, she's adorable!" Teddy squealed, and then clapped her hand over her mouth when Sabrina mewled in protest. "Crap, too loud. But holy shit, she's so cute. Can I steal her?"

Teddy wasn't surprised to see Braun, but the others were.

"Um." Autumn frowned at Braun, staying by the door. "What?"

Zoe looked at me, at Braun, and then at Teddy, who was positively gooey with glee holding Sabrina. "For real, though. What? Who's he?"

"That's Braun, dum-dum," Teddy said, in a soft, squeaky, singsong, baby-talk voice. "That's Mommy's new man. Yeah, isn't he? That's the sexy nerd with the magic dick. Yes it is. That magic dick made you, didn't it? Yes it did."

"Ohmygod, Teddy, stop." Autumn made a face of visible disgust. "Just...stop."

Teddy stuck her tongue out, and kept talking in the singsong voice. "It's been scientifically proven that high-pitched singsong voices appeal to babies."

"I call bullshit," Zoe said.

"It's true!" Teddy insisted. "They hear it better, and they like it. The higher pitch and the singsong calms them. There's a reason people instinctively talk to babies like that."

Autumn came to my side, opposite Teddy and Braun. "What's going on, Lizzy? Last I knew, you hadn't seen, talked to, or even texted Braun since the day you found out you were pregnant."

"I hadn't." I pointed a finger at Teddy. "I went into labor at the showing, and my clients called Teddy, because she was closest. Everyone else was at showings all over the place, while Teddy was at the office. Teddy called Braun, and apparently Braun showed up."

Teddy heard everything. "You were always in love with him, and I knew it. When you came back from telling him you were pregnant and didn't want to be with him, you looked like you'd just sucked on a dirty gym sock. And the whole fucking pregnancy, you were moping around when you thought we weren't looking, staring off into space and sighing all dramatically."

"I was *not* moping," I snapped.

"You were a little mopey," Autumn said. "I just assumed it was a pregnancy thing."

"You were, boss," Zoe said. "The dramatic sighs were real, too. It was super obvious you were thinking about something deep."

I groaned. "I had no idea I was even doing that."

"You'd space out for minutes at a time, staring out the window, looking all pensive," Teddy said, moving up next to Autumn and transferring Sabrina to her.

"For real?" I thought back, trying to remember. "I did that?"

"All the time." She smiled at me affectionately. "It was always him, and I knew it. You weren't going to do anything about it, you big scaredy-cat, so I did it for you."

I squeezed her hand. "Thank you, Teddy."

She eyed Braun, and then me. "So…did it work? Are you…?" she trailed off, pointing from me to Braun.

I reached out and took Braun's hand. "Yeah, it worked."

She squealed, clapped her hands and jumped up and down. "Yes! I thought for sure you'd send him packing." She did a dance around the little, over-crowded room. "I did it, I did it, oh yeah."

Zoe intercepted her, grabbed her by the arms. "Teddy, you spaz. Chill."

Teddy made a grumpy face. "No. I'm happy. I fixed our boss."

"You fixed me," I echoed, laughing. But then I glanced at Braun, and realized that there was no way I could have gone through that delivery without him, and that I couldn't fathom facing what was coming, becoming a mother, on my own. "Yeah, you certainly helped."

Autumn was swaying slowly side to side, looking distant, emotional. I saw a tear roll down her cheek, and she abruptly moved toward Zoe—there was a baby transfer, and then Autumn was gone, out the door without a word of explanation.

I frowned at Zoe. "What the hell was that?"

Zoe was carefully expressionless. "That was…that was not my story to tell."

"Zoe."

She shook her head. "No, Lizzy. That's Autumn's story, not mine. Some things are too personal, you know? It's old, and she'll be fine, so don't worry."

Zoe and Autumn had been through the wringer, I knew that much. Turbulent, chaotic childhood, rough and tumble journey to adulthood. There was a lot I knew I didn't know, that I had a feeling no one knew, and apparently one of Autumn's secrets had to do with babies.

I could guess, but I would rather wait until I could get Autumn alone.

The nurse floated in, then. "All right, Mom needs to rest, guys. Dad, you can stay, I'll bring a blanket and pillow for you for when you want to lay down. That chair there folds out into a bed. Ladies, you can come back tomorrow, but for now, Mama needs rest, and so does baby."

There was a flurry of goodbyes and hugs and kisses, and then we were alone. The nurse did some checks on me, went through some explainers about diapers and blankets and call buttons...once my girls had left, I was suddenly so tired I couldn't see straight, much less absorb information.

I looked up at Braun. "I hope you got all that. I'm too tired to think, all of a sudden."

He brushed my cheek with his thumb. "I've got it."

"Do you want me to take the baby so you can get some rest?" The nurse helped me settle her into the cart-cradle. "Once you go home, you won't have us to take her. So, it really would be a good idea to take this opportunity to get some good rest. What you went through was a major trauma to your body, and you need rest to recover."

I gazed at Sabrina, and then at Braun—for the first time, I realized he looked possibly even more tired than I was. "Yeah, I think that's a good idea."

"Okay. When she's ready to eat again, we'll bring her in." The nurse went to the blinds and shut them, darkening the room, then went to the light switches and turned most of them off, and suddenly the room was darkened enough that I could sleep. "Get some rest." She pointed at Braun. "She needs her space, so don't try to get in that bed with her, Mister."

He frowned in amusement. "Of course not."

She shrugged. "You'd be surprised what we see. Anyway. Sleep well. Baby should sleep for a while, now that she's eaten."

When she was gone, Braun helped lower the upper half of the bed so I could lay flat.

"I know she said to give me space," I said, looking up at Braun, "but...would you sit with me and hold my hand until I fall asleep?" That, asking him to sit with me, to hold my hand, admitting I needed him...that was harder than admitting I loved him.

"Of course." He settled on the edge of the bed, took both of my hands in his.

I fell asleep within minutes. I woke up briefly, a

little while later, and Braun had pulled the fold-out chair next to my bed, and was lying in it on his side, curled up in a too-small space, sleeping.

He was still holding my hand.

EPILOGUE

I CLOSED THE DOOR TO THE NURSERY AS QUIETLY AS I COULD. Tiptoeing out, I rubbed my face with both hands, exhaustion rifling through me.

I swayed on my feet in the hallway, reeling. She was a hungry girl, my Sabrina. She was also completely nocturnal, it seemed. She did her best eating and pooping in the middle of the night. Braun handled the diaper changes, and god bless him for that, but feeding her kept me awake half the night, if not more.

I heard voices—last I knew, it was just me and Braun here. But, I recognized Laurel's voice right away.

I pushed away my exhaustion and went to see why Laurel was here at…whatever time it was. I had no clue. Morning? Night? Evening? Who was I, anyway? I hadn't changed out of the sweatpants I was wearing in at least a week, hadn't worn a bra in even longer, since all I did all day and all night was feed Sabrina. When had I last bathed? No clue. The last meal I'd eaten was…I couldn't remember. Something in the middle of the night, warmed up leftover takeout that Braun had brought while I was feeding her.

When I arrived in the living room of my condo—after what seemed like an endless walk—Laurel was sitting at my island talking to Braun, who was standing near the door, holding my Louis Vuitton overnight bag.

I frowned. "You going somewhere, with my bag?"

He smiled. "Yes. Well, *we* are."

I blinked, not comprehending. "We are? Where? Why?"

"How about you trust me? It's a surprise."

"Braun…I'm filthy. I've been wearing these clothes for at least a week. I'm exhausted, dead on my feet."

"I know." He just smiled. "And like I said, just… try to trust me."

"How long?"

"Just overnight."

"But…Sabrina."

Laurel came to stand in front of me. "You have milk pumped and frozen, yes?"

"Yeah. Apparently I'm, like, a super milk machine, because I'm full even after she's eaten both sides."

"And there's formula, right?"

"Well, yeah."

She held my arms. "I've got it." She rubbed up and down my biceps. "I've done this, remember? Almost every night for the last year, I take care of my neighbor's son, and I started when he was no older than Sabrina is now. She's over six weeks old, she's healthy, and you need a break. Just for tonight. Trust me, and more importantly, trust *him*." She indicated Braun with a jerk of her head. Then, she leaned closer to me, whispering conspiratorially. "Also, I happen to know you got the all clear to get jiggy with it, if you know what I mean. And I'm guessing you both have needs that need seeing to." She winked. "I packed your bag myself, so you know you're covered."

I swallowed. "A whole night?"

"One night. We can come back tomorrow morning, whenever." Braun stood waiting, patient and calm. "So. Let's go."

"Like this? Shouldn't I change?"

"Nope." He indicated the roof. "Did you know I had a helipad installed up there?"

"You did not."

"I did. So, *get to the chopper, now!*" He said the last part in a funny but accurate impression of Arnold Schwarzenegger.

I sighed. "Okay, fine. Just let me grab my phone and purse."

"Nope, you don't need a thing." He took my hand and tugged me to the exit. "Just come with me."

"Okay, okay." I turned back to Laurel. "She just went down, she's got a full belly and clean diaper, so she should sleep for a few hours."

"I've got it, Lizzy. I can do this. Just relax. Enjoy it, okay?" She blew me a kiss. "Have fun, kids!"

I laughed, but then Braun was tugging me onto the elevator. Which went *up*, instead of down. "You actually had a helicopter landing pad installed on the roof?"

"I sure did."

"How is that even possible? Is that legal?"

He shrugged. "My guy said he got it all covered with local ordinances. I trust him."

"You're crazy."

"The closest place to land was like ten minutes away," he said, waving a hand. "The whole point of the damn thing was so that my commute to and from LA would be as quick and easy as possible. So now, I land and I'm home, both places."

"We're going to your building in LA?"

He nodded. "Yeah. I've got a little surprise for you there."

"When have you had time for a surprise?"

He chuckled. "The nice thing about being stupid rich is that I can pay people to do just about anything I want. I tell someone what I want, and it gets done. Pay them well enough, and you can be sure it gets done right, too." He put a hand to the small of my back as the doors opened—sure enough, there was a small, sleek helicopter on a helipad. "Ever been in one?"

I shook my head. "Nope. Always wanted to, though."

He led me to the aircraft, which was powered down. The pilot climbed down from the cockpit as we approached and opened the passenger door, revealing white leather as luxurious as in his Rolls Royce.

"This thing is pretty sweet," I said, unable to stop grinning.

"It is, though, isn't it? Only room for four, but it's light and fast. I'm a die-hard car guy, but this is the way to travel, I'm telling you."

He handed me up and into the cabin, climbed up in after me, and buckled me up, then handed me a headset.

A moment later, I heard the pilot's voice in my ears. "Ready, sir?"

"Roger, Roger." Braun grinned at me. "I still get a kick out of that. His name is actually Roger."

The pilot grinned and shook his head. "He thinks he's funny. Like he's the first to think of that."

I couldn't help a laugh. "He does think he's funny. And to be fair, usually, he is."

Roger began flipping switches, checking each action against a checklist on a clipboard; I heard the engine overhead begin to whine, felt power begin to thrum, vibrating the seat. And then the volume of the whine became a roar, and the sense of power was palpable and enormous, and the shadow of the spinning rotors became a solid blur. Another moment, and I watched Roger wiggle in his seat, adjust his headset, flex his fingers and grasp the control sticks; he feathered them, and we almost imperceptibly rose, and then a little more, and then there was a sense of weightlessness as our upward velocity increased. I reached out and grabbed Braun's hand as the windows showed our altitude—very, very high. This wasn't at all like an airplane. The feeling of being at the mercy of the aircraft and physics and the pilot was more immediate and visceral, and I didn't mind admitting to myself that I was more than a little scared.

"Quite a ride, huh?" Braun said, grinning at me.

"Uh-huh," I mumbled.

"Scared?"

"Yep."

We were blasting forward, then, nose tilting down, and were packing on velocity with every second, until the seaside was blurring underneath us and somehow the speed, while exhilarating, wasn't as scary as the slower ascent.

I relaxed a little, my death grip on Braun's hand easing. He was utterly at ease, watching out the window once in a while, but mostly watching me. The trip was short—a fraction of the time it would have taken to drive from my Malibu condo to LA. We stayed high as we entered LA airspace, angling across the maze of towers and high-rises; the vantage point of LA from here was breathtaking. We pinpointed a building, and it grew larger as we drew closer, our altitude and speed bleeding off gradually, until we were directly above the big yellow H.

"Wait till the rotors stop," Braun told me. "Don't want to get knocked over. The prop wash is powerful."

I heard and felt the reverse of startup—the roar descending into a whine, and then into silence.

"You're good to go, sir," Roger said.

"Thank you, Roger," Braun said. "We're in for the night, so you can go until tomorrow. We'll probably want to head back up to Malibu around eleven or so, at the latest."

"Sounds good, sir." Roger smiled at me. "Pleasure flying you, ma'am."

"It was a marvelous ride, Roger. Thank you for making my first trip in a helicopter a pleasant one."

He nodded, giving me a quick salute that spoke of his military service. "Glad it was a good one. See you tomorrow morning. Have a good evening."

Braun opened his door and slid out, held the door in one hand and helped me down with the other. He had my bag on his shoulder, and he closed the door behind me. The rotors were still slowly spinning. I couldn't see much of the rooftop from here—the helipad was at the highest point of the building, with the rest of the rooftop hidden from view. There was a doorway at the far end of the pad, a utilitarian metal service door; Braun led me to it, opened it and ushered me through—it opened to an enclosure big enough for three or four people at most, with elevator doors standing open. There were only two buttons, a P and an H; the doors closed, and I felt the brief, gentle descent. A pause, and the doors shushed open, revealing a spacious, airy penthouse living room; the far wall was entirely floor-to-ceiling windows, of course, the ceiling miles and miles overhead, also glass from wall to midway overhead, where it transitioned to exposed, industrial rafters. Polished cherrywood floors ran for acres in every direction, leading from the interior wall where the elevator was across to the kitchen. White cabinets, stainless steel appliances, a huge island with a butcher-block countertop made from the same cherrywood as the floors, but matte rather than the high-polish gloss of the floors, the vertical surface of the island a pale gray, with six industrial-style stools, wood tops and polished metal. There was a breakfast nook against the window-wall, and beyond that, a huge table to seat ten, chairs on one side and a bench on the other, underneath the glass part of the ceiling. Opposite the dining table from the kitchen, a huge handwoven oriental rug framed an overstuffed cream leather sectional, matching ottoman, a glassed-in gas fireplace with a mind-bogglingly gargantuan flat screen

TV. The whole space was open, airy, flooded with natural light. A hallway near the elevator led to what I assumed was the bedroom suite, and a couple other doors—an office, probably, a workout room maybe.

"It's amazing," I said, taking it all in. "Breathtaking."

"Thanks." He looked around. "I designed it."

"You never cease to amaze me."

"Want to see the rest?"

"Absolutely."

The hallway dead-ended at the master suite, with an office on the window side, and a huge exercise room opposite with mirrors on the walls, top-of-the-line free weight equipment, kettlebells, a few machines, a treadmill, and a stationary bike. The master suite was almost entirely glass, the bed framed underneath a canopy of glass, showing the sunset-glowing vista of downtown LA. The headboard of the bed was the wall itself, quilted and stuffed like a couch-back, and on the other side of the freestanding wall-headboard, the bathroom. A stonework shower, double vanities, all the usual luxury amenities.

I frowned at Braun. "The thought and design in this bathroom is stunning, Braun, but..."

He seemed to be restraining a smirk. "But what, Lizzy?"

"I don't mean to be critical, but...there's no bathtub." I was fighting disappointment, to be honest. "A good soaking tub is essential."

He was definitely hiding a smirk. "Hold that thought while I show you the roof."

"The roof?"

He extended his hand to me, and I let him take my hand and pull me out of the master suite. "By the way, all the glass is dimmable, which cost a fortune, so if it's a crazy bright, hot day, it can tint to take the edge off the glare. And in the master suite, it's mirrored glass, so we can see out but we have total privacy. Just so you're not worried about a peeping Tom with a telescope somewhere."

"That must have cost a fortune."

He chuckled. "Oh boy, did it ever. Worth it, though."

I nodded, breathing a sigh as we went out through the main living area again. "I agree—the overall effect is absolutely stunning."

"I've been dabbling in design and architecture," Braun said. "Taking some online classes. It's fun, and a really exciting challenge. My next venture might be a construction company, doing everything in house from architecture to subcontracting."

"Oh, just dabbling in architecture," I deadpanned, "as one does."

He chuckled, leading me through a door beside the elevator, which led to a small foyer with...another elevator. This one also featured two buttons, an R and a P. He pressed the R, the doors closed, and we ascended briefly. When the doors opened, my breath stalled.

We were at a lower level than the helipad; the pad was above us, the wall of it forming the backdrop of this outdoor space. The wall was shiplapped in white wood, with a handmade wood pergola overhead, strung with small Edison bulbs. The floor was outdoor decking, a soft gray, with fringed rugs underneath hand-carved oak furniture with thick white cushions—a big couch, a loveseat kitty corner, and another couch opposite the other, a low coffee table between.

The piece de resistance, however, was the tub. Beyond the seating area, a small set of stairs lead down to a free-standing copper soaking tub. It was framed on two sides by high walls, the rear side the stairs up to the sitting area, the fourth side open to the air, facing the hills of LA.

"This was the trickiest part to design, and I had to have some help. I wanted to make sure it was all but impossible to see the tub from anywhere, yet still have a one-of-a-kind view." He led me down to it, and from here, all of LA was gone, behind the walls, hidden from view, and all you could see were hills and suburbs and roofs.

I turned to stare at Braun. "An outdoor tub, on the roof?"

He grinned, pleased with himself. "Yes, ma'am. Your very own private rooftop soaking tub. I've personally been to every vantage point in a half-mile radius, and this particular spot is invisible unless you're here, on this roof. I've sat in it, without water, just to test the view, and let me tell you, it's…amazing."

"You did this?" I blinked hard. "For me?"

"It was finished just this week." He smiled. "So, it was a little white lie, but all the time I said I was at work, I was actually here, overseeing this. And working, remotely. But mainly overseeing this build."

I swallowed hard. "You built me a rooftop soaking tub."

"I did."

"We're here so I can take a bath, aren't we?"

He nodded. "You've been such a warrior, these last six weeks, taking care of our baby girl, and I just…I felt like you needed a quick getaway. I know you won't leave her for long, but I figure, this, at least, is a little… spa day, just for you. I had one of my assistants set me up with all sorts of bath…stuff. Bath bombs and fancy salts and bubbles." He gestured at one of the walls, which featured a dozen small drawers, then at the opposite wall, which was a built-in shelf with huge white bath sheets. "Towels, obviously, the biggest and softest I could find."

An artful spiral of copper piping emerged from the floor on the other side of the tub from the stairs, becoming a massive faucet with industrial-style metal knobs trimmed in red rubber for hot water and blue rubber for cold. On the wall with the towel racks, a pair of hooks, meant to hold a robe.

"This is amazing." I took his hands. "I mean, it's...I don't have words. I've been dreaming of a long hot bath for weeks."

"I know." He smiled, bent to kiss me softly, chastely. "I know you tried to take a bath the other day, while she was napping, but she woke up hungry and that was that. I wanted you to have a moment or two to yourself." He kissed me again. "So, I have a chef coming, and he's going to make us some pizzas in the brick oven I had made up there. And we're going to sit here and eat pizza, and then you're going to sit in that tub and have a glass of wine."

"What will you be doing while I'm in the tub?" I asked, letting my eyes ask the question behind the question.

"Watching you, of course."

"You're gonna watch me take a bath?"

"Yeah."

"Why not get in with me?"

He tucked my hair behind my ear. "Because I want that soak to be all about *you*." He let his hands wrap around my waist. "Trust me, I have plans for you for after the bath. Don't you worry about that."

He was true to his word—I'd missed it the first time, but part of the rooftop seating area was a brick pizza oven built into the space, along with a grill and a pair of small refrigerators, one for drinks and the other for chilled snacks, like cheese, olives, and meat. He personally prepared us a little snack board while the chef, a jovial New Yorker, tossed dough with a showy flourish, chattering at us in a practiced patter. It was entertainment itself, watching him make the pizzas, and I found myself truly relaxing for the first time in weeks.

Our lives had been a frantic barrage of learning how to be parents when we barely knew each other, really, changing diapers and feeding and holding and rocking, washing onesies when she had blowouts, gagging over the smell. We dozed when she did, and Braun was gone a day or two each week, checking on his various business endeavors when they needed his personal presence—and overseeing the rooftop renovation, apparently.

Yet, despite the chaos of merging our lives and learning to be parents, it was...beautiful. It was good. We were together. We had each other, and we were learning. I wasn't doing it alone. When I woke up in the middle of the night to feed her, Braun was there. He'd bring me snacks while I was nursing, and he'd stay awake with me, read to me, turn on shows on the iPad for me.

He was *with* me.

He was mine, and I was his. It wasn't perfect, but it was *working*. It was succeeding.

Now, sitting on the couch outside his—*our*—new rooftop deck, eating absolutely incredible brick oven pizza, sipping sparkling water, watching the sunset, watching evening fall and lights twinkle on, being next to him and alone was just so…*nice*—I missed Sabrina, badly, and a part of me felt guilty for not missing her more, for being so glad to have this time alone, but I knew how much I needed it, how much *we* needed it.

While we ate the pizza, Vinny, the chef, made something elaborate out of dark chocolate mousse and handmade ganache and some sort of sweet cream filling. It was indulgently delicious, and I could've eaten myself sick on it; fortunately, Vinny only made one portion each, because I don't think I'd have had the self-control to stop eating it, had there been more.

Dessert in our bellies, Vinny said goodbye, and we were finally alone.

I just sat for a moment, enjoying the peace, the quiet, the solitude.

Braun pressed a kiss to my temple. "Why don't you go into the bedroom and put on a robe while I draw the bath for you. What's your favorite scent?"

I was giddy with excitement at the prospect of a bath. "Lavender," I said, without hesitation. "Lavender bath bombs are my absolute favorite."

He nodded. "Lavender. Got it. You go get ready, okay?"

I was grinning ear to ear. "Thank you, Braun. This whole thing is so thoughtful and amazing."

"You haven't even had the bath yet."

"For dinner, for bringing me here, for getting Laurel to watch Sabrina."

"We need time alone," he said. "You've taken to motherhood like a duck to water, but you deserve a little time off."

"Like a duck to water, huh?"

"You're a natural, is all I meant." He stood with me, faced me, nose to nose. "I don't mean you're anything like a duck."

"Quack quack," I murmured, smiling up at him. "I know what you meant."

He tapped my nose. "Go, before I start kissing you and can't stop."

I lifted up, touching my lips to his. "I wouldn't complain."

"No?"

I ran my hands up his chest, over his shirt. "I haven't been kissed in damn near a year, Braun. Much less anything else."

"Me neither," he said, and his lips grazed mine, a teasing kiss. "I watched the video of you so, so many times. Looked at those pictures of you and…fantasized about you. Tried to remember in detail each moment we spent together."

"Same here," I said.

He tucked his hands under the hem of my T-shirt, which was stained with baby spit-up and probably other less savory things, touching skin. "This was about you getting to relax and take a bath," he said. "I want you, more than I can even say, but Lizzy, I just want you to—"

I grabbed the hem of his shirt and tugged it up. "I know, Braun. I know. And I admit I want a bath more than almost anything." His chest bare, I scoured his flesh greedily, hungrily relearning the feel of his skin and his muscle, the angles and planes of him. "*Almost* anything."

His hands ran up my bare back, under the shirt, lifting it bit by bit. "Almost, huh?"

I slid the button of his jeans open, lowered the zipper. "There's *one* thing I want more, right this moment, than a bath."

"And what would that one thing be?" he asked, his voice husky.

I reached into his underwear and clasped a hand around his erection, groaning at the thick hot steel of him in my fist. "This."

He moaned. "God*damn*, but I've missed the way you touch me."

"Get me naked, Braun."

I didn't have to tell him twice. He peeled my shirt off, and my milk-heavy, swollen breasts bounced free and swayed, aching. Not from being swollen, this time, but from the ache of needing his touch. I received it, immediately—his hands palmed my breasts, lifted, cupped, kneaded.

I gasped at his touch, sensitive. "Careful," I whispered, groaning. "You might get some milk droplets."

He laughed, pinched my nipple, and indeed a bead of milk dotted the tip. He licked it off, and smirked. "Yum."

I laughed, and the laugh turned to a gasp as he knelt in front of me. "Oh please, Braun. Please. *Please*."

His eyes were hooded, heavy-lidded as he curled his fingers in the waistband of my sweatpants. Boring, stained, unfashionable, embarrassingly Mom-ish plain gray give-up-on-life sweatpants. He drew them down, and I stepped out of them, feeling self-conscious about the fact that I hadn't really even tried yet to get back to my prepregnancy body, which now featured stretch marks on my belly and waist and above my hipbones.

I was wearing the worst possible underwear, too—plain black briefs, from Target. Because who had time or energy for fancy panties when you're nursing an infant a billion times a day and changing diapers and barely sleeping?

Yet, Braun's dark gaze spoke of only one thing: desire.

Not just lust, not just horny, lecherous need for sex.

Desire.

For *me*.

His hands roamed up my thighs, and his eyes stayed on mine, occasionally flicking over my curves. Which were now, admittedly, a bit curvier than the last time he'd seen me naked.

In this context, at least.

He cupped my hips, and his lips touched my skin there, and then he pressed another delicate, tender kiss to the stretch marks. "Beautiful."

I swallowed. "Braun…"

He kissed my belly. "Beautiful. So beautiful."

I shook my head. "Not like I used to be."

"No," he agreed. "More than ever."

"How can you think that?"

He kissed my other hip, and the marks there as well, and then his hands were cupping my ass and tracing the line of my underwear around under my buttock and inward. "Because I love you. Because I'm attracted to you—to *you*, to who you are and to what you look like. And you're more beautiful now than the last time I had my hands and mouth on you. I want you more than ever, Liz. So don't spend a single second being self-conscious. Be proud. You're a mother. A warrior. A powerful woman who carried a human being inside you. That's a miracle, and you're a marvel, and I'm so incredibly proud of you."

I blinked hard. "Don't make me cry, dammit," I whispered, half laughing and half sobbing. "I want to have an orgasm, not a sob-fest." I cupped his face as he rested his chin on my stomach, gazing up at me. "But thank you. That means more to me than I can even say."

"An orgasm, you say?" He traced a finger around the leg of my panties again, this time up from my thigh to beside my core. "Then we might need to get these off you."

I pushed them down. "Please, please, please."

"Please, what, my love?"

I stepped out of the underwear and stood naked in front of him, there on the roof. I truly didn't care in that moment if anyone could see us—let them look. I had more important things to care about.

I caressed my fingers into his hair, widened my stance, and pulled his face to me. "Make me come, Braun, please. I need to come so bad. It's been so long. Please."

He flicked his tongue against me. "Like this?"

I groaned. "Fuck yes. That. More of that. Don't tease me, don't draw it out. Just make me come. Please."

He gave me exactly what I was pleading for—his tongue, in an immediate assault, hard and fast, and he certainly hadn't forgotten how I like in the intervening months. Within seconds, I was aching, and in another minute, I was shaking, and he slid two fingers into me and supported me with his other hand around my backside and licked me into oblivion.

My legs gave out at the peak of my orgasm, and he caught me, settled me on the couch, lying back against it, and he knelt in front of me and draped my thighs over his shoulders and went back to my sex, and this time he was slow, thorough, methodical, teasing. He took his time bringing me to a second climax, and that one was infinitely more powerful than the previous, and when it was over and I was lying limp and wrung-out, he moved to sit beside me. Kissed me on the breast, the chin, the cheek.

"I'm gonna go run your bath," he said.

"Unh-uh," I murmured a negative. "Not yet you're not."

"No?"

"Nope." I gathered my energy and sat up. "My turn."

He blinked at me. "We can wait—"

"Maybe you can," I said, helping him out of his jeans. "But I can't."

"Well, when you put it like that…" He grabbed his jeans off the floor and rummaged in one of the back pockets, from which he produced a folded string of condoms. "I came prepared."

I took them from him and set them aside. "Good thing you did." I pulled his underwear down, exposing his manhood. "But we won't be needing those just yet."

He swallowed hard. "Oh no?"

I twisted to face him, sliding my fist on his length. "Nope."

"We have to use one," he said.

"I know." I twisted my fist around the plump head. "And we will. But for what I had in mind, we don't need one."

"Lizzy," he said, swallowing hard again as I pumped him with one hand, and then both. "Ohh god."

"You got to taste me," I said, licking my lips. "Now it's my turn. I want to taste you."

"Shit," he groaned. "Just…be careful."

I laughed. "Be careful? Of what?"

"Of the fact that I haven't even done anything to myself in months, so I may just explode the moment you put your mouth on me. I'm close right now, and you've been touching me for a matter of seconds."

I grinned. "Oh. I see." I bit my lip as I bent over him. "Well. How about you let me worry about that? You just sit there and enjoy it."

"I like the way you think."

"I figured you'd be on board with that."

I fit him into my mouth, pulsing my fists around his base, and he groaned. I pushed my tongue against his springy flesh as I took him deeper and cupped his sac in one hand while twisting around his girth with the other. He moaned, head back, eyes closed, hands tangled in my hair.

"Holy fuck, Liz, that feels like heaven."

"Mmmm."

I backed away, and licked him, tongue running around the tip, then over it, and then around the rim under the head, and then up the length, and then I turned my head sideways and took his length sideways in my mouth and ran my lips up him, until I reached then head once more and went over him, taking him into my lips and to the back of my throat.

And then I took him in earnest, then, pumping up and down with my mouth and massaging his balls and pulsing my other hand on his root until hips began to move, and then he was groaning nonstop, wordless snarls of ecstasy as I brought him to the edge, and took him over.

He blasted into my mouth, and I swallowed, swallowed, pumped him for more and swallowed that too, and he was groaning my name now, chanting my name as he came and came.

Finished, finally, he pulled me away. "Holy shit, Liz."

I rested my cheek on his thigh and looked at him. "I love you, you know."

He palmed my face, thumb grazing in circles. "I Love you." He laughed. "And not just because of the blowjob. Although that's love-worthy in and of itself."

"I'm so, *so* glad Teddy called you," I said. "I can't imagine doing any of this alone." I sighed, laughing ruefully. "I honestly don't know what I was thinking."

"You could have done it alone," he said. "You're plenty capable. But you won't ever have to."

I just lay there, my face on his thigh, inches from his slack manhood, enjoying the feel of him, the scent of him, the heat and the realness of him, the intimacy of closeness.

We didn't need to talk. He gazed at me, at the view beyond, and I rested, eyes closed, not quite dozing, but drifting idly.

I toyed with him, after a while, wanting him again. This time, I wanted him inside me. And I wanted him to take his time, to last as long as he could. I traced him, twisted, flipped him this way and that, gently, affectionately, playfully taking my time bringing him to arousal. He just watched, a happy smile on his face.

After a while, he was fully erect. It was full dark by this time, a clear night with a full moon. The city was bright, the night warm. I fisted him, pumping him until he groaned.

"Enough," he gasped. "I need you. I need to be inside you."

Sitting up, I ripped a condom from the string, opened it, withdrew the ring of latex. "Funny, I was just thing the same thing."

"You were, huh?"

I rolled it onto him, and then swung my thigh over to straddle him. He sat up higher, caressing my hips up to my breasts as I rose up on my knees, grasped him and guided him to my opening. He kissed my breasts, hands gripping the taut globes of my ass; I notched him inside me, hesitated.

"Ready, babe?" I asked.

He blinked, head turning to the side. "Babe."

I laughed. "Huh. That was accidental. Never used one of those endearments in my life."

"I like it."

I circled my hips with just the head of him nestled inside me. "Me too." Bent to catch his face in my hands, kissed him, deep and slow. "Baby. Honey. Love. Darling," I whispered each word.

"Sweetheart." He caressed me everywhere, his hands roaming my body, relearning the feel of me, re-memorizing my curves under his hands.

I let my hips flex, back and forth, then circle, teasing us both. "Braun, my love."

He gazed up at me. "Liz...I need you."

"You need me?"

"So bad."

"You need to be inside me?"

"God, please."

I was upright on my knees on the couch, straddling him, facing him, breasts draped against his face, hands in his hair and on his jaw. I sank a little lower. "That's what you want?"

He groaned, a desperate sound. "Fuck yes. That, please. I need to be deeper."

"You need to be...deeper?" I rolled my hips, sliding the inch or two of him that was in me through my sex. "Like that?"

"More."

I clung to his shoulders for balance and lifted up, so he nearly slid out of me, and then lowered myself onto him, one...two...three inches of him.

"More." He gripped my hips. "All the way, Liz. Please."

"Maybe you should just...*take* what you need."

He flexed up into me, pulled me down. I went, sinking down hard onto him. I screamed, and captured the scream with his mouth, and then we were off, moving together. I lifted, and he drew away, and then I was slamming down and he was driving up, and I was so full of him, aching with the massive thick intrusion of him within me, and it felt so good after so long apart from him that I wept with the beauty of it.

It was slow.

Ages, we roiled together.

For an eternity, I took him as deep as he could go within me, and for that eternity, I kissed him breathlessly, and he whispered my name into the kiss.

When I felt him lose the thread of control, his hips flexing helplessly, his groans coming ragged, I slid a hand between our bodies and helped myself along, and his hands were fierce and strong, jerking me down onto him, and I felt him throb inside me. I squeezed with all that I had, and then the clamping heat inside me began to billow, to crash, and I was clenching around him helplessly and I was crying into his kiss, weeping his name, weeping *Iloveyou* over and over.

We came with lightning heat, shattering bliss, united, in synch.

Again and again, and again, we crashed together, exploding together, until there was nothing left but gasping and sweating together, stilled, my forehead to his.

I sat on him, then, glutted on him, hugging him as I quaked through the afterglow.

I pulled back to look into his eyes. "I don't want to take a bath alone."

"Okay."

"You and me, and a bottle of champagne. That's what I want."

"You just sit here and relax," he said. "I'll get it all set up."

He ran the bath, turning on the hot water and letting it run till it steamed, and then closed the drain and added cold water until he deemed the temperature acceptable. He sorted through various drawers until he found the bath bomb he wanted, unwrapped it, tossed it in. One of the other drawers contained thick white candles; he arranged a good half dozen in clusters on one side of the tub, retrieved a lighter from a different drawer, lit them all. Came back up

and got a bottle of champagne from the outdoor re-
frigerator, uncorked with a *pop*. Poured us each a
glass.

He helped me to my feet, gave me my flute.
"Ready?"

I smiled at him, happier than I could ever remember being. "More than ready."

He led me down to the tub. I splashed a hand
through the water, and it was the perfect temperature
for a bath—just barely too hot. I got in first, gingerly,
slowly lowering myself into the water with hisses and
gasps. And then I was fully immersed, and Braun got
in next.

For a moment, we just sat in the piping hot water, staring out at the magical view.

Then Braun extended his champagne flute to
me. "A toast—to amazing sex, unexpected love, and
a baby that's changed both of our lives...for the infinitely better."

I laughed, clinked my glass against his. "I'll drink
to that—to amazing sex, unexpected love, and a baby
that's changed both of our lives...for the infinitely
better. And I'll add one thing: to us."

"To us."

We sipped, and I sighed in pleasure at my first
taste of alcohol since I found out I was pregnant.

We luxuriated in that tub until the water went
cool, let some out and refilled it with more hot water,

watching the moon rise huge overhead. LA around us; we just sat, not talking, smiling at each other.

Later, we dried off in huge towels that were nearly the size of a king bed comforter, went to the bedroom and made love in his huge bed—*our* huge bed.

He had a flatscreen TV cunningly hidden in the floor, so that at a push of a button, it rose from the floor at the foot of the bed, and we watched a comedy special, and I fell asleep in Braun's arms, replete with love.

I woke up in the middle of the night, out of habit—Sabrina always woke at around three wanting to eat, and my body had adapted.

I stole out of bed and found Braun's phone. Dialed Laurel's cell number—he had her saved in his phone under her full name, Laurel McGillis.

"Hello?" Her voice was soft, quiet.

"Hey, Laur—it's me."

"Oh, hey, babe. You have a good evening?"

"The absolute best." I heard the smile in my own voice, felt it on my face. "Best night ever. Thank you, so much."

"Oh, no problem. Your daughter is an absolute doll, you know that. Give her the bottle and she just stares up at you with those big brown eyes. She's a darling."

"You'd be a good mom, Laurel, you know that?"

She sighed. "Yeah. Maybe. I don't know that there's any man out there who can handle me, though."

"There is. We just have to find him for you."

"Maybe I need an ad of my own."

I snorted. "I mean hey, it worked for me." I felt my heart twist, melt. "Laurel, I need to say thank you, big time."

"You already did."

"No, not for staying with Sabrina." I swallowed. "For putting my real number in that ad. You changed my life."

She let out a breath. "I didn't anticipate any of this, that's for damn sure."

"Who could have? But nonetheless, if you hadn't, I wouldn't have Braun, and Braun is…"

"He's great. Even I can say that, and I've not met too many men I can say are truly amazing. But he's one of them. You snagged a keeper, Lizzy."

"I did." I laughed. "I might even become Elizabeth Bennet for him."

"For real?"

"I can't imagine life without him, so yeah. It just makes sense." I heard Sabrina squawk sleepily. "I'll let you go. I just wanted to say that—thanks for giving us this time. And thank you so, so, so much for being dumbass enough to put my real number in that ad." I laughed. "I may just return the favor."

"You better not!" She stopped laughing abruptly. "Although…it *did* work for you."

"Maybe we should experiment on someone else."

"Autumn," Laurel said, immediately. "She needs a man. She's uptight. I don't think she gets enough dick. She needs some of that magical dick."

"I don't disagree."

"You're serious?" she said, laughing. "For real?"

I cackled. "I mean, yeah? It did work for me. We tweak the ad for her, but…yeah. It could work."

"You're crazy." I heard Sabrina squawk again, and then patting as Laurel burped her. "I love it. Let's do it!"

"I'm in." I yawned. "And if it works again for her, we do it for you. Hell, we could get all of us men this way."

"Let's talk later. You should be sleeping. And this little one," and here she transitioned to a lovey soft baby-talk voice, "is just…about…asleep."

"Alright. Later, then."

"Later, boss."

I hung up, and went back to bed. I lay on my side, sleepy but not ready to go back to sleep yet. I stared at Braun for a while, marveling at the unexpected turn my life had taken, and how lucky I'd been that he had taken the chance on that ad.

Beautiful, successful single woman, 40, seeks

attractive male billionaire to impregnate her the old-fashioned way. No strings. NOT seeking sugar daddy. Validation required. Serious inquiries only, please.

Who knew those five sentences, twenty-eight words would so completely change the course of my life?

I fell asleep, facing Braun, full of joy in a way I hadn't known was possible.

THE END

Big Girls Do It:
Boxed Set
Married
On Christmas
Pregnant

Rock Stars Do It:
Harder
Dirty
Forever

From the world of *Big Girls* and *Rock Stars*:
Big Love Abroad

Biker Billionaire:
Wild Ride

The Falling Series:
Falling Into You
Falling Into Us
Falling Under
Falling Away
Falling For Colton

The Ever Trilogy:
Forever & Always
After Forever
Saving Forever

The world of *Wounded:*
Wounded
Captured

The world of *Stripped:*
Stripped
Trashed

The world of *Alpha:*
Alpha
Beta
Omega
Harris: Alpha One Security Book 1
Thresh: Alpha One Security Book 2
Duke Alpha One Security Book 3
Puck: Alpha One Security Book 4
Lear: Alpha One Security Book 5
Anselm: Alpha One Security Book 6

The Houri Legends:
Jack and Djinn
Djinn and Tonic

The Madame X Series:
Madame X
Exposed
Exiled

The Black Room
(With Jade London):
Door One

Door Two

Door Three

Door Four

Door Five

Door Six

Door Seven

Door Eight

The One Series
The Long Way Home

Where the Heart Is

There's No Place Like Home

Badd Brothers:
Badd Motherf*cker

Badd Ass

Badd to the Bone

Good Girl Gone Badd

Badd Luck

Badd Mojo

Big Badd Wolf

Badd Boy

Badd Kitty

Badd Business

Badd Medicine

Badd Daddy

Dad Bod Contracting:
Hammered
Drilled
Nailed
Screwed

Fifty States of Love:
Pregnant in Pennsylvania
Cowboy in Colorado
Married in Michigan

Goode Girls
For a Goode Time Call…
Not So Goode
Goode to Be Bad
A Real Good Time
Goode Vibrations

Standalone titles:
Yours
The Cabin

Non-Fiction titles:

You Can Do It

You Can Do It: Strength

You Can Do It: Fasting

Jack Wilder Titles:

The Missionary

JJ Wilder Titles:

Ark

To be informed of new releases, special offers, and other Jasinda news, sign up for Jasinda's email newsletter.